M000284043

OVER THE
EDGE

Also available by Kathleen Bryant

Beginning with Breakfast
Almost Innocent
Sheep's Clothing
Kokopelli's Gift
A Time to Love
Ancient Secrets (writing as Kate Bradley)

Nonfiction Titles

Moon Spotlight Sedona
Moon Spotlight Navajo & Hopi Country
Moon Phoenix, Scottsdale & Sedona
Moon Four Corners
Moon Grand Canyon
Sedona & Red Rock Country
The Four Corners: Timeless Lands of the Southwest
Sedona: Treasure of the Southwest
Western National Parks' Lodges Cookbook

OVER THE EDGE

A NOVEL

KATHLEEN BRYANT

CROOKED LANE

NEW YORK

Copyright © 2024 by Kathleen M. Bryant

Published in the United States by Crooked Lane Books, an imprint of The Quick Brown Fox & Company LLC.

Crooked Lane Books and its logo are trademarks of The Quick Brown Fox & Company LLC.

Library of Congress Catalog-in-Publication data available upon request.

ISBN (hardcover): 978-1-63910-754-4
ISBN (ebook): 978-1-63910-759-9

Cover design by Nicole Lecht

Printed in the United States.

www.crookedlanebooks.com

Crooked Lane Books
34 West 27th St., 10th Floor
New York, NY 10001

First Edition: June 2024

10 9 8 7 6 5 4 3 2 1

To Richard, for making life more
wonderful

CHAPTER

1

E ARLY MORNING SUN warmed the sandstone cliffs around
me, and from behind closed eyelids I sensed the orange
glow. Even now, a promise of late June's heat lit the edges of
the breeze that brushed across my cheek and stirred the hair
slipping from the loose twist I'd managed that morning in
the dark. Hoping to ease into the meditation I'd skipped in
order to get to my new job on time, I exhaled, then slowly
breathed in the familiar tang of juniper and iron-rich dirt,
along with a hint of the smoldering sage Teejay had used to
greet the sun.

A towhee trilled and buzzed and, for a moment, I felt
older than the juniper, nearly as ancient as the rocks, with a
deep sense of belonging as though I knew how to shape a
piece of chert or follow a mule deer on silent bare feet. Part of
me recognized this feeling was key to fixing the brokenness
that had brought me here to Sedona. Then I saw *him* again,
real but not real, a slim and sinewy man scrambling over the
red sandstone toward a spiral petroglyph and—quick as a
flipped switch—the line between observer and participant
blurred. Panicked, I pulled myself back from the vision and
drew a shaky breath.

"Oh, wow. So cool. You getting this, Sarah? Yoga on the rocks—I'm gonna Instagram it."

The voice yanked me firmly into the present. My eyes snapped open. Thirty-nine years old and auditioning for a seasonal gig as a tour guide, here I was in a nameless red rock canyon with two middle-aged suburbanites seeking adventure (so long as it didn't require too much hiking or involve too many bugs), a Jeep painted the bright blue of a desert sky, and last, but certainly not least, Teejay, fellow guide and local poster boy for the exotic-but-approachable western male. He looked, I realized, a lot like the man from my vision.

"There's no cell service!"

Missy's wail floated up from below. She was the younger of the two women, or at least dressed that way, in a loose tank top and cutoffs so brief they made her tree pose iffy for social media sharing. Sarah was more modestly clad in long black leggings she would certainly come to regret as soon as the sun started angling deeper into the small box canyon.

"Del, would you take a shot of the three of us, please?" Sarah called up.

"On my way." Regretful the respite from our chatty passengers was over so soon, I unwound from a half-lotus and brushed the red dirt from my bare legs, hearing Teejay's rich chuckle. The ledge gave me a bird's eye view of the women mugging for photographs.

I started back down the steep route I'd taken to my perch, thinking that if I'd been a college student on summer break, instead of a grown-up on a career break, this would be the perfect job. After all, I was getting paid to visit Sedona's backcountry, a pastime that had become almost obsessive for me, and in the company of the local heartthrob. Friends had assured me leading Jeep tours offered the most money I could hope for in Sedona's tourist economy. I needed the cash. Journalists didn't get pensions, and disgraced reporters were more likely to get a swift kick out the door.

Slowing to negotiate a section of loose rock, aware the small stones would skitter like ball bearings if I wasn't careful, I paused to gauge the remaining route down to the canyon floor. Though I couldn't be positive from nearly thirty feet away, I was pretty sure Missy's red-lacquered fingertips had wound themselves around Teejay's bicep. In that moment, it hit me I would never rake in the tips he counted on to cover the rent for his RV space along Oak Creek.

This was my second week of ride-alongs, learning different routes and memorizing Teejay's relaxed patter over the intercom as he pointed out sights or patiently explained why the rocks were red. Blue Sky Expeditions was one of a handful of off-road excursion companies that advertised adventure with racks of brochures in hotel lobbies and gift shops. What distinguished ours from the rest was its cover photo of Teejay—a brilliant bit of marketing from Blue Sky's otherwise lackadaisical owner.

Even now, standing among the pale dried grasses and chaparral, Teejay was a match for his cover shot, wearing jeans so worn they were almost white and a plaid shirt with its sleeves torn off. He carried his two-way radio at his hip like a gunslinger, but he'd removed his concha-trimmed gambler's hat for Sarah's photo, his black hair pulled back neatly, then wrapped with a leather cord, emphasizing his cheekbones. Imitation—or in this case, cultural appropriation—was the sincerest form of flattery. Though he might look like a filmmaker's idea of a modern Navajo, I happened to know Teejay was the grandson of Italian immigrants to the Midwest and that his given name was Timothy Joseph Mattea. Other than that, he was something of a mystery, and I assumed that, like many Sedona transplants, myself included, he preferred to leave the past in the past.

"You coming, Delilah?"

Only Teejay called me by my full name. I resisted the temptation to needle him back. Though we'd become friends—*sort of*—before I signed on with Blue Sky, he was now essentially my supervisor, and I'd learned the hard way not to let professional relationships turn personal.

"Almost there." My right boot launched a stone over the edge.

The sharp thud reverberated across the canyon, and I glanced up to see a human form disappear around a blockish boulder. Before I had time to worry my visions were becoming full-blown hallucinations, my gaze landed on a shadowy alcove. I paused to allow my eyes to adjust and saw it wasn't an alcove after all, though I knew the ancients had once sheltered deeper in this box canyon, leaving behind a small masonry room and a roasting pit.

The sun, stronger now, lit the higher ledge and the shadow that shouldn't be there, its edges soft and organic against the fractured rock. Instinct—and memory—knotted my stomach. The shadow looked like . . .

"Hey, Delilah! Time to go."

I scrambled the rest of the way down on shaky legs, numbly accepting the phone Sarah handed me and taking the requested photo. Teejay had replaced his hat, but even though the flat brim shaded his eyes, I could tell he registered my distress. I shook my head slightly, and he seemed to get the message.

"What's next?" Missy whipped out our brochure from her waist pack and waved it in my direction. "We've done the sage smudging and sunrise ceremony. Are we going to a vortex? We need to be back at the resort for our herbal wraps by ten."

"Um," I offered, grateful when Teejay stepped in.

"We can make a quick stop at the Chimney Rock vortex. It's powerful. Photogenic, too."

He shot me a warning look, and I played along. First, no vortex waited at Chimney Rock, only a relatively short Jeep ride and a quick return to Missy and Sarah's hotel. And second, Teejay was more likely to tell tourists the only vortexes in Sedona were the magnetic forces that pulled people's credit cards from their wallets. I tended to agree, though I had a feeling Steve Nicholson, Blue Sky's owner and a childhood friend of mine, wouldn't endorse that line, no matter how hands-off his style.

Teejay let the women walk ahead, their voices fading as they neared the tall stand of cottonwoods that screened the canyon from anyone traveling by on the dirt forest road. Below the trees, two or three vehicles could squeeze in next to an earthen stock tank. The dried-up tank, a few strands of rusted barbed wire, and some grayed and splintered wood from an old cattle chute were the only signs of the site's historic use as a corral. Though the box canyon didn't offer a thrill ride or a scenic panorama like Soldiers Pass or Chicken Point, where larger tour companies operated, it suited our small outfit's reputation for focusing on personal reflection and cultural history.

"What's wrong?" Teejay asked quietly when the women were out of sight.

"There's something—*someone*—up there." I nodded toward the cliff. "Next to that lone piñon. It looks like fabric."

He squinted at the ledge. "Campsite? Sleeping bag or backpack, maybe?"

"Too far from town, don't you think?"

Sedona was surrounded by thousands of acres of Coconino National Forest, which allowed at-large camping for two weeks at a stretch, a limit sometimes overlooked by enforcement rangers, who had their hands full with things like wildcat tours, trash dumping, and resource damage. Thus, the local unhoused population stayed almost invisible, many choosing hidden spots near neighborhoods, where they could easily walk or hitch to find food, water, or a place to clean up.

"We better check it out." Teejay's wary expression reflected my own reluctance to investigate the nonshadow, but in his case, duty won. He handed over the keys. "Get the binoculars out of the Jeep. And see if you can convince Missy and Sarah to stay there."

"Ha. I'll try."

As I approached, the women's voices rose. With the imposed quiet of the sunrise ceremony behind them, they seemed impatient for the next stage in their adventure. Between the Jeep and the tank, currently a rain-parched basin of cracked clay, I spotted a plastic grocery bag impaled in a patch of catclaw bushes, a sight so common our drivers joked about crumpled plastic being Arizona's official cactus flower. Inspired, I gave Missy and Sarah a lame excuse about needing a couple of minutes to clean up some trash I'd found deeper in the canyon and asked them to wait a little longer. They looked skeptical, so I also mentioned rattlesnakes. Their wide-eyed expressions reassured me they'd stick close by.

I walked back into the canyon with the binoculars slung across my torso, catching up to Teejay, who'd already scrambled halfway up to the ledge where I'd been sitting. We climbed the last few yards without speaking. I lifted the binoculars and focused across the canyon. No spiral petroglyph. No ancient warrior. *But that pile of rags—*

The ground swayed below my feet as my legs turned rubbery. Teejay grabbed the waistband of my cargo shorts to steady me, taking the binoculars with his other hand.

My heartbeat whooshed loudly in my ears, muffling my voice. "You don't need to look. He's dead."

I read the question on his lips. "Who?"

"I'm pretty sure it's Franklin." The flaming red hair and bushy beard were unmistakable. "Looks like he fell. His head—" My throat felt too thick to get the words out.

Teejay lifted the binoculars anyway. He focused, and the moment he recognized the old army jacket, the red hair, his fingers tightened. He handed back the binoculars, his face grim, and pulled out his radio. "Go back to the Jeep and get them out of here."

The buzzing in my ears receded, and the sound of women's voices floated up. I scanned the trail below. Missy and Sarah were making their way slowly back into the canyon, poking under rocks and bushes with a pair of long branches.

"What the hell are they doing?"

"Scaring snakes, I think."

He snorted. "Don't say anything to them. I'll radio dispatch and wait here for the rescue crew."

"I'll drive them around the loop." I referred to a network of unpaved forest roads that circled west before leading back to Sedona. "Less likely we'll run into any emergency vehicles."

"Good plan." He looked toward the opposite ledge, assessing, and I remembered Teejay was an experienced climber, often called on to assist the county's backcountry rescue team. "They'll probably send a chopper to short-haul him out."

He was already on the radio as I started to pick my way back down for the second time that morning. Still a bit wobbly, I placed a palm on the canyon wall to steady myself and took one last glance backward. I tried to pinpoint a route leading from the canyon trail to the ledge where Franklin's body lay. He must have slipped trying to find a way up.

It was an accident, of course. How could it be anything else?

*　*　*

After dropping Missy and Sarah at their hotel, I returned the Jeep to Blue Sky's modest headquarters. Sightseeing tours had morphed into a multimillion-dollar industry over the years, with mom-and-pop businesses consolidating or selling out to corporate owners. Blue Sky Expeditions hung on with a handful of drivers and a ragtag fleet. The larger outfitters boasted comfortable guest reception centers in Uptown's tourist hub; Blue Sky's call center and garage were crammed into a small concrete block building a half mile up Airport Road in West Sedona.

Our drivers typically used the time between tours to clean their vehicles, but when I reached for a hose to sluice off the red dust, Arnulfo Flores, the company mechanic, took it from me, shaking his head.

"I'll wash it." He was a man of few words, but his brown eyes were sympathetic. Apparently, the news had traveled.

When I opened the door that connected the garage to the call center via a wide hallway, the clamor of voices and ringing phones rolled toward me like a physical force. More shaken than I wanted to admit, I stopped to lean against the counter that served as our break area and wondered again what the hell I was doing here.

Not just here at Blue Sky, but *here*, in Sedona. As a child, I'd found freedom and refuge in the red rock canyons and buttes. As an adult, I understood escape wasn't that easy. Trouble seemed to follow me, as silent-footed as a mountain lion.

I straightened and pasted on a smile for Megan Ramirez, Blue Sky's youngest driver, who stopped to hug me briefly on her way to the garage.

"You okay, Del?" Her bouncy dark-brown ponytail brushed my cheek as she stepped back and peered at me.

I nodded.

"Gina told me what happened. I'm taking over Teejay's Schnebly Hill tour. Only four guests today—plenty of room for you to ride along, blow out the jitters." She jangled a set of keys as though to entice me.

"Thanks, but I think I'll stick around here. Grab a training manual, brush up on my geology."

She wrinkled her nose. "As Evan would say"—she pitched her voice lower and added a drawl—"a degree from MSU—*making shit up*—doesn't cut it here."

"Hey now, little sister, no bad-mouthing me behind my back."

Caught like a pair of naughty schoolkids, we spun around as Evan Zeigler, retired Forest Service ranger turned tour guide, strolled down the hallway to refill his insulated mug from the coffee maker on the counter. Drawing on his decades of experience, Evan had helped Teejay assemble the ridiculously fat three-ring binder of training materials that covered everything from archaeology to first aid.

Like a lot of people who watched Jeep guides zipping around in rainbow-colored vehicles as they regaled tourists with true facts and tall tales, I'd assumed landing the job would be a snap. The competition turned out to be fierce, but lucky for me, I had connections. I'd known Steve Nicholson, Blue Sky's absentee owner, since childhood. What I hadn't known was the connection could have just as easily worked against me. Steve put a minimum of effort into the business his grandparents had started, spending most of his time kiteboarding on Maui and leaving day-to-day decisions to Teejay, the company manager in all but name.

While Teejay acted as boss, Evan, with his silver hair and military posture, was our unofficial role model. Born and raised in east Texas, he'd worked all over the West as a Forest Service botanist. He dressed the part, sticking to ranger-esque garb, favoring a western-style straw hat, his sage green cargo pants and khaki shirts always neatly pressed. During my first few days on the job, I'd shadowed him to learn the names of spring wildflowers before they faded under the June sun. I'd also learned his patient demeanor was spiked with a wicked sense of humor.

"You okay, Del?" He unconsciously echoed Megan. "I've seen some crazy stuff out there in the canyons, but a dead body sure does top 'em all."

"I'm fine." I waved at Megan as she departed, then gratefully accepted the cup of coffee Evan held out. My nerves didn't need the caffeine, but the familiar scent was a comfort.

"Let Gina know if you want to go on a ride-along later. I'm heading out in a few minutes, but Sam will be in soon."

I nodded, leaving him there doctoring his coffee with the hazelnut syrup he kept in a small flask tucked in his shirt pocket. At least that was what I assumed the caramel-colored liquid was. I'd seen no sign Evan was drinking on the job but plenty of evidence that anything left in the break area was fair game for moochers or practical jokers.

High in spirits but low on cash, Blue Sky's drivers worked on rotation and depended on tips to supplement a basic hourly wage. Teejay assigned routes based on seniority, so whenever he decided I was ready to go solo, I'd be awarded the bottom rotation and the fifth Jeep, a ten-year-old Wrangler Arnulfo was doing his best to reanimate.

Phones trilled as I carried my coffee toward the front office, where Gina Lambert—lead dispatcher, bookkeeper, and all-around office mom—held court. Two other employees worked behind the reception counter: Harmony, whose ash-blond hair sported pink streaks (the third pastel shade since we'd started orientation together less than a month ago) and Chase, a student at Northern Arizona University who helped handle phone reservations during summer months.

Behind the reception counter, racks displayed our signature blue bandannas, logo T-shirts, and refillable water bottles. Our cramped waiting area with its blanket-padded bench was homey—if your idea of "home" was the men's dorm at Northern Arizona University. Outside, a shaded patio offered additional seating at a wooden picnic table. The setup was minimally comfortable for drivers hanging around to be assigned a tour, less so for customers. This far from the Uptown tourist track, walk-ins were rare. More often, we picked up guests at their hotels or met them at The Market, a West Sedona epicenter for locals and visitors alike.

I pulled the heavy training manual from a shelf below the reception counter and settled onto the bench to reread the geology section, but Teejay's enthusiasm for Permian seas and sand dunes couldn't penetrate my fog of distraction. When the ringing phones and geology jargon got too much for me, I headed outside into the midday heat.

Even in the shade, a deep breath didn't so much clear the head as turn thoughts to ash. I'd found an extra pair of binoculars in the garage, using them now to watch helicopters and biplanes back-and-forth noisily from Airport Mesa, a flat-topped butte that defined West Sedona's southern boundary. Earlier, I'd spotted a search-and-rescue helicopter bearing northwest across the cloudless blue sky, guessing it was headed for the box canyon.

How had Franklin ended up in such a remote spot?

One of Sedona's chronically homeless, Franklin was a familiar sight along the three-mile stretch of 89A between the library and The Market, toting his possessions in grocery bags, usually bareheaded and often barefoot, no matter the weather. Tall and straight, his skin reddened almost the shade of his beard, he'd become something of an iconic figure to young starry-eyed seekers on Sedona pilgrimages. But Franklin didn't own a vehicle, and the box canyon was fifteen miles from town, a mere speck among the complex contours and folds along the Mogollon Rim, a two-hundred-mile escarpment marking the edge of the Colorado Plateau.

Thoughts of his gruesome demise squelched my appetite, but Gina's mothering impulses kicked in, and she sent me out to pick up sandwiches for everyone. After lunch, I tried texting Teejay, but he was either not answering or beyond cell phone reach. By late afternoon, when he still hadn't returned, I started filling out an incident report.

It was after four when I looked up to see a silver SUV circling around to the garage, its driver wearing the blaze orange of Yavapai County's search-and-rescue team. I was out the doorway before Teejay had finished thanking the YCSO volunteer for the ride.

"What happened out there today?"

He held up a hand. "Hang on, Delilah. I'd rather talk to everybody at once. Round them up for me, okay? I'll be in Steve's office."

He looked weary, and I held back my questions as I followed him inside. We all still referred to the small office at the end of the hallway as Steve's, though his visits to Sedona were rare. I hadn't seen my old friend since my Aunt Claire's memorial service. Teejay flipped on the lights and tossed his hat onto the desk. Arnulfo had already gone home for the day, but through the window that looked into the garage and out the open bay, I spotted Megan's Grand Cherokee rolling up.

I waved her inside before walking toward the front office, interrupting Evan and Sam Curry, seasonal driver and career student, who were bargaining for the last can of Red Bull.

Gina instructed Chase to take over the phones, and the rest of us crowded into Steve's office to hear what Teejay had to say.

Briefly, he recounted how the recovery team had extricated Franklin's body from the ledge. After years of reporting grisly scenes from traffic accidents to violent encounters, I could easily picture the missing details: the smells, the flies, the shocking derangement of the human body.

"How long was he out there?" The question came from Sam, who'd gone so pale his freckles stood out even more than usual, his hazel eyes troubled.

"A couple days maybe. The vultures and other scavengers—"

Megan made a face. "Got it. Say no more."

I thought back to recent sunrise tours, a boisterous family of four yesterday, and this morning, Missy and Sarah, who weren't exactly walking in silence. My mind went to the shadow I'd seen disappearing behind a boulder. Vultures liked to sun their wings in the morning, and ravens were a common sight any time of day. I'd rather believe the shadow was a large bird and not a hallucination.

"Accident?"

Someone gasped at Evan's question—not me, though I felt shock and then guilt, maybe because I hadn't considered Franklin mattered enough for anyone to harm him, or maybe because I tried not to think about him at all, preferring to give him a wide berth whenever I saw him around town.

"The investigators won't be sure until the ME performs the autopsy." Teejay's expression was grim. "But right now, they're treating it as a suspicious death."

"*Suspicious?*"

Drivers and dispatchers spoke over each other. Teejay held up a palm and the voices stilled. "The box canyon is off limits until the sheriff clears it. That means no tours."

Gina groaned, then her cheeks pinked. "I'm sorry. I don't mean to be unfeeling, but that's our exclusive. How long before we can get back in there?"

Being able to offer the box canyon tours, in addition to the standard routes we shared with larger outfitters, was key to Blue Sky's survival—we all knew that. The big Jeep companies pitched wild rides; we promised a sense of the wild. Our permit from the Forest Service allotted only ten tours to the canyon each week. Keeping visitation to a minimum limited impact and granted our guests a sense of discovery. I had a personal attachment to this approach because it made me feel less like I was climbing aboard Sedona's tourism juggernaut when I signed on to become Blue Sky's newest driver.

Teejay shrugged. "Can't say. That's up to the sheriff."

This time everyone groaned.

"The Forest Service can't yank our permit, can they?" Sam fidgeted in his chair.

"We're pretty solid with the ranger district." Teejay nodded toward Evan. "But there'll be gossip about this, and I don't want to find out any of it started here." He paused to look at each of us, but it felt like his gaze lingered on me.

For a few uncomfortable seconds, no one spoke. Sam looked at his well-worn hiking boots. Evan stared out the window to the garage, his jaw clenched.

At last, Harmony broke the silence, tears making her pale gray eyes seem even vaguer. "Can't we do a ceremony or something?"

"For Franklin?

"Um . . . yes. Of course. And for the canyon, to clear the negative energies."

"Sure." Teejay's voice was gentle. "But not until the sheriff's released the scene, okay? We safeguard the box canyon like it's ours, so this feels personal, but we need to step back and let the sheriff do his job. Ours is to take care of our clients." He turned toward Sam and Evan. "Don't you two have tours?"

"Leaving now, Boss." Evan's drawl signaled the assembled group that it was time to move on.

"Gina?" Lips pursed, she turned to face Teejay. "Can you fill in Chase? Send him back if he has questions."

"Sure." She joined the exodus.

Sam and Evan headed for the garage, already running late for their sunset tours. Megan followed the other women, muttering something about checking on last-minute reservations for the weekend. At five thirty, the front door would be locked and the phones switched over to an answering system. Their voices faded, leaving me alone with Teejay in the office.

I picked up the incident report I'd left on his desk and handed it to him. "What weren't you saying?"

"That obvious?" He scanned the half-finished report, blew out a sigh, and rubbed his temples, pulling a few strands of dark hair from the leather wrap. "Franklin was shot."

My breath stuttered. "That's why he fell?"

"Looks that way. The investigators didn't find a blood trail. Only footprints—the couple of dozen you and I and our tour guests left behind."

I tried to imagine it, Franklin running from some unknown assailant, then realizing he was trapped in the shallow canyon. He must have scrambled up the sandstone, seeking a hiding place, trying to gain higher ground. As soon as I pictured the desperate scene, I remembered something. "When was the last time you saw him?"

"Two nights ago. Wednesday, at the party in Lee Canyon."

"Me too. The timing fits."

"Not here, okay?" The look on his face told me he'd already considered this, probably even talked to the detectives about it. "I can meet you at The Market in about an hour, after I finish up. Thanks, by the way." He held up the report.

"No problem."

During my orientation, I'd learned that drivers filled out incident reports for everything from degraded road conditions to illegal dumping. Finding a dead body had to qualify as an incident.

Before I could say anything else, Chase Bradley poked his blond head inside the doorway. "Hey, Teejay. Got a minute?"

Clean cut and neatly dressed in a blue polo and dark slacks, Chase was the first college student I'd met with his own business cards, printed with his stock introduction line—"Chase, like the bank." When he looked my way, he quickly masked his expression, but not before I caught a flash of resentment. He'd applied for my job. I suspected he would have been good at it, too, after spending the last two summers fielding phone calls and handling dispatch.

I closed the office door and left them to it, lingering in the hallway for a moment before deciding to slink through the garage without saying good night. Out of the corner of my eye, I could see Teejay had drawn the blinds of the connecting window. Normally, I'd be curious about their conversation and feeling awkward about taking a job I wasn't entirely sure I wanted. But the news that Franklin had been murdered crowded everything else from my mind.

During the short drive home, I thought back to Wednesday evening. Teejay, Evan, Sam, and I had joined a convoy of Jeep drivers recruited to shuttle a crowd over Forest Service roads northwest of Sedona to Lee Ranch, a private inholding at the mouth of Lee Canyon. That night our passengers weren't vacationing families but a cross-section of Sedona's movers and shakers—city and county officials, the district ranger, nonprofit leaders, Chamber of Commerce members, and a local developer, Jack Lyman, who couldn't stop grinning at the prospect of riches headed his way.

The event was a kick-off celebration for a multipronged land exchange that would put a hundred-odd acres, ranched by two generations of the Lee family, into public ownership. The flip side of the trade was The Flats, a large parcel of US Forest Service land along the highway west of the city. The local newspaper called the trade a win-win-win. As a private inholding, the ranch blocked public access to Lee Canyon like a cork in a bottle. Once Lee Ranch was added to the forest, a gorgeous red rock canyon with significant historic and prehistoric value would become accessible to the public. Five acres of forest land along Highway 89A would be retained for a new ranger station and visitor center, while the rest of The Flats would transform into a golf resort to be annexed by the city as a source of tax revenue. The Lee Ranch trade neatly ticked off all the boxes, aiming to please preservationists, politicians, developers, and forest-loving locals.

That evening, while sunset painted the cliffs in shades of orange and gold, local VIPs had wandered among easels displaying charts and renderings, drinking champagne or Perrier out of red plastic cups. It was an odd sort of homecoming for me. Back in the day, my aunt Claire had been part of the Lees' social circle, but this was the first time I'd seen the ranch in over twenty years, and the golden glow made the outlying ramshackle buildings look like the movie backdrop they'd once been. The old ranch house was festooned in tiny white lights, and the swimming pool reflected a fat yellow moon rising above burnished cliffs.

After sunset, we'd shuttled the passengers—happy and flushed from goodwill, sparkling wine, June's high desert heat, or all of the above—over dusty Forest Service roads back to their waiting cars, leaving the Lees, their live-in caregiver, and a small catering staff. It was nearly nine when the last Jeep drove away.

I was still putting the timeline together as I pulled into my driveway and parked. Sometime later that moonlit night, Franklin had ended up five miles away in the box canyon, where he encountered his murderer. The next day passed without anyone noticing his absence. And then, this morning, I found him.

CHAPTER

2

CURIOUS TO HEAR how Teejay remembered the evening of the party, I showered quickly, swapping my shirt and cargo shorts for a blue cotton slip dress. I loosely braided my hair—dark red and wet from the shower—and headed out the doorway.

In the mid-1970s, my aunt had used her Hollywood earnings to buy a large lot on the edge of Soldier Wash. She designed the house herself, tucking it into the native piñons and junipers at the end of a looping gravel drive. When she died of cancer two years back, I'd inherited the small slump-block house and a 1962 Willys Jeep Wagon that'd somehow survived pack rats despite being parked for decades in my aunt's former horse barn. The horse barn's loft was now my home. I wasn't yet a teenager when Claire had converted the loft into a studio apartment for her friend and property manager, a gangly old cowboy named Henry Grisom. It was Henry who taught me how to drive the Willys when I was fifteen, a skill my taxi-hailing parents hadn't considered important.

Nearly twenty-five years later, I could still catch a whiff of his pipe smoke as I opened the wagon's door. The Willys had no air-conditioning. What it did have was a voracious appetite for oil, along with a balky shifter and a large steering wheel that made driving Blue Sky's Jeeps seem like child's play. Its tan paint was scratched and faded but without a speck of rust, and I owned it free and clear. Windows open, I rolled down Soldiers Pass Road, letting the warm breeze blow away the tendrils of dread that had crept over me since learning Franklin had been shot.

I drove to the back of the strip mall that hosted The Market, Sedona's natural foods store and unofficial community hub. Though the store had changed owners and locations many times through the years, it continued to draw several subsets of locals, from the health-conscious to the spiritually conscious, people who wouldn't blink at shelling out five bucks for a bottle of designer water, and those who were here for the free Wi-Fi. I parked near the loading docks and garbage bins, where the Willys' capricious reverse gear wouldn't embarrass me.

On my way around the building, I spotted a small figure huddled in a patch of shade—Franklin's ex-girlfriend. I often saw her pushing her banged-up old Schwinn along the sidewalk, though sometimes she'd stash it in the brush along the margins of West Sedona, where she could bum a cup of coffee at The Market or wash up in a gas station restroom. A few times I'd given her a lift to one of the churches where an unhoused person might find food and kindness.

Crazy Jane, locals called her, but I didn't know if Jane was her real name, or if some Yeats fan had saddled her with it. Like the Crazy Jane in the poems, she sometimes sounded wise (once she'd warned me to save seeds). Most of the time, however, her mutterings didn't make sense, and she scared the tourists. A few months back, I'd been an unwilling observer when Jane and Franklin had a rousing argument in the drugstore parking lot. I hadn't seen them together since.

My steps slowed. I didn't want to be the one to tell her about Franklin's death. She might react badly, or she might not react at all. But Jane, who probably knew Franklin better than anyone, deserved to get the news straight up instead of churned through Sedona's well-oiled gossip mill.

She stood as I approached, her eyes pale blue against her sun-weathered face. Teejay once told me she was a longtime local, but if she'd been around during the summers when I visited my aunt, I didn't remember her. Though her dark blond hair was streaked with gray, she wore it in pigtails, like a child. She was dressed in cutoffs, a faded purple T-shirt, and a pair of plastic flip-flops, with a worn blue daypack slung over her shoulders.

"I haven't seen him." Her voice wobbled with emotion.

Her words stopped me in my tracks. "Franklin?"

"He's gone. Found and lost." Her hands fidgeted with the straps of her pack. A faded tattoo peeped out from beneath one sleeve, and both arms were covered with long scratches. *Defensive wounds?*

Questions whirled through my head like a roulette wheel before rattling to a stop. "When did you see him last, Jane?"

"Here." She turned away, her gaze tracking a mammoth SUV with tinted windows, its occupants likely seeking an extra-large parking spot.

I tried to reel her back in. "At The Market? When?"

She glanced at me briefly, but her eyes were unfocused, her head shaking side to side. I inched closer, as though I were approaching a skittish horse. *Careful. Don't spook her.* "How long ago did you see Franklin?"

"The green man is looking for him. I have to tell him."

Her gaze slid away again. I pitched my voice even lower, angling sideways so I wasn't looking at her head-on. "Would you like some water or coffee? I'll get something for us, and then we can sit and talk here in the shade."

I waited for her reply, sharing her view across the rows of parked cars, watching as a white pickup entered the lot.

When I turned back, Jane was gone.

I wandered The Market's aisles, looking right and left for a glimpse of Jane's purple T-shirt. The store was crowded with after-work shoppers pushing carts and tourists grabbing snacks for sunset picnics. Thirty-odd years ago, a psychic had set Sedona's future in motion by identifying a handful of energy vortexes. Yet it was the town's *social* vortexes—The Market and the local post office—where gossip swirled and rumors emanated to all corners of Red Rock Country, from West Sedona to Uptown and south to the Village of Oak Creek. I tuned into the snippets of conversation as I passed. Apparently, the news about Franklin's death hadn't traveled this way. *Yet.*

Jane was nowhere to be found, so I settled for a yogurt smoothie from the juice bar. As I waited for my order, the middle-aged woman next to me complained at length to the barista about the deleterious effects of mercury retrograde on the cash register. Behind her, a pair of tourists fidgeted impatiently, rolling their eyes and lifting their phones to record the moment. I stepped out of camera range.

By the time I joined Teejay, he was already halfway through a burrito and a pint of local brew. He offered to buy me a beer too, but I lifted my smoothie cup. "Got mine."

He looked around at the mostly occupied tables and chairs. "Okay if we move outside?"

I nodded, thinking if Teejay wanted to curtail gossip about Franklin's death, he picked an odd place to meet. The Market was the closest thing Sedona had to a public square. Even with his black hair matted with sweat, his jeans and boots dusty, Teejay drew admiring glances from nearby customers, women and men alike. As he led the way to the shaded patio, weaving around the metal tables and chairs with his easy stride, it struck me again how much he resembled the ancient cliff dweller who kept intruding on my dreams.

Thanks to the persistent heat, the patio was only sparsely occupied. We chose a four-top and sat at right angles, where we could both take in the views. Because Arizona refused to follow the rest of the country into daylight savings time, golden hour arrived early. Late afternoon sun burnished the buff-colored cliffs on the eastern horizon and streaked across the familiar flat top of Airport Mesa. Halfway down the mesa, tiny figures swarmed over an orange-red saddle of sandstone, a vortex site that drew people like iron filings to a magnet every sunset.

Teejay leaned in so we wouldn't be overheard. "You smell like soap. Man, I could use a shower."

His gaze skimmed my face, and my fingers itched to cover my jawline, a reflexive gesture I've struggled to unlearn. More out of habit than anything else, I'd braided my damp hair to hang over one shoulder, the dark red waves mostly hiding the pale line etched from chin to ear. I'd known Teejay long enough to assume he'd noticed the scar, though he hadn't asked how it got there. Since I'd started working at Blue Sky, we'd shifted into a strictly professional mode.

Today's events had shaken that a bit, the shared experience drawing around us like a curtain. I swept it aside with an attempt at humor. "I practically live in the shower now. More than thirty percent humidity, and my swamp cooler is useless."

Teejay followed my cue. "Just wait till the *real* monsoon kicks in."

Monsoon jokes were standard fare. Years ago, the weather service had proclaimed June fifteenth the official annual start to Arizona's monsoon season. Mother Nature hadn't gotten the memo. We'd passed mid-June a week ago, yet the average dew point remained stubbornly below fifty. Evan started an office pool, worth a couple hundred dollars last time I checked, the entire kitty awarded to whoever came closest to guessing the date of the first measurable rain. Though the irony was lost to everyone but me, I'd put my money on my mother's birthday, July fifth. Teejay picked July fifteenth, which struck me as unduly pessimistic.

Despite my attempt at small talk, his gaze stayed focused on me. "You doing okay?" he asked.

"Fine. How about you?"

"First time I've pulled a broken body off a cliff that wasn't there by accident. And since it happened on our turf . . ." He shook his head, as if to erase the image.

"Why there? I mean, you must have thought about motive, or talked to the investigators about it."

He ignored my question for one of his own. "What made you look up today?"

I hesitated. No way was I going to tell him my attention was drawn by someone who didn't exist, an imaginary figure who kept appearing in my dreams and now, it seemed, when my eyes were wide open. "I thought I saw something move." True enough. "Maybe a raven or a vulture."

"Not a person?"

I shook my head, but he continued to watch me closely. My thoughts had been circling around this since I'd left Blue Sky's headquarters. "What was Franklin doing at the party in Lee Canyon? Did he get there in one of the Jeeps?"

My passengers had included Sedona's mayor and several Yavapai County commissioners. Franklin, who favored a battered army jacket paired with jeans or sometimes a rakishly tied sarong, would have stood out like a lump of clay among jewels.

Teejay's brow furrowed. "Maybe he hitched a ride with one of the rangers."

"Maybe." A contingent of uniformed Forest Service employees had been there to make sure tipsy guests didn't stumble into a rattlesnake or wander off with a potsherd or two.

"You could ask your buddy, Ryan Driscoll. He was there."

His voice was neutral, yet I felt my muscles tense. "I've known Ryan since I was six. His parents were part of the Lees' social circle, like my aunt. We went to barbecues at the ranch. While the adults smoked and drank, the kids swam in the pool or rode horses around the canyon."

"Nice."

"Yes. It was."

I focused on my smoothie, already watery from the lingering heat. I didn't know why I was feeling defensive, maybe because Teejay had made my childhood sound privileged. Maybe I felt defensive because it *was* privileged, something I'd recognized even then. With celebrity guests and movie people, the Lees had turned Sedona into a little Hollywood, at least for a couple of decades, until audiences for westerns dried up like tumbleweeds. My aunt, a prop artist and matte painter, had successfully transitioned from movies to fine art. Whittaker Lee, a stuntman and aspiring actor, hadn't been as lucky. When I was a kid, a ghost of glamour had still infused the ranch and its technicolor cliffs, but I'd been far more interested in climbing around the canyon's prehistoric Indian ruins, looking for arrowheads and potsherds.

Teejay's voice brought me back. "Driscoll was at the box canyon today, asking questions about our recent tours, who the guests were, what times we were there, that sort of thing."

"Ryan's the senior enforcement ranger. It may be the sheriff's investigation, but the box canyon is the Forest Service's jurisdiction."

"Yeah, everybody was there today—air rescue, the ropes team, detectives, scene techs . . ."

Teejay's gaze wandered to the sidewalk, where a pair of women who could've been Missy and Sarah's doppelgängers were photographing themselves next to a larger-than-life statue of Merlin. They were absorbed in their own conversation, but I lowered my voice and chose my words carefully.

"I saw Franklin talking to Barbara Lee that night. She didn't look happy."

"You ever see Barbara look happy?"

"Well, no, but . . ."

He shrugged. "Franklin probably crashed the party."

"Awkward," I agreed. "Especially since he liked to carry on about industrial tourism, resource exploitation, that sort of thing." He'd hold court here at The Market or at the brewery, another popular local hangout. Sedona's horde of young idealists seemed to regard the older man as a role model, buying him coffee or beer in exchange for his views. "Maybe he pissed someone off about the land trade."

Teejay drained his glass, leaned back. "How well did you know Franklin?"

"I met him once. Here. I was minding my own business when he sat down next to me and announced that all of us with red hair and green eyes were descended from Vikings." I left out the rest, the part where he'd reached over and lifted my hair away from my face, smirking as he said, *Do you think hiding the scar on your cheek will keep people from seeing the scars inside?*

If Franklin had wanted to shock me, he'd succeeded. I'd frozen like a startled doe. Now, I couldn't even remember how I extricated myself from the encounter, but I'd avoided Franklin like the flu ever since. Belatedly, I realized the obvious: The combination of seduction and menace had reminded me of the predator who'd ended my career and nearly my life. I felt Teejay's gaze and pushed the thought away.

"Franklin liked to ruffle feathers. But he's not the wild-eyed revolutionary most people take him for, and generally being an asshole wasn't reason enough to get him killed." Teejay crossed his arms. "Let's wait and see what the sheriff's office says before we point fingers."

"I'm not accusing anyone." I straightened in my seat, surprised we were arguing. An inner voice warned me to be careful: Teejay was essentially my supervisor at a job I needed more than wanted. The words tumbled out anyway. "Maybe I'm just uneasy at seeing another piece of my childhood changing. You've lived here, what, fifteen years now? Long enough to remember the days when locals outnumbered tourists. Do you really think the trade is a good thing?"

"Almost twenty." He rubbed his forehead and sighed heavily. "As far as land exchanges go, it could be worse. Adding Lee Canyon to the national forest could be good for Blue Sky's business."

I didn't have a reason to be disappointed in Teejay, but I was. "You sound like the Chamber of Commerce."

"You sound like Franklin." He switched to a softer tone. "Most of our passengers haven't been off a paved road before. Some haven't looked twice at a bird or a sunset. Letting people see and feel what's at stake is worth a thousand lectures about conservation."

I swallowed my arguments. We were silent for a few moments, watching the last band of golden light lift from the top of Munds Mountain. Finally, Teejay spoke. "Franklin's death might not have anything to do with the party or the land trade."

"Right." I kept my expression neutral, but my reporter's instinct was hard to beat down. Money was always a popular motive for murder, and for the right people, the land trade promised to be a financial windfall. Was it really that far-fetched to consider the possibility someone might find Frank-lin's rabble-rousing threatening? Someone like Jack Lyman, the life of the Lee Ranch party?

I shifted. The metal chair was hard and uncomfortable through the thin cotton of my sundress, and questions continued to poke at me, like an invisible cactus spine under the skin. Maybe that was why I wanted to poke back. I was about to ask Teejay if he'd seen Franklin leave the party when red and blue lights strobed the twilight, stealing my attention.

Two city patrol cars rolled into place on opposite ends of the lot as a small figure zigzagged through the parked cars toward the building's rear. A white SUV, striped with the Yavapai County Sheriff's brown-and-gold logo, pulled in to block that route. Before the runner could change direction, a Forest Service pickup swerved into the lot, tires complaining. Doors slammed, and several uniformed officers converged on the would-be fugitive. I recognized her pigtails and purple T-shirt.

"That's Jane." I pushed back my chair and stood. "They're going to arrest her."

"Hold up." Teejay reached out, his fingers lightly circling my wrist. "Think twice before you jump into the middle of it."

I pulled my hand free, spinning to look at him, surprised at the hot sting of tears pressing against my eyelids. The flashing lights had triggered me. Overreacting was a common PTSD symptom. I released a slow breath, then inhaled, but my voice wobbled anyway. "I saw her earlier. I don't think she knows about Franklin yet. They might misread the situation."

"All right. We'll walk over, see what's going on. Okay?"

His gaze was steady, and I calmed. I took another deep breath. "Okay."

As we wound through a gathering crowd kept in check by a handful of city cops, I picked out a familiar broad-shouldered figure and headed that way. Like me, Ryan Driscoll had moved back to Sedona after years away. Now he was one of the two law enforcement officers or LEOs assigned to the forest's Red Rock District, a jurisdiction that covered over a half million acres. In his khaki uniform shirt and straw Stetson, he looked even taller, a duty belt worn low on his narrow hips.

His smile of recognition was tempered by the palm he held outward. "Far enough, Boston. This isn't your beat."

I halted. Ryan started calling me that the summer I turned six, when my parents deemed me old enough to fly across the country by myself to stay with my father's sister. During the school year that followed, I'd worked hard to lose the accent, but when I showed up at Aunt Claire's the next summer, the name had already stuck. I'd forgiven Ryan for the nickname—he was, after all, the first boy I'd ever kissed. But the jab about my "beat" stung a bit, since he knew more than anyone what sent me running back to Sedona.

"What's going on, Driscoll?" Teejay asked.

Ryan's gray eyes narrowed as he took in the pair of us. He straightened to his full height. "We're detaining a person of interest in Franklin Johnson's murder."

Johnson. It was the first I'd heard Franklin's last name, and I wondered what else I didn't know about him.

"Are they charging her?" I watched, powerless to help, while Jane struggled with the deputies attempting to restrain her. I wasn't aware my muscles had tensed in empathy until Teejay brushed my wrist, a touch so light it might have been accidental.

"No, they just want to talk to her, but she's a flight risk." Ryan's tone was softer now, minus the formal edge he'd taken with Teejay.

Unexpectedly, Jane sat down hard on the asphalt, pulling one of the deputies off balance. Ryan rushed over to help, leaving me standing with Teejay at the front of the circle of onlookers. Jane looked toward me and wailed, a sound of wounded betrayal.

"No—" My protest was lost to the lump in my throat as two deputies marched her to the waiting SUV. Ryan glanced my way, then spoke quietly to the men as they loaded Jane into the back seat. He watched, hands on hips, as the white SUV turned west onto the highway, the city police cars falling in behind.

Ryan turned back to the curious crowd. "Go home, folks."

I recognized a few faces and overheard some grumblings about storm troopers and excessive force, but most wandered back to their cars and grocery carts. I waited, Teejay at my side, as Ryan approached.

"You too, Boston. They're taking her to the county jail for questioning. If they don't charge her, she'll be out later tonight. I'll drive her back to Sedona myself."

I searched Ryan's face before he turned to shoo away lingering bystanders. As a Forest Service LEO, his duties ran more to issuing parking citations or reporting resource damage; he might not have reason to be as cynical as I was about witness rights during a criminal investigation. But at least Ryan had some experience dealing with Sedona's chronically homeless campers. I had a gnawing suspicion Jane might need all the help she could get.

"Where'd you park?" Teejay's question interrupted my thoughts.

"Around back."

"I'll walk with you."

His solicitude was unnecessary, and I was about to say so, then decided to seize this chance to continue our discussion.

As we passed the spot where I'd talked to Jane earlier, I asked, "Did you see Franklin leave the party?"

Teejay sighed loudly. "I'm not going to tell you to let this go—"

"But?"

"—but let the law look after Franklin."

"Of course." My words were flat. We'd reached the wagon, and I unlocked the door and turned to face him. A solitary light beamed down on the loading dock, leaving his face shadowed.

"I'm serious, Delilah. The box canyon is off limits until the sheriff clears it. That means no sunrise tour tomorrow." I heard more than saw the smile teasing the corners of his mouth. "Sleep in while you can because when you start leading tours, you'll wonder where the days go."

With his reminder that my probationary period wouldn't last forever, I mumbled a good night and climbed into the driver's seat. For a few weeks now, I'd been content to study training materials, attend workshops, and shadow the more experienced drivers on their routes, marking time until I had to decide: Was Sedona my home, or was it only another place to hide?

CHAPTER

3

SLEEP WAS A struggle I often lost. When dreams took me back to the city, I'd mentally retrace my steps through Sedona's backcountry until the rhythm of the trail lulled me. Sometimes I'd get up and meditate or sit outside on the landing, watching the shadows in Soldier Wash until I convinced myself that here, among the rocks and junipers, the darkness held nothing to fear.

Now, Franklin's death challenged that notion. I couldn't convince myself Jane was guilty, and that meant his killer was still out there. *Somewhere.*

By itself, that thought might have kept me awake, my reporter's curiosity picking at it like a puzzle box to be teased open. But the patrol cars' flashing lights had triggered something deeper, and my mind was darting from past to present, reliving late-night callouts, remembering the atmosphere of violence, thinking of *him*, the monster in all my nightmares.

I forced myself to focus on the suspicious *tick-tick-tick* coming from the loft's rooftop swamp cooler, a boxy contraption that used evaporated moisture to cool the air. It was simple but efficient—until the weather turned humid. I hoped the old beast would survive until September, when summer would start to release its grip. Next, I constructed shopping lists in my head, for the hardware store, for groceries. But as I drifted toward half sleep, my mental discipline relaxed, and my thoughts returned to the party at Lee Ranch, watching Franklin arguing with Barbara, handing her something. Or taking something? I tried to sharpen the memory.

Then a single, stray, seemingly mundane detail popped into my mind and stayed there—the plastic bag I spotted this morning, ensnared by catclaw bushes at the mouth of the box canyon.

Part of Blue Sky's agreement with the Forest Service was to keep the box canyon litter-free; I'd meant to take the bag when I left with Missy and Sarah. Between the shock of finding Franklin dead and my haste to whisk our guests away from the scene, I'd forgotten. The bag was from a local store, the red logo and bold script a common sight. But I'd logged enough hours at crime scenes to understand anything nearby was potential evidence—a tossed cigarette butt might reveal DNA, a fast-food wrapper could lead to security camera footage, and so on.

It was pure speculation to think the bag was the same one I saw Franklin holding out to Barbara. My imagination— overactive and untrustworthy since that awful night three years ago—might have filled in the details. Mostly awake now, I swung my legs out of bed and sat up.

I gripped my phone, hesitating. It wasn't yet midnight. *Should I crawl back in bed, try to sleep? Or call it in?* I knew the number for the ranger station by heart, but I also knew no one would answer this time of night. Emergency calls went to the fire dispatcher's office—and they had bigger problems now that fire season was underway. Better to call the sheriff's office—their techs had probably picked the bag up earlier.

Probably.

I came up with a plan, not necessarily a good one, but it was late, and I wasn't thinking clearly. I'd drive out there and check, since I knew exactly where to look. If the bag was still there, I'd leave it alone, drive to a spot where there was cell service, and make the call to the county.

Then, conscience clear, I could return home and go to sleep at last.

*   *   *

My aunt's house was dark when I backed the Willys out of the barn. My renters were a young couple who'd relocated from Silicon Valley to Chandler when their company pulled up stakes. Cash-flush after selling their Bay Area house, they'd offered to buy Claire's as a weekend getaway. I'd persuaded them to rent instead, while I stayed in the loft apartment and tried to figure out my situation. But their Red Rock Fever had cooled, and they hadn't visited in almost a month. I tried not to think longingly of the air-conditioning as I rolled past, gravel crunching under the tires.

Even on a Friday night, Sedona shuttered early, and I cruised through all green lights without needing to downshift. Outside of town, it was darker, and I scanned the highway's shoulder for the Forest Service road that led toward the canyon-cut backcountry below Bear Mountain. When I was a kid, the turnoff was marked by a pair of gnarled trees, a juniper and a piñon, standing on either side of 89A like sentinels. Locals had called the route Two Trees Road—until ADOT widened the highway to four lanes and cut down the trees early one morning while Sedona slept.

I slowed to make the turn onto what was now officially Red Canyon Road, though a few droll quipsters still referred to it as No Trees Road. After a couple of miles, the gravel surface changed to dirt. I turned the wheel to avoid a rock,

and the wagon's headlights glinted off a pair of eyes shining
from the roadside, probably a coyote, though one night last
fall, on my way home from a sunset hike, I'd seen a mountain
lion leap across the road in a single bound, illuminated so
briefly by the headlights that it seemed almost a dream. For
me, this was the true magic of Sedona—not vortexes or UFO
sightings or chakra activations, but the numinous encounters
with the natural world and the wave of sheer awe that swept
over me nearly every time I entered the landscape.

A couple of miles more and I turned again, onto an even
narrower dirt road. Here, far from the heat island of pavement and buildings, the air was cooler against my bare arms.
Though I could smell the red rock dust pluming behind me,
I kept the windows rolled down and felt the knots between
my shoulder blades unravel.

The gibbous moon hung low in the sky, an eerie pump-
kin color, hazed by a wildfire burning in the Kaibab National
Forest, a few miles south of Grand Canyon. In June, fire danger was a given: thunderstorms produced lightning, but rain
evaporated before reaching the parched ground. After our
wet winter, the fuel load was heavy in northern Arizona's for-
ests and grasslands, and initially fire managers had allowed
the Antelope Fire to burn to reduce undergrowth. But this
afternoon, stronger winds had whipped up the flames, and
firefighters were now hustling to keep it from reaching the
national park.

Even smoke-dimmed, the moon cast enough light for me
to distinguish the layers of the cliffs below Bear Mountain
and the Mogollon Rim. My grasp of geology might be limited, but I knew enough to feel humbled as I neared the stony
forms shaped by eons of seas and deserts. Faced with that
immensity of time, chasing after a stray bit of trash seemed
a fool's errand.

I parked along the road a few yards from the two-track approach to the box canyon. The Willys would have cleared the track's high crown, but I didn't fancy backing the wagon around in the dark. My phone was zipped into a pocket of my cargo shorts, and I left it there as I headed down the track, confident moonlight was enough to keep me from tripping over a rock . . . or a rattlesnake.

When I got to the cottonwoods, I realized my mistake. The moon was still behind the cliffs, and the dry tank was a black void, the undergrowth of catclaw, saltbush, and manzanita indistinguishable from the canyon's deep shadow. Crime scene tape fluttered from branches and brush as cooler air flowed down canyon, the landscape's nightly exhalation. I'd hoped the white plastic would stand out like a ghost, but I didn't see the bag where I thought it should be. I scanned left and right, reluctant to impair my night vision with the light from my phone.

I waited, hoping my eyes would continue to adjust, feeling my skin tighten at the sound of the wind stirring the cottonwood leaves. I was just starting to reach for my phone to illuminate the deeper shadows when I heard footsteps.

Freezing like a cottontail, counting on the darkness to hide me, I stared past the tank to the two-track.

"Hey, Boston. A little late for a hike, even for you."

I relaxed at the familiar voice and started walking out of the shadows to meet him. "Hey yourself, Ryan. A little late to be working—even for you."

We were close enough now that I could see he was still in uniform but hatless, his badge glinting in the moonlight. Like me, Ryan had walked up the track without a flashlight, though he probably had one clipped onto his bulky duty belt.

"Long day, that's for sure. The sheriff's investigators finished this afternoon, but I'll have another look tomorrow before releasing the scene." He nodded toward the canyon, the trail still blocked by the strands of tape. "Thought I'd drive around the loop on my way back toward town, check for illegal campfires. We went from Stage One to Stage Two when the Antelope Fire flared up."

"So I heard." Stage One prohibited campfires and generators outside developed campgrounds. Stage Two was even more restrictive. Though fire bans were typical for June, the hasty implementation indicated how serious this year's risk was.

"I spotted the Willys. That vehicle is a hazard, you know."

I laughed at the ongoing joke. Every time I ran into Ryan around town, he tried to convince me to sell him the old wagon. The Willys was awkward, ugly even, with its dull tan paint and desert pinstriping. Still, it reminded me of happier times, when Claire and I would crowd onto the blanket-covered bench seat, and Henry would drive us into the backcountry, scraping through mesquite bosques and bouncing along cattle trails for a picnic or hike. Those memories outweighed the inconvenience of worn gears and manual steering.

"I didn't hear your truck."

"Trick of the wind, maybe. I pulled over as soon as my headlights picked out the Willys. Thought you might need help."

I nodded. He looked like a hero—tall, blond, and broad-shouldered—though I figured his riding to my rescue wasn't as likely as trying to bust me over sneaking into a restricted area. Good thing I'd decided to stay on the right side of the tape.

Thinking of minor transgressions reminded me of all the summer nights I'd crept out my bedroom window to join a pack of local kids, usually at the Posse Grounds, Sedona's oldest town park. Later, as soon as a couple of the boys in our crowd earned their driver's licenses, we'd head for Oak Creek or drive up Airport Mesa to see the town's lights sprinkled below. Those places still existed, but the magic was lost in the crowds of tourists.

As though he'd read my mind, Ryan said, "I miss those summers when we were kids. What was it your aunt used to call us?"

"The Wild Jackaloons."

He chuckled. "That's right. Remember that night we piled in the back of Steve's pickup to steal apples by the creek? Old man Cooley started shooting, probably thought we were deer, and put a pellet through the windshield." His smile flashed white.

"Dan Cooley saved us from green-apple bellyaches."

"Yeah, I guess."

The teasing note turned speculative, and my breath caught. I knew Ryan was thinking about a different night; during the summer I turned fifteen and he'd talked me into riding my bike to our favorite swimming hole. I'd expected to join the rest of the Jackaloons, only to find him waiting there alone. That fall, I returned to school feeling like I'd grown up.

But the following year, Ryan was sneaking off to skinny-dip with Cooley's granddaughter, and I went back east early. Neither Ryan nor I had ever married, and I'd occasionally wondered what might have happened if that hadn't turned out to be the last summer I lived with Claire. I was glad the dim light hid the heat rising in my cheeks, and I tried to reestablish a lighthearted tone.

"You were such a delinquent. Naturally, you'd become a cop."

"Yeah, well." He shrugged, his grin lopsided. "I've been working for the Forest Service fifteen years now, over half that in law enforcement. Since my dreams of being a cowboy were shattered, it was the next best thing."

I knew Ryan well enough to understand he was only partly joking. His great-grandparents had homesteaded along lower Oak Creek, downstream from what would become Red Rock State Park. In the late nineties, his parents had moved to Texas after selling the family ranch. Now its ridgelines were scattered with McMansions elbowing for views of Cathedral Rock.

It wasn't just idle curiosity that had me asking, "Who bought your family's ranch and developed it? Was Jack Lyman around back then?"

Ryan shook his head. "Nope, and I gotta wonder where you're going with this, Boston. Lyman showed up the year after the economy crashed, snapped up a lot of property for cents on the dollar, and rode out the downturn."

"And now his name is plastered all over town—work trucks, real estate signs, a commercial plaza. When the land trade goes through, he'll multiply his investment. A lucky man."

"Jack Lyman makes his own luck. Been to Cooley's orchard since you got back?"

"Orchard?" The word was as bitter in my mouth as the memory of green apples. "It's a subdivision."

"Exactly. After Lyman's crew prepped the site, the city inspector noticed a couple of building envelopes had expanded into the floodplain. Lyman switched back to the original plans, but the inspector started checking up more often, slowing down permits. So Jack offered the guy a job."

"Make a friend of your enemy. Clever." My thoughts raced. Everyone in Sedona knew Franklin on sight. But did Jack Lyman know him as a friend . . . or an enemy? I was about to ask, but Ryan wasn't finished with his story.

"It didn't end there. A couple of weeks after the inspector burned his bridges with the city and went to work for Lyman Construction, Jack called him into his office and fired him."

He paused to make sure he had my attention. "My point is, if you're going after Jack Lyman, don't let him see you coming."

"Noted." Was I really that obvious? Or was Ryan already thinking along similar lines and wanting me to butt out? That would be the wise move, but I was as stubborn as the Willys' second gear.

"Lyman isn't the only one who benefits from the land exchange," he pointed out.

"Of course not. The Lees get cash, and the Forest Service gets a fancy new visitor center."

"Whitt's been throwing good money after bad for years now, so yeah, he needs this deal. As for the Forest Service . . ." He scoffed. "The agreement everyone toasted Wednesday night is nonbinding. We've got months of surveys and NEPA studies to get through. One little thing could sink the deal. A funding shortfall. A forgotten easement. An endangered wildflower."

"Franklin getting shot?"

After a few beats of silence, he asked, "Teejay tell you that?"

I kept my mouth closed, knowing how important the Forest Service permit was to Blue Sky, reluctant to turn up the heat on the simmering antagonism between the two men.

Ryan rubbed a hand through his hair. "I don't mean to sound callous. I'm just saying if there's a way to screw this up, the Forest Circus will find it."

"You're in favor of the trade?" Teejay, and now Ryan. Was I the only one who harbored doubts? I was about to venture my opinion when he reached out and settled his hand over my upper arm.

"Listen."

I stilled. The warmth of his fingers made me realize how the air had cooled around us, how late it must be getting. I slowed my breath and strained to hear something besides my heart pounding in my ears.

His voice was low. "Pack rats probably."

"There's a big midden on the other side of the tank. I hope they're not launching a foray to the Willys."

He released my arm, breaking the spell, and we started walking back toward the road in unspoken agreement. The pack rat nest in the no-go patch of prickly pear and cat-claw reminded me why I was there. I was about to tell Ryan about the plastic bag when he broached the subject himself.

"You didn't answer my question before. What brings you here in the middle of the night? I hope I'm wrong, but it seems like you're looking for trouble."

"Not really." I hedged. "I saw a grocery bag stuck in the brush this morning, and I wanted to make sure the investigators picked it up. Probably nothing, but . . ."

"Yeah, that bag could've been blowing around for weeks. But if that's what's keeping you awake, you can rest easy. I watched an evidence tech collect it and label it."

My relief was tinged with a flush of guilt. I'd have crossed the scene tape to search if Ryan hadn't arrived. Something occurred to me. "You said you'd drive Jane back, but she's not with you, is she?"

"Nope." He kept his attention on the uneven track.

"Tell me the sheriff didn't charge her. What do they think—she biked fifteen miles in the dark to shoot Franklin, then rode back into town?"

He sighed and turned to face me. The moonlight was brighter here, but his expression was unreadable. "They haven't charged her. Not yet, anyway. But since she's a flight risk, they can hold her for a day or two, see if she settles down and starts talking sense."

"She may be"—I searched for the right word—"*eccentric*, but she's harmless, you know that."

"Yeah. Thing is, family members, girlfriends, boy-friends . . . they're always the most likely suspects. The sheriff's just playing the odds, and anyway, she might know something."

He started down the two-track again, and I followed. This would be the time to tell him about the conversation I had with Jane earlier, but something stopped me. Maybe I considered Ryan more of a compliance officer than a detective. Or maybe I was having second thoughts about getting involved. Then I flashed on Jane spending the weekend in a jail cell and felt a chill I couldn't attribute to the down-canyon breeze.

"Will you keep me posted?"

He took his time answering. "Sure. As long as you promise not to stalk Jack Lyman." When I didn't respond, he stopped and turned. "I'm going out on a limb for you here. Tell me you won't mess up another investigation."

The chill deepened, freezing my voice.

"I'm sorry. That was a cheap shot. What happened to you back east. If you ever want to talk . . ." He trailed off. "I meant to say that at Claire's service, but it was the wrong time."

It still felt like the wrong time. Ryan's wry humor and easy jokes were comforting reminders of a shared childhood. The possibility of introducing a new level to our relatively uncomplicated friendship made me uneasy, and it occurred to me now I'd been keeping him at arm's length for just that reason. Still, he was my oldest friend in Sedona, and I couldn't shut him out completely. I sighed. "I wish I'd come back sooner, spent more time with Claire before she died."

"You were here when it mattered most. She didn't die alone."

I'd heard those words so many times from Claire's friends and acquaintances that they'd become more cliché than comfort. I started to thank him anyway, but my throat closed. I nodded, then continued down my side of the track, the hump of brittle grass between us as we walked. Gradually, the lump in my throat eased, and I forced myself to reengage.

"I've been putting off going through her things. Too final, I guess. Instead, I go back to the places she took me to. Trails, rock formations, ruins. The ones I can still find, anyway."

"I can help you find the ruins. I still check on 'em, make sure they're okay. Next to handing out parking tickets, it's my job."

I heard the smile in his voice. Part of me—the twelve-year-old girl who'd never had a best friend—wanted to tell him everything. But the adult me—the one whose errors in judgment ended in disaster—felt uncomfortable confiding in anyone. Among a long list of PTSD symptoms, my therapist had warned me of "impaired social interactions." But which part of me was off? The sharer or the shielder?

Searching for a middle ground, I landed on something Ryan could help with. I needed to know if the images that kept surfacing in my mind—the rock art spiral, the cliff dweller—were half-forgotten memories . . . or *something* I couldn't explain. Years had passed since I'd explored Sedona's canyons with my aunt. A memory lapse was only natural. Though I wanted to trust Ryan, he'd never known the real reason my parents sent me to live with my aunt every summer, so I was careful with my words.

"Claire once took me to some rock art that was really special. I keep hoping I'll run into it in a side canyon somewhere."

"You don't recall the location?"

"Since the attack, my memories have been—" I made a wobbling gesture with my hand.

"Damn." We'd reached the road where our vehicles were parked, but he made no move to leave. "Sorry to hear that, Boston. The rock art—tell me what you remember."

"A spiral petroglyph. At least that's how I picture it, pecked into the rock."

"That helps pin down—"

"Which side of the creek," we finished, almost in unison.

"Because on this side of the creek, most of the rock art is painted on—pictographs—and on the other side, most is pecked or incised," I said, pleased I remembered this detail from the Blue Sky training materials.

"You've been brushing up on local archaeology."

"Enough to keep from making a total fool of myself once I start leading tours." Now that the subject had shifted into safer territory, I could feel my armor soften.

"Can't have you spinning tall tales to entertain the sightseers. Come with me on some hikes, and I'll give you the official Driscoll curriculum, untainted by touristy BS. Maybe we'll find the place you're thinking of."

"Okay, I'd like that." I tried to call up an image of the spiral. "The glyph I'm thinking of was large, maybe with some people or animals around it."

"Anthropomorphs and zoomorphs."

"*Gesundheit.*"

He laughed. "If you want to dazzle them, Boston, you've gotta learn the lingo."

"Something you picked up working for the Forest Service?"

"Long before that, purely self-taught. Welcome to my alma mater, the school of hard rocks." He swept his arms wide before resting his hands on his hips. I chuckled, but the gesture drew my attention to the gun snapped into his duty belt, reminding me a man had died little more than a stone's throw from where we were standing. And here we were, flirting. My amusement vanished.

Were we flirting? Ryan and I had been thick as thieves until that summer when things got awkward. Now I felt awkward again, but for entirely different reasons.

"I guess I'll see you around." I turned to get in the wagon.

"Stay out of trouble, Boston." His words held a lilt of amusement, but I heard a warning. I put the Willys in gear and rolled away. When I glanced at the mirror, he was still standing on the dirt road watching me, bathed in the red glow of the taillights.

* * *

After my midnight misadventure, I found the loft unbearably hot and stuffy. I tossed the wagon's keys onto the kitchen counter, then started opening windows, my mind buzzing from the conversation with Ryan. Sleep was out of the question.

My stomach grumbled, a reminder I'd barely eaten all day. I made a sandwich and ate standing over the sink, too hungry to take the time to sit at the small table I more often used as a desk. Cramped as it was, the loft was larger than my studio apartment in Boston, a bolt-hole used only when I wasn't glued to my computer in the clamorous newsroom or out chasing a story. The last big story, the one I hoped would get me a Pulitzer or at least a promotion, led me instead into a hell of my own making. I'd corresponded with a killer, and then—certain I understood him better than anyone, including the detectives on the case—I'd built my own trap and stepped inside.

I swallowed hard. Was I about to make a similar mistake?

Three years ago, after I'd been stitched up and sent home, I'd dutifully attended weeks of employer-provided therapy. My editor stood by me, even when details about how I'd interfered with a case began to leak. But then came the memory lapses, the errors, the erosion of skills that had once been second nature to me. When the merger happened, I'd been in the first wave of layoffs. There was no way to prove wrongful termination, even if I'd wanted to—losing my job was only a minor penance for my survivor's guilt.

I was newly unemployed, drinking hard, and wallowing in self-pity when my father called, his voice cracking as he broke the news about Claire. He didn't have to explain he'd chosen to preserve my mother's fragile hold on normalcy over helping his sister, and it wouldn't have mattered. I started looking for a plane ticket to Arizona moments after we ended the call.

When I got to Sedona, Claire's cancer was stage four, and she spent most of her days in bed. I spent mine taking care of the house and yard, both long neglected, and trying to coax her to eat, as though the right food might stave off her inexorable decline. When she died less than six months later, I began the grieving process all over again. At first, I'd blamed my father for waiting too long to make that phone call, but then I acknowledged I'd been too wrapped up in my own problems to realize how seriously ill Claire had become.

Survivor's guilt, round two: a knife blade that bit as sharply as the first, even though this time the scars were only figurative. While my aunt was slowly dying, I was beginning to return to life. Caring for her helped me find my center again, and as I explored Sedona's canyons and cliffs, I began to reclaim the sense of innocence I'd lost since my childhood.

I'd been a terrible therapy client. But somehow I'd come away with enough self-awareness to understand now that Jane was my mirror, showing me what I could have become if my father hadn't called. One stupid choice and life can go sideways, like a car sliding out around a curve. A series of stupid choices and it's almost impossible to get control of the wheel again.

Was I projecting? *Probably.*

Was I deluding myself to think I could keep her from crashing? *Maybe.*

Or maybe the lump in my stomach was from scarfing down a peanut butter sandwich too quickly, and the urge to help Jane was me trying to prove I was still capable of teasing out the truth of a story and writing it in a way people would understand.

I drank a large glass of water and thought about the last time I'd seen Franklin alive. During the party at Lee Ranch, officials and business owners had mixed with members of the Sierra Club and other local nonprofits, all smiling (some wider than others) as they toasted the signed agreement to initiate the exchange.

I'd found the conviviality among usual foes a bit forced, though the alcohol had helped smooth the edges. Behind the champagne toasts, a different drama had been bubbling:

Someone gave Franklin a ride to Lee Ranch.

Franklin and Barbara Lee had argued.

Later that same night, Franklin was killed.

Teejay might not see a connection, but I did. All three parties—the Forest Service, the Lees, and Jack Lyman—stood to gain from the land exchange. But the developer had the most to gain—or lose, if Franklin raised hell about the trade.

Ryan hinted Whittaker needed cash. If the Lees didn't pay for the booze and Jeep shuttles, who did? After years of budget cutbacks, I doubted the Forest Service had a slush fund for sparkling wine and hors d'oeuvres. The nonprofits might have drummed up donations from their members or from local businesses. But a mental snapshot of Jack Lyman, the poster boy for largesse, flashed in my mind.

Roughly half of the guests, mostly the enviros, had lined up for the ranger-guided walks to the canyon's ruins and pictograph panel. The rest, including Lyman, clustered by the pool, where caterers filled glasses and passed trays of appetizers as people chatted and laughed. Along with the other drivers, I was hanging out closer to the bunkhouse where we'd parked, near enough to watch Lyman hold court.

"Razzle-dazzle in the desert," another Jeep driver commented behind me, his tone a combination of awe and sarcasm. I wasn't sure if he was referring to the party or to Jack Lyman himself, flashing smiles and shaking hands as he directed people toward the poster-sized renderings of the proposed development.

The Lee Ranch of my memories had always combined rustic adventure with glamour—riding and exploring the surrounding canyon, then cooling off in the pool while grilled steaks and Coppertone lotion scented the air. At the center of it, Whittaker Lee had been larger than life, an honest-to-goodness cowboy and movie star, full of stories and booming laughter. On Wednesday night, however, Whittaker had lingered like a silent shadow on the fringes of the party. When I saw him, my gaze automatically searched the crowd of happy faces until I found Barbara. Dressed in a long white caftan, her chandelier earrings glittering, she was every bit as elegant and beautiful as I remembered but, like her husband, keeping to the sidelines.

She was by herself in the shade of the carport when I saw Franklin approach her. Their brief but intense exchange ended with him reaching into the pocket of his faded army jacket to offer her a small parcel, loosely wrapped in a grocery store bag. Even thirty feet away, I recognized the white plastic, the red logo. She'd shooed him off before scanning the crowd. She was about to glance in my direction when Evan grabbed my elbow and steered me toward the food. When I looked over again, both Barbara and Franklin were gone.

Before it was time to start shuttling guests back to town, I'd taken a few minutes to look over the proposed build-out for The Flats. The site plans had been enlarged, mounted on foamcore, and stamped with the Lyman Land Company logo. That's when it hit me. The trade-off for preserving Lee Ranch would be to transform the western approach to Sedona from an open piñon-juniper woodland into an ocean of rooftops and parking lots. The renderings re-envisioned The Flats, where the old town dump used to be, as an epicenter of lodging, shopping, and recreation more stylish and much larger than Uptown, putting most locals literally and figuratively in the middle. The plan was more Scottsdale—the ritzy resort town east of Phoenix—than Sedona. The new western gateway would be great for business . . . and I hated it. Yet no one else seemed to share my opinion.

Except, perhaps, for Franklin.

When he had an audience, Franklin liked to peddle conspiracy theories or knock conformist lifestyles. I'd pegged him as just another Sedona eccentric, more talk than walk, but I'd been biased against him ever since he'd diagnosed the scars on my psyche. Was Franklin's preachy back-to-nature spiel grounded in genuine environmentalism? He spent hours at the library reading or using the public computers. Maybe he'd stumbled onto something that might throw a wrench in the Lee Ranch trade.

I drained my glass of water and glanced at the small table across from the kitchen, where the *Sedona News* rested on top of a pile of bills. The biweekly "*Snooze*" would have landed on people's driveways a couple of hours before we discovered Franklin's body. I wanted to learn more before the rumor mill cranked into gear or the newspaper ran the official story.

This issue's front page included a puff piece on the proposed western gateway, with a sidebar about Jack

Lyman—army vet, successful businessman, and proud doggy daddy to a smiling yellow Labrador. I shoved aside the paper to reach for my laptop, taking it outside to the landing at the top of the stairs, where I'd squeezed in a bistro table and chairs.

I started with a quick dive into federal land exchanges, confirming Ryan's comments about the lengthy process. A proposed trade in Minnesota failed because it impacted threatened species. In Colorado, another ground to a halt due to lawsuits claiming the US Forest Service had favored developers over local conservationists. But I found no whispers of objection to the Lee Ranch trade, which would preserve the homestead and surrounding canyon as open space. Even if Jack Lyman had sweetened the deal or pressured the Lees, why would Franklin care?

More to the point, why would someone want to silence him?

Though Johnson was a common surname, I had skills and a secret weapon. When the paper where I'd climbed the ranks from fact-checker to investigative reporter was gobbled up by a corporate newsgroup, I'd lost my job. But somewhere in the shuffle, the IT department's regular purge of invalid passwords had faltered, and I still had access to the archives, databases, and search tools I'd used as a journalist.

My laptop glowed bluish-white in the dark. My neighbors slept peacefully, their houses mostly hidden behind trees and brush. I was poised to reenter the rabbit hole, but why? To champion Jane? To find justice for Franklin? To take a stand against the forces eating away at the Sedona I remembered? I was done tilting at windmills. But driving a Jeep full of tourists around the red rocks didn't feel like a career move, and digging for information was something I was good at.

The cursor winked at me, and I typed in my password.

CHAPTER

4

THE MOON CLIMBED overhead as I worked. Mosquitoes, encouraged by the heavy pre-monsoonal air, buzzed lazily around my face. I got up for a glass of water and a sage bundle Teejay had given me, meant for loftier purposes than warding off insects. The fragrant smoke wafted while I settled in for round two.

Greater Sedona straddled two counties, with the Village of Oak Creek and West Sedona in Yavapai County, Uptown in Coconino. Franklin's name was buried in a Coconino County Sheriff's report, published in the Flagstaff newspaper a dozen years earlier.

"Gotcha."

A black-and-white photo showed a younger Franklin, barely recognizable minus the wild red locks and beard, here trimmed into a neat Van Dyke that revealed a pointed chin and lips shaped like a Cupid's bow. Per the report, "A man was questioned for loitering at an Oak Creek Canyon campground. He gave a false name, but one of the deputies recognized him as Frank Johnson, an occasional overnight guest at the county jail."

I smiled at the touch of humor. I'd cut my journalistic teeth on council meetings and crime reports, welcoming even the smallest opportunity for levity. The brief paragraph concluded, "Additional names appeared on prescription bottles in Mr. Johnson's possession, and he was arrested for suspected fraud."

A mournful cry broke through my focus, like a lost kitten calling for its mother. The Gambel's quail who made their home in the surrounding brush were starting to rouse, and I looked up from the screen to note a faint glow on the eastern horizon. I stood and stretched, torn between coffee and the opportunity to grab a couple of hours of sleep before it was time to report to Blue Sky's headquarters. Prescription fraud wasn't necessarily a gateway to murder, yet the lightness in my chest told me I was on the right track. Add in the cool, fresh morning air, and I was out the moment my head hit the pillow.

"Good morning, Del! Ready for another day in paradise?"

Gina Lambert, petite and perky, was always first behind the reception counter, handing out assignments and inspirational tropes. What she didn't know was paradise had a snake, and Franklin's death was more than an inconvenient accident. Since I couldn't enlighten her, I smiled at her relentless cheerfulness.

She tipped her cap of chestnut-colored curls toward her computer screen. Her red dress and carefully applied lipstick confirmed today was Saturday. Every week without fail, Gina met her girlfriends for lunch, all enthusiastic members of the Red Rockin' Grannies, a local dance troupe for women of a certain age.

"You're riding with Teejay again today," she reminded me. "The Schnebly Hill tour at ten."

"How many?"

"Four. Weekenders from Tucson. Mom and dad plus two kids, ten and twelve. The age of questions—better brush up."

Her smile was teasing. "Teejay says you'll take the lead on this one."

My satisfaction at a successful night of online digging faded. Twelve-year-olds were brutal, not only sharp with questions but also quick to sense weak spots.

"Then at one, there's the wedding party. Eight people."

"Wait—the bride that wanted a Native American blessing before her big day tomorrow? Has the sheriff cleared the box canyon already?"

Gina groaned. "I'll check. If the canyon is still off limits, I'll offer the bride some alternatives." She scrolled through the scheduling spreadsheet—a complex grid of tours, times, and drivers—while muttering under her breath.

She glanced up. "Teejay's in a mood today. He started the coffee and disappeared. Don't say anything until I get this sorted."

"Okay. Run it by Evan. He'd know if a switch would create any issues with the Forest Service."

"Two steps ahead of you." She reached toward the phone, then paused to pull an envelope from the shelf below the counter. "Hold on, Del—you forgot to pick up your check last night."

I'd been in such a hurry to get away I'd forgotten the number one reason I was here—a paycheck. Gina apologized, explaining payroll lagged a week. "The next check will be better. You'll get the bonus for shuttling guests to Lee Ranch."

"Jack Lyman ponied up for that, right?" I was only guessing, but Gina nodded as she reached for the phone again, eager to get on with her calls. I persisted. "Why *us*? Pink Jeep Tours could have handled that crowd without even half their fleet."

She shrugged, already dialing. "He's Teejay's landlord."

I sent her a quick smile to cover my surprise and waved the envelope in silent thanks. The coffee smelled fresh, so I stopped in the hallway long enough to fill up. I'd learned no one messed with Teejay's scratched and dented steel mug, waiting by the coffee maker, but after mine went astray a few times, I'd used bright pink nail polish to embellish it with flowers. Problem solved.

I took both mugs into the garage, where I found him peering under the hood of one of the company's older Wranglers. Arnulfo had mad skills, but Teejay knew his way around an engine compartment and insisted drivers do their own pre-tour inspections. His frown was ominous—the Jeep was the one assigned to me as soon as my training period ended.

"Morning, Delilah." He straightened and wiped his hands on an oil-spotted rag before reaching for his coffee. His gaze met mine, searching. "You ready to lead this one? We're picking them up at Juniper Lodge." He named a resort a few miles up Oak Creek Canyon.

"Ready." I aimed for convincing, then ruined it with my next words. "If you test my geology on the way." Though driving one of our customized Wranglers was easy compared to the Willys, maintaining a relaxed but informative narration while bouncing over ruts and rocks was more challenging than it looked, *and* I'd be doing so under Teejay's watchful gaze. Asking him about Jack Lyman would have to wait.

We ran the gauntlet of souvenir shops and galleries that lined both sides of the highway through Uptown. On a busy weekend, jaywalkers and drivers creeping along in search of parking spots could create backups for miles, and timing was crucial for our excursion up Schnebly Hill Road, a route shared by a half dozen outfitters. The goal was to space out tours so guests felt like they were discovering the old wagon route for themselves, not eating dust in a parade of Jeeps.

Lucky for us, the morning traffic was sparse, and within minutes we were entering the leafy shade of Oak Creek Canyon. Here, the air was still cool, and I was glad for the long-sleeved shirt I'd buttoned up over my tank top. The geology refresher turned out to be unnecessary. The Batemans had spent the previous afternoon in Slide Rock State Park, so I let ten-year-old Maddy and her older brother Paul teach me about spring-fed Oak Creek and its fault-formed canyon. They talked over each other as they described sliding down the creek's smooth and slippery sandstone chute.

I turned up the intercom when we left pavement and started grinding up Schnebly Hill Road, a tooth-rattling, spine-jarring route. I split my concentration between avoiding rocks and projecting my voice over the engine noise. At twelve, Paul was already a budding scientist, peppering me with questions that went way beyond the usual "Why are the rocks red?" For his benefit, I slowed to point out the different geological layers that dominated Mitten Ridge, a spectrum from dark brownish red to coppery orange.

Everyone scrambled out to explore the Cowpies, a cluster of aptly but unfortunately named sandstone mounds that overlooked Bear Wallow Canyon before it yawned open to a wide view of Airport Mesa. From this distance, the planes looked like toys, and the kids watched, transfixed, as one circled to land on the short runway.

Paul and Maddy zigzagged in front as we crossed the rolling slickrock, slowing to funnel onto the trail that led back to the Jeep. A bright green collared lizard darted in front of us on its hind legs, like a mini-velociraptor, and Maddy squealed with delight. Belatedly, I realized I'd been neglecting the parents, but when I turned to include them, I saw they were holding hands and grinning like two people who'd won the lottery.

"Great kids." I meant it.

"We like them." The deadpan delivery signaled a well-used quip. Chris and Lori Bateman elbowed each other and giggled. I caught up with the kids, leaving Teejay to follow the parents at a discreet distance.

Being outdoors seemed to thaw him—the hard lines of his jaw had unclenched, and he hiked with his usual loose-limbed stride. I tried to match his ease, to focus on the moment, not worry about my job performance or brood over Franklin.

After our return to the lodge, I helped Lori Bateman check under the back seats for the flotsam that often got left behind in the wake of our younger passengers. She slipped a generous tip into my hand. I offered half to Teejay, but he shook his head.

"Not bad." He counted the bills before handing them back to me. "You can buy lunch."

We stopped at Indian Gardens to order from the deli, carrying our sandwiches through to the patio out back. Only three other tables were occupied, a mix of locals and out-of-towners enjoying the food and tree-shaded setting. I savored the quiet and refused to wolf down my sandwich the way Teejay was doing.

"So," he said between bites. "What's the verdict?"

"You're asking me?" I'd expected a more formal job review, and the question caught me off guard.

"After yesterday, I wasn't sure you'd stick it out, but it seemed like you had fun this morning. Ready to solo next week?"

"Yes." I cleared my throat, hoping that would explain why my response sounded weak. "My throat's a little sore from talking so much, but yeah, it was fun."

"Good. This weekend's your last chance to shadow the other drivers. As of Monday, you're officially done with probation. Arnulfo should have your Jeep ready by then."

He offered me the small bowl of extra lemon slices he'd requested and nodded toward my nail polish-embellished mug. The barista, wearing a DON'T BE TRASHY T-shirt, had refilled it with a mint-Tulsi blend and a wink.

"Squeeze some into your tea. It helps. And don't look so worried. Yesterday spooked me too, but happy guests like the Batemans are more likely than dead bodies."

"Have you heard anything from the sheriff's office?"

He frowned as he chewed his last bite of sandwich. Gauging his reaction, I continued, "This may not be important, but . . . I noticed a plastic bag stuck in the bushes near the parking area yesterday. Ryan said he saw a scene tech pick it up."

An expression—guilt? embarrassment?—chased briefly across his features before he nodded. "I meant to grab it after the tour yesterday. You talked to Driscoll this morning?"

To head off any impression I was in the habit of chatting with Ryan over breakfast, I started to launch into a humorous recap of my late-night journey, then clamped my lips shut. The radio squawked loudly, drawing the attention of the other customers. Teejay scooped it up and stepped a few feet away before responding, keeping his voice low. He returned almost immediately.

"That was Chase-like-the-bank." He drained his iced tea and gestured toward my sandwich. "Wrap that up for later. We need to go."

*   *   *

As I threaded through Uptown traffic, Teejay filled me in. The sheriff's office still hadn't cleared the box canyon, and the bride-to-be wasn't answering her phone. After leaving numerous voice mails and texts, Gina had gone for lunch with her girlfriends. In the meantime, per Chase's panicked dispatch, Bridezilla had landed.

Harmony shot Teejay a rescue-me look the moment we entered the office to a chaotic scrum of voices and bodies. I looked for the bride, mascara trailing down her cheeks in a goth-goes-circus look, sobbing about her wedding weekend being ruined. Phones rang unanswered in the background while a trio of young women dressed in pink T-shirts tried to soothe their friend, and two large guys who looked like brothers folded themselves onto the padded bench, muttering darkly about missing lunch. Harmony was doing her best to live up to her name, and Chase—the coward—had escaped under an ear-covering headset to handle dispatch.

Adding to the confusion, the wedding party had driven directly from the rehearsal with three additional last-minute guests in tow, a pair of gray-faced ushers who'd clearly over-done the previous night's stag party, and the groom's mother, who was sneaking wide-eyed glances at her son. He leaned forward, elbows on the reception counter, hands supporting his head, comforted by the only calm person in the crowd, presumably the best man.

I dashed behind the counter and grabbed a ringing phone, leaving Teejay to take charge. I hadn't been cross-trained for reservations, but I'd picked up a few standard responses through osmosis.

By the time I hung up, Gina had returned from lunch, using what I thought of as her Mom Voice to reestablish order. Teejay had already deployed his uncanny charm to convince the bride—who gazed through teary eyelashes at him like she might consider abandoning the wedding alto-gether, if only he suggested it—that an alternate destination would be even more awesome and spiritual than her original choice.

Harmony and I watched the well-oiled teamwork. She hid a whisper behind her be-ringed fingers. "Not an auspicious start to a pre-wedding blessing. I wish I'd worn my tourmaline today."

Her other hand touched her sternum. Reaching for the missing pendant? Energy tapping? I wasn't sure which remedy might apply here, and I didn't ask. As a kid, I'd been more into horses than healing crystals, and Sedona's reinvention as a New Age mecca was just one more reason the town now seemed unfamiliar to me.

Within minutes, Gina had consulted the scheduling grid, assigned a second Jeep to the expanded group, instructed Chase to track down Sam, and persuaded Evan, on his way back from a creekside tour, to skip lunch. I left my half sandwich in the refrigerator for Evan, and Teejay left the decision to me: I could ride along with the wedding party, or I could shadow Megan Ramirez on her history tour for the afternoon.

Bridezilla, or a retired couple from Red Wing, Minnesota, who were interested in Sedona's apple-growing past?

"I'll go with Megan."

"Chicken." Still grinning, he turned back to the group crowding the front office, handing out reusable water bottles and Blue Sky bandannas to appease them while they awaited Evan's arrival.

I slipped out to the garage, the door chiming softly behind me. Arnulfo had gone for lunch, but Megan was checking over her ride, a clean garage towel draped over her shoulders to protect her crisp white blouse. I felt rumpled and windblown in comparison, the back of my tank top damp from the Jeep's stiff upholstery.

"Still crazy in there?" she asked.

"Yep. Thought you might need help with the grandparents."

Megan's smile was conspiratorial. Since her history tour traveled on pavement and carried fewer passengers, she usually drove the blissfully air-conditioned Grand Cherokee everyone called Gramps, not only for its elderly status but also because it was grandfathered in when the Forest Service decreed outfitters use open touring Jeeps.

After the mayhem in the office, settling into the contoured leather felt like a guilty pleasure. Once we were rolling down Cook's Hill, Megan's laughter bubbled over. "If anyone can tame Bridezilla, it'll be Teejay."

"He does have a way with the ladies." I kept the observation neutral.

"Yep. Harmony told me last week a woman from Florida called in for a private 'Teejay tour.' Or sometimes they'll ask for *that guy* on the brochure." She shot me a quick sideways glance before entering the double roundabout intersection everyone still referred to as the Y. "But he's not just another pretty face. He gets people right away. If I had half his skills, I'd double my tips and transfer to NAU."

With her encyclopedic knowledge of local history, it was easy to forget Megan hadn't yet completed her courses at the JC in Clarkdale, which she'd decided was more affordable than starting at Flagstaff's Northern Arizona University. "What would you study?"

"Anthropology. I'd like to be a curator at the Heard in Phoenix. Or"—her expression turned dreamy—"the museum in Mexico City."

"What do your parents think?" I was rooting for Megan's dreams, but her roots in the Verde Valley ran deep. Her mother's forebears included one of Sedona's early lawmen.

Her father's helped establish the first irrigation ditches along lower Oak Creek. A few months back, his mother—Megan's beloved *abuelita*—had been diagnosed with breast cancer, a further blow to her ambitions. Megan and her cousins had rallied to keep the family business running smoothly.

"They want me and my sister to take over the nursery. Anyway, right now I'm getting paid to be outdoors, and that's good, right?"

"Definitely." Being on the land all day, seeing the natural world change from hour to hour and season to season, was my idea of therapy. I thought about being Megan's age again as we passed among monuments whose names I'd learned as a girl—Twin Buttes, the Nuns, Bell Rock. If I could rewind my life, would I still choose journalism? I'd loved the hunt, fleshing out a story from bits of information or interviews— until my drive to go deeper and bigger had turned me into the hunted. Sedona was my safe space, filled with happy childhood memories, bright blue skies, and red rocks shaped like teapots and elephants.

Did I really want to spoil that by looking for Franklin's killer? A chill washed over me, and I reached to turn down the AC.

"Here we are." Megan pulled into the circular drive of a fauxdobe B-and-B. I popped inside to fetch the Warners, retired farmers who were treating their grandson to an Arizona adventure for his seventh birthday. Tow-headed and freckled, he bounced in the back seat between them, as Megan struggled to capture his attention with anecdotes about filming locations and historic sites.

John Wayne and Jimmy Stewart didn't impress him, but a surprise cameo at Sedona's history museum saved the day. We were strolling through the museum's heritage apple orchard when a rattlesnake sent us a warning, the dry buzz like windblown leaves. Megan calmly called a snake wrangler, while I wrangled the grandson, eager to get a rattlesnake selfie with the new phone his grandparents had given him.

Megan ushered us inside, and we safely watched from a window as the snake expert, dressed like a cowboy, corralled the five-foot-long diamondback and used a grabber tool to whisk him away. As soon as the coast was clear, I excused myself. During my first day on the job, Megan had offered blunt sisterly advice: "Drink plenty of water and never pass up a bathroom."

On my return from the museum's facilities, an elderly volunteer docent mistook me for a visitor, and I didn't correct her. Dressed in a pink pantsuit, bent nearly double with age, she led me to a poster for *Angel and the Badman*, a 1947 John Wayne flick. My attention strayed to a small photo almost lost in a collage of movie memorabilia.

"Is this from *Howling at the Moon*?" I asked when she paused for a breath.

"Why, yes." She peered up at me over half-frame readers. "It was a television comedy series about a disgraced newspaperman who moved his family out west. Not very successful, I'm afraid."

A disgraced journalist, ha-ha. The irony wasn't lost on me, but something else had captured my attention. "The girl leaning against the wagon wheel . . . could that be Barbara Lee?"

"Barbie Bellamy then. She played the role of the middle daughter."

"Wow. She looks so young."

"Actually," her voice dropped to a whisper, "she was twenty-one. They made her look younger, like Ingrid Bergman in *Joan of Arc*." She leaned closer, and I caught a whiff of lavender. "Barbara was expecting in this photo. What a scandal. Everyone in America believed she was fifteen and, since Whittaker was playing the role of her father, well . . ." She clicked her tongue against her teeth. "Biggest fuss since Joan Crawford came here to film *Johnny Guitar.*"

Before she could switch to juicy tales about Crawford and her costars, I asked about the Lees' marriage. My chatty guide clammed up. I followed her gaze to the doorway; the grandson was waving his arms to get my attention. I thanked her and rejoined Megan's tour, though my thoughts kept circling back to the Lees.

* * *

Despite the sizzling mid-June heat, the reservation lines buzzed all afternoon. More than once, Gina commented how my probation couldn't end soon enough. I hoped my smiles and nods hid how much I'd rather be snooping around Lee Ranch. Evan and Teejay still hadn't returned from Bridezilla's blessing ceremony, so Gina slotted me into another short scenic tour with Megan, and after that, Sam's golden-hour hike up Doe Mesa.

Initially, I'd been less than impressed by Sam Curry, a six-year senior from San Diego State with a head of golden-brown curls and a done-it-all demeanor. He affected pitch-black sunglasses and faux-distressed safari clothes with—inexplicably—a diver's knife strapped around his right calf. But his too-cool-for-school attitude melted on the trail, and he was great with kids.

I acted as sweep, lagging far enough behind to evade conversation, yet close enough to keep an eye on our guests, a boisterous family of six from Phoenix. The dad, dressed in a white Diamondbacks T-shirt, joked they'd driven to Sedona to cool off.

The older kids rolled their eyes, but one of the youngsters pronounced solemnly, "It's a dry heat," winning a smile from his father.

Their voices faded as I fell back, distracted by the seductive fragrance of cliffrose. I found the vanilla-flowered shrubs on a rocky slope and paused for a breather. The long night was finally catching up to me. After four tours, I had no more pleasantries or fascinating interpretive tidbits to offer. Information swirled through my brain but short-circuited before the words could reach my mouth.

I topped out onto the mesa, slightly winded and perspiring freely. This was *so not* a dry heat. Thunderclouds poked above the eastern horizon, tantalizing but distant. A faint brown haze hovered to the north, the Antelope Fire creeping closer to the Grand Canyon. The monsoon was taking its time riding to the rescue.

I spotted our group a few yards away, Sam kneeling in the red dirt beside a sprawling prickly pear cactus piled with grayed sticks. The impressive pack rat nest had inspired an impromptu lesson about the ways plants and animals adapted to the desert. I swatted at no-see-ums and willed Sam to start walking again so I could generate enough breeze to lose the bugs and cool down.

At last we began working our way around the edge of the mesa. The homes and businesses of West Sedona looked like scattered thumbtacks among the piñon-juniper woodland below Capitol Butte, the red forms of Bell Rock and Courthouse peeking up in the distance. Our guests stopped frequently for awed exclamations. First-time visitor or longtime local, anyone could catch Red Rock Fever—struck senseless by the breath-stealing scenery, the spiritual vibe, the artsy shops. The side effect was an unbalanced economy, with the cost of living exceeding service job wages. Not for the first time, I considered myself fortunate to have Claire's property and a decent employer in a place where people like Franklin and Jane foundered—literally—on the rocks.

Screeches and laughter interrupted my thoughts. White-throated swifts whistled past us like miniature dive bombers as they pursued insects. Sam urged the group onward. Now Bear Mountain dominated the views, a 6,500-foot peak eroded from the red and gold cliffs along the edge of the Colorado Plateau. While Sam identified the canyons hidden in the mountainside's shadowed folds, I tried seeing the landscape through Franklin's eyes. One long sandstone fin stretched toward Doe Mesa like a bony come-hither finger. Somewhere beyond it, the box canyon lay hidden in a maze of stone.

Franklin knew better than to head into a waterless landscape in June, when midday temperatures often passed the century mark. Miles of rugged dirt roads separated Lee Ranch from the box canyon. What—or who—had lured him to such a remote spot?

Lost in thought, I didn't realize how far I'd fallen behind until I heard Sam shout at me from a couple of switchbacks below. I hurried to catch up. By the time we waved goodbye to our tired and happy guests, the temperature had dropped to a tolerable ninety degrees, and the faraway cloudbank had dissolved into pale blue sky. I grabbed a garage towel to help Sam clean our ride, but he took it from my hand and shook his head.

I was impressed by the unexpected kindness, until he said, "You look like I dragged you behind the Jeep. I don't want Teejay on my ass for breaking the rookie. He's been on a tear since—"

"Yeah, I know." My thoughts returned to the day before, the shock of finding Franklin's body. *Teejay.* I still hadn't found a spare moment to ask him about Jack Lyman. I tossed Sam the towel, and he caught it one-handed. "Thanks, Sam. I'll be inside if you change your mind."

On my way down the hall, I peeked into Steve's empty office, then turned and nearly crashed into Gina. We laughed over who was most startled, and she explained she'd stayed behind to restore order after the whirlwind day.

"Is Teejay around?"

Gina shook her head, jangling her favorite gold hoop earrings, which she put back on every evening when she'd finished answering phones. "He took his Jeep to the car wash to get it detailed. The ushers couldn't hold it together on the bumpy roads. Too much partying last night." She wrinkled her nose. "At least they were both in the same vehicle."

"Ew. Glad I missed it."

"Better hope they do a thorough job because he wants you with him on the sunrise tour tomorrow."

The tour started at seven, but we started earlier to ready the Jeep for our guests. "The sheriff released the canyon?"

"As of twenty minutes ago. They wanted that Forest Service cop to check it again. He stopped by to give us the all-clear."

"Ryan Driscoll?"

"Tall? Blond? Looks like a young Patrick Swayze?" She arched a meticulously penciled eyebrow. "I do appreciate a man in uniform. He said he'd wait for you out back. Lucky girl."

"We're old friends," I called after her as she left. Which didn't explain why I spent several minutes in the bathroom splashing cool water over my face and fluffing my hat hair.

CHAPTER

5

B Y THE TIME I walked around to the employee parking area, Gina's white Lexus was gone. Ryan leaned against the Willys, six-feet-something and seemingly impervious to the heat, his khaki epaulet shirt crisp, his regulation straw Stetson shading his gray eyes. He straightened as I approached, removing the hat and smoothing a hand over his hair. A few blond waves resisted, making him less authoritative. I thought of Gina's swoon and couldn't help smiling.

"Hey, Boston. I came by to let you all know the canyon is cleared for tours."

"Our office manager told me. She was dazzled and surprised by the in-person visit. We don't normally get this level of attention from the ranger district."

He put on his best aw-shucks smile. "Seems like a nice lady."

"Gina's a pistol. She's the boss of us all, signs our checks and keeps the business end of things running smoothly."

"While Steve Nicholson is off surfing in Hawaii."

"Kiteboarding."

"Whatever." He waved a hand dismissively. "He's over forty. Time to grow up and move on. We used to call him

Nichol-head for a reason. Gets the family business handed to him, and he couldn't care less."

I bit back a reply, not for Steve's sake, but because at thirty-nine, I wasn't sure what grown-up meant either.

Ryan wasn't finished. "Most of the old gang left for bigger towns and better jobs. You probably heard my sisters stayed in Texas with my folks."

I nodded. Ryan's comment explained why I didn't see old friends whenever I picked up my mail at the post office. "How about Sarah Simms? Or her brother Pete?"

"Now *that's* a juicy tale. Pete became a pastor. Sister Sarah moved to Vegas, started working as a call girl, living proof preachers can't save 'em all. But I always hoped you'd find your way back."

Deep dimples bracketed his smile, a flutter in my midsection reminding me I'd found it irresistible at fifteen. I changed the subject.

"Any news about Jane? They'll have to charge her or release her soon."

"Maybe. There's some back-and-forth between the sheriff's office and the magistrate. They're hoping to make her a ward of the state, straighten her out enough to answer questions." He rubbed the back of his head. "She's indoors, three meals a day, might not be such a bad thing."

"Can I see her?"

Surprise crossed his face. "Family only. Detectives are trying to track them down." His gaze sharpened. "You think she'd talk to you?"

I was still reluctant to tell Ryan about the encounter I'd had with Jane outside The Market, at least not until I worked out what her ramblings meant, if anything. "She might. I've given her a ride now and then, but I can't say we've ever had a real conversation. She loses the thread. You know."

"Yeah, I do." He shook his head. "Don't get your hopes up. She's got all the signs of meth use, and her cognitive issues might be permanent."

My heart sank. Even if Jane were freed from jail, she might never be free from the consequences of her choices. Then I remembered the scratches on her arms. From a struggle? Or from meth-induced hallucinations? I thought about the crime report I'd found last night. It was a leap from forging prescriptions to selling street drugs, but in twelve years, anything could happen. Everyone assumed Franklin had been Jane's boyfriend, but maybe he was her dealer.

"Franklin and Jane were campers—you must have had previous encounters with them. Do you think he was selling drugs?"

Ryan sighed. "We do sweeps with other agencies, but our priority is looking for campfires, not drugs. It's a tinderbox out there. We keep an eye on the larger encampments, follow up on complaints about trash buildup or disorderly behavior. If Franklin hid a meth lab somewhere on the forest, I'd sure like to find it."

"Did you talk to him that night at the party?"

He shrugged. "The archaeologist had us standing around to keep an eye on the ruins and rock art. Didn't even realize Franklin was there until Teejay told the sheriff's investigators."

"The detectives don't know how Franklin got to the ranch?"

"Maybe you should ask Teejay about that."

"He said to ask you. I was near the end of the pack, and Franklin wasn't in any of the Jeeps ahead of me. Maybe he cadged a ride from one of the forest rangers."

"Help him crash Jack Lyman's party? Not a chance."

I told him I'd seen Franklin arguing with Barbara. "It looked like he was trying to pass her something."

He cocked an eyebrow. "Drugs?"

"I don't know." I was already sorry I brought it up. "Do you think I should call the sheriff, offer to make a statement?"

"You could, but there's no time like the present. Step into my office." He nodded toward his pickup, a white F-150 emblazoned with the USFS shield, parked a few feet from the Willys. When I hesitated, he walked over and opened the passenger door. "I'm not trying to pull your leg, Boston. It's a multiagency investigation."

I stepped up to the passenger seat. The truck was a few years old but spotless, except for the ubiquitous red dust coating the dash and center console. A pump shotgun was racked in the window behind the seats. The side windows were down, but Ryan turned on the AC anyway, and a blast of funky humidity hit me in the face before the blowing air started to cool. He turned his phone on to record the time and date.

Stripped down to bare facts, the moment between Barbara and Franklin seemed smaller, the coincidence of the bag even more tenuous. Ryan's expression didn't reveal the slightest hint of skepticism, yet I started to doubt myself. Yesterday I'd seen an eight-hundred-year-old cliff dweller. How could I trust my own eyes? Yet I didn't speak up when Ryan declared that he would type the report and send it that night.

"You talk to anyone about this? Teejay?"

"No." I felt my muscles tense. "He warned us not to say anything that might fuel gossip."

"Is that right?"

His tone held an edge, and I wondered, not for the first time, why he and Teejay were snarly around each other, like a pair of circling coyotes. Ryan and his coworkers kept tabs on our permit compliance, and that made our friendship awkward. Or had I gotten it the wrong way around? Maybe my friendship with one of the Forest Service's law enforcement officers was the reason Teejay had hired me.

"If we're done—" I began, at the same time as Ryan reached to turn down the AC, his hand brushing my bare knee.

"Doing anything tonight?"

The words dropped into the sudden quiet and stopped me as I reached for the door handle. I blinked to fight back an eye roll. *Did men never get how much we hate that question?* But maybe I was flattering myself, and my efforts to keep him at arm's length weren't only unnecessary but also hindering our long friendship.

"Yes," I said at last, my voice firmer than my resolve. "Crashing. I'm beat."

"Come on—it's the weekend. We could drive to the airport vista. Walk a bit, leave the crowds behind, catch the sunset."

I couldn't help smiling at his persistence. "My Saturday nights are like everyone else's Wednesdays. Now that the box canyon is open again, I need to roll out at dark-thirty tomorrow. Can I take a rain check?"

"I'd say yes, but the monsoon'll be late this year." His dimples flashed again, but his gray eyes were serious. "I hope you won't keep me waiting that long."

A spark of electricity went through me. Alarm or attraction? I did the only wise thing and retreated, bidding Ryan good night and stepping from the confines of the cab before I could change my mind.

As I got into the Willys, I spotted Teejay driving up Airport Road, Jeep gleaming from the wash and detailing. Evan wasn't far behind, which meant I'd be unlikely to have a chance to probe Teejay about Jack Lyman—his landlord and my likeliest suspect. No doubt the guys would relish regaling me with tales of Bridezilla's blessing ceremony, but then Tee-jay might ask why Ryan was hanging around to talk to me, a question I wasn't quite sure how to answer.

By the time I backed the Willys out and circled the build-ing, Ryan's white truck was already heading up the mesa, and the Jeeps were rolling into the garage. I pasted on a cheer-ful smile and waved as I passed the open bay, feeling Teejay and Evan's stares on the back of my neck as I turned toward home.

*   *   *

Slow to wake, I blinked at the light streaming into the loft. Sunday's predawn glow already had a yellow cast, which meant I'd overslept. Anxiety propelled me out of bed, and I hobbled around the loft pulling on shorts and the first clean shirt I encountered. I coiled the messy braid I'd slept in and crammed on my wide-brimmed hat to keep it in place.

No time to investigate why my alarm hadn't sounded—probably user error. I shoved the phone in the pocket of my cargo shorts and grabbed an apple on the way out. My heart raced as I drove down Soldiers Pass Road, and not only because I was late. Today I'd be returning to the box canyon in the light of day, facing the cliff where Franklin died.

When I pulled behind the building to park, I saw Teejay scraping something from the rear of one of the Jeeps. As I approached, he gestured toward the rest of our small fleet, all sporting oval black-and-white bumper stickers that read "Don't PHX Sedona."

Someone's idea of a joke? Immediately, I thought of the land trade, then Sam. Joke or not, the hard set of Teejay's jaw told me he was unamused. I knelt to help remove the sticky residue, but he shook his head. "We need to roll. Evan can work on the rest when he gets in."

His hat shaded his eyes, but his expression was tight, the famous charm nowhere to be seen. On the plus side, he'd filled my travel mug with coffee, and it was waiting for me in the Jeep.

"You drive." He tossed me the keys.

His attention stayed on the road as I drove through Uptown, deserted at this early hour. Thanks to the caffeine easing into my bloodstream and the soothing green canopy of leaves as we made our way up Oak Creek Canyon, my anxiety about the box canyon started to fade. I wanted to ask how he felt about returning to the scene of Franklin's death, but a sideways glance had me thinking better of it.

A group of four men waited outside their rented cabin along Oak Creek—father, grandfather, and two thirty-something sons, here for a weekend of fishing and hiking. Mindful of the fire restrictions, Teejay saged them in the gravel driveway. The older men elbowed each other and joked, Grandpa grumbling about turning into a crystal cruncher. The younger of the two sons flushed, and I gathered he'd organized the outing.

The sage bundle's pungent scent faded as we made our way west. The sky was already bright, the sun's rays gilding the top of the dome-shaped peak that presided over West Sedona, adding a convincing touch to its official name— Capitol Butte. A few old-timers still referred to it as Grayback, and newer residents liked to call it Thunder Mountain, which had a romantic cachet despite a debatable attribution to Walt Disney.

Because of the early hour, Teejay kept the intercom off and sat with the men in the back, engaging with them about the passing scenery in a way that was more conversation than rehearsed spiel. Though I couldn't distinguish his words over the sound of the engine, I knew he usually spent this part of the drive introducing Sedona's backcountry, describing how the network of canyons had provided humans with food and shelter for thousands of years, from paleolithic hunters to the Yavapai who'd hidden here when the US Army forcibly removed the tribe in 1875.

The men's voices hushed when I stopped and turned off the engine to allow a small squadron of javelinas—a half-dozen adults and three piglings—to cross Boynton Pass Road into the mixture of juniper and grasslands below Bear Mountain. Morning light spilled down the mountainside and turned the parched grasses into a foamy pale gold. Famously nearsighted, the collared peccaries seemed unaware of our presence. So long as we stayed quiet, they wouldn't scatter.

All four men leaned out the side of the Jeep, cameras and phones tracking the animals weaving their way around saltbush and soaptree yucca. Teejay's breath stirred the loose strands of my hair as he leaned forward to whisper in my ear, "Good thing we're not in a canoe."

I chuckled quietly, feeling the residual tension leave my shoulders at last. The javelinas disappeared behind a rotund one-seed juniper, and the men settled back in their seats. We traveled the remaining miles to the box canyon in companionable silence.

I parked next to the earthen tank. The crime scene tape had vanished. Teejay led the way into the canyon, and I brought up the rear, surreptitiously munching my breakfast apple, slowing to examine the sandy trail. Wind had erased signs of Friday's evidence-recovery efforts, and the only tracks besides our own were the lace-like ribbons left by insects and birds.

Cliffs rose around us protectively as we neared the heart of the box canyon. The canyon walls still blocked the sun's rays, and the stone radiated the night's coolness. I tucked the apple core into a pocket. Ahead of me, the men spoke in soft rumbles as they admired the layers of orangey reds and tans, streaked with dark tapestries of desert varnish.

The trail ended in a garden of stone, scattered pieces from a giant's game. One blockish hoodoo looked like an elephant's head and trunk; another rose from the canyon floor like a giant stone mushroom. Both were social media stars. The usual challenge was getting our photo-snapping guests to look outside the frame and take in the microcosm hidden within the canyon's embrace: the prickly tangles of catclaw and fairy duster, the resinous scent of piñon and juniper, the dry rustles of lizards and birds. On cue, a canyon wren's descending flutelike call echoed off the stone walls, and the men fell silent again.

After the last note faded, Teejay began reading from the Navajo Blessingway. This time, there were no mutterings about woo-woo stuff, and even the grumbling grandfather listened attentively as we gathered to sit among the scattered rocks.

"In beauty I walk . . ."

Teejay's warm baritone transported me back to the morning in early spring when he'd first brought me here. Moisture from winter rains still lingered in the air, and the manzanita had been jeweled with tiny pink-and-white blooms. We'd continued toward the canyon's back wall, crunching over the scree at the base of the cliffs and scraping past a brushy oasis growing beneath a seep. I pulled aside a branch and froze. A five-foot-long snakelike pictograph, white against the red sandstone, "crawled" from a vertical seam toward a crumbling masonry granary tucked into the alcove beyond.

The magical sight reminded me of exploring the canyons when I was a kid, and emotions rolled through me in waves—the thrill of discovery, the ache of Claire's absence, the eerie sense that if I followed the snake, I'd slip through time. Then Teejay broke the spell, drawing my attention to a sizable mound of blackened earth and fire-cracked rock—an agave roasting pit, likely used by Yavapai families who'd found refuge here long after the granary's builders had left. He pointed out the smoke-stained cliffs, the scattered charcoal pictographs, and my storm of emotions settled into the worry I'd say or do something that might reveal too much, or that might give him the impression our friendly hike was something more. I knew I was still a mess—the moment of déjà vu proved it.

My fears were unfounded. The outing had been an audition for the job offer that came a few weeks later. Now that Teejay was my boss, the boundaries were clear, and that day seemed as long ago as the canyon's ancient past, screened from prying eyes by the undergrowth, present but unacknowledged.

"In old age wandering on a trail of beauty, living again, may I walk. My words will be beautiful." After closing the prayer with a wren-like melody on his cedar flute, Teejay directed the men to spend a few minutes in quiet contemplation.

I sat on a coffee-table-sized slab of Coconino sandstone, broken from the cliffs so long ago that wind and weather had softened its edges. *Time*—millions of years to lay down each thickness of tidal flats, sand dunes, and seafloor, all recorded in stone. Could the canyon walls also absorb human events and emotions? Not a trace remained of the intense activity two days ago, yet the atmosphere felt changed, as though something in the canyon's rich warp and weft had been torn.

Can Teejay feel it too?

He sat on a chunk of limestone a few feet away, his lashes dark against his tanned skin, his face as calm as a Buddha's.

He held one hand at his heart, the other on the stone in a gesture of connection.

Embarrassed I was staring, I shut my eyes and exhaled slowly, trying to focus, but Franklin's last moments flashed through my mind. Why *here*? The narrow trail ended where we were sitting, about a half mile from the tank. On the rare occasions when Teejay led guests to the alcove at the back of the canyon, he varied the approach to avoid wearing down a distinct path. Even an experienced hiker might dismiss the faint traces as game trails.

I itched to explore for evidence of a campsite, but surely Ryan Driscoll had already done that. I gave up any pretense at meditation and opened my eyes to scan the canyon walls.

Geology made a giant staircase, with some layers prone to forming cliffs, others to slopes. Backcountry hikers knew to look along seams or fractures for a route up, often hidden by scrubby growth that appeared to spring out of solid stone. But on this side of the canyon, the shale slope ended at a sheer rock face, with no sign of a likely ascent.

My gaze went higher, above the ledge where I'd spotted Franklin's body. Call it my imagination, a hallucination, or another symptom of my quirky mental circuitry, but I'd "seen" a figure on that cliff.

I'd assumed Franklin scaled the cliffs to get away from someone in pursuit. What if he was climbing down instead? Pines grew along the canyon's high rim, the curved spire we called the Giant's Claw rising from the head of the canyon like a sentinel. Was there an upper route between the box canyon and Lee Ranch?

A sense of rightness rushed through me like a drug. I couldn't wait to run my theory past Teejay. But when I glanced at him again, my excitement drained. The circles under his eyes were almost as dark as his lashes, and new creases emphasized his sharp cheekbones. Steve Nicholson had left him responsible for Blue Sky's shoestring operation, and our livelihood depended on being able to bring guests here. If I shared my suspicions, the sheriff might close the box canyon again. What would be worse—being proved right or being wrong?

* * *

After we returned our guests to their cabin, Teejay joined me in the front of the Jeep. Oak Creek Canyon was still quiet, a tunnel of green leaves and rocky cliffs. Campers had emerged from their tents, and breakfast smells wafted through the trees. Though grills were off limits under Stage Two restrictions, a few savvy folks had come prepared with Coleman stoves. The rest would be lining up at the Indian Gardens deli counter for breakfast or driving into town.

I glanced over. "Remember how we were wondering if someone gave Franklin a ride after the party? What if he hiked to the box canyon?"

He frowned. "The box canyon is another five or six miles from town."

"And if he hiked cross-country, away from the roads?"

"Three, four miles maybe—if you could find a direct route. The Lees ran cattle for decades, so there's a lot of erosion, some deep arroyos. It would be a hard hike in daylight. At night . . ." He shook his head. "Nah. It would be easier to stick to the roads, even though it's a couple miles farther."

I slowed for a curve, then again for the string of cars and trucks inching their way toward Uptown. I didn't want to let go of my theory. "I think the two canyons are pretty close together as the raven flies. What if Franklin went *over*, not around? The moon was almost full that night. He could have skirted above all the ditches and brush, maybe along a slickrock bench or over a saddle. It would be shorter and faster."

"You talk to anyone else about this?"

"I didn't think of it until this morning when I looked at the cliffs." Persuasively, I added, "A topo map might help us pinpoint any feasible routes."

"Sure. I can get you the USGS quad when we get back." He glanced at his cell phone as I nudged the Jeep another car length forward. "But first, we pick up guests for the Schnebly Hill tour. After that, I want you to shadow the other drivers. Check with Gina to see who's got room. Tomorrow you'll be heading out on your own."

Absently, I agreed, still thinking about my theory. Even if I'd figured out *how* Franklin traveled to the box canyon, I still didn't know *why*. When the string of brake lights ahead of me flashed alarmingly, I went on alert for jaywalkers or road hazards, relaxing when I realized our parade of vehicles had slowed because, five cars ahead, someone was simultaneously driving and shooting video of Snoopy Rock. "Now that's multitasking."

"Maybe not for long." Teejay nodded toward a black-and-white police car approaching in the other lane, its turret lights flashing. "Let's go around."

I had just enough space to make a quick right, taking a series of narrow side streets to bypass the congestion. By the time we made it back to headquarters, Megan had arrived for her first tour, and a hint of lingering incense told me that Harmony—lucky girl—had managed to fit in an early morning yoga class. She and Gina were already working the phones, and Chase-like-the-bank was settling in next to them as he chatted with Evan, who leaned against the counter with his ever-present cup of coffee.

Teejay scanned the group. "Where's Sam?"

"Late," Evan drawled. "As usual."

Gina interrupted to tell us the family who reserved the Schnebly Hill tour had canceled moments before. "I rescheduled them for this afternoon. They're on their way to the urgent care clinic." She fought with a grin and lost. "Getting a fishhook removed from dad's ear."

I winced. "That'll smart."

"Happens all the time," Megan assured me.

"Not as often as unfortunate encounters with cacti," Evan chimed in.

Chase snickered. "Remember that guy who couldn't sit down after backing into a prickly pear? His wife cradled him like a baby while Teejay used tweezers."

Between calls, a lively discussion ensued about the strangest injury sustained before, during, or after a tour. Evan took the prize with his tale about stopping a Jeep to pick up a middle-aged man wandering naked along Dry Creek Road. Dazed, his skin reddened from sunburn, he told Evan he'd gotten lost overnight while investigating lights from a UFO. He still had a set of night-vision goggles draped around his neck. Evan had delivered him to the ER, modestly wrapped in one of the Mexican blankets we kept stashed under the seats for chilly mornings and evenings.

"Did he ask Kenneth what the frequency was?" Gina's question caused Evan to spit out his coffee, but the rest of us looked at each other blankly.

"No," Evan managed to choke out, "but he did say an alien drugged him and stole his pants."

"Definitely weird," Megan pronounced. "Even for Sedona."

We were nodding our heads in agreement when Sam pulled in, preceded by the distinctive rattle of his vintage VW Bug. At the same moment, the phones started ringing again, and I overheard Chase patiently explaining Sedona was a town, not a national park, and no, Stage Two fire restrictions didn't mean everything had closed.

The other drivers drifted off, and after pausing to refill my water bottle, I headed down the hallway toward the office, thinking Teejay might have already found that topo for me. About to knock on the doorframe, I stopped short. He was deep in conversation with Evan, their heads bent over paperwork spread across the desk. Even from across the room, I recognized the incident reports folder. Teejay looked up and saw me lurking. He scooped the forms back into the folder as Evan straightened, his expression unreadable.

"Sorry, guys. Is this a good time to get that map?"

"Later. Meantime, Evan's got empty seats on the creek tour. Why don't you ride along?"

"Okay, sure. We'll talk when I get back?" The desk phone started ringing, drowning out my question, and since he was already reaching for the receiver, I gave up and followed Evan to the garage.

CHAPTER

6

THE BREEZE SWIRLED through the open Jeep and tugged at my hair as we curved down Upper Red Rock Loop Road. The two couples seated behind me chatted about jobs and home states, awkward small talk that changed to *oohs* and *ahhs* as we rounded the next turn to a sweeping view of Cathedral Rock. Evan pulled over so our passengers could admire the graceful reddish sandstone spires rising from the valley.

When we arrived at Red Rock Crossing, the parking lot was packed, but he eased into a magically empty spot shaded by an immense cottonwood. "I bribed the concessioner." His dry delivery made it impossible to tell if he was serious or if his parking karma was that good.

Our guests gathered their water bottles and daypacks, and we followed him down a gentle slope to Oak Creek. Clear water meandered over a broad bed of pinkish-red sandstone, sculpted and smoothed by ages of sediment-laden flows. When conditions were right, the shallow pools reflected Cathedral Rock like a mirror. Today, the pools swarmed with people splashing and wading to beat the midday heat.

After the requisite selfies, we followed a dirt path upstream, hiking over and around tangled tree roots and river cobbles carried by past floods. Dense riparian vegetation allowed peekaboo views of the creek and cliffs. I dodged a long blackberry cane, its green fruit just starting to blush, remembering a summer morning long ago when Claire and I had set out for the creek at dawn to beat the crowds, only to find birds had beaten us to the berries.

Bored by small talk and disappointed none of our guests were taking advantage of Evan's encyclopedic knowledge of plants, I let my thoughts wander. Why hadn't Franklin returned to Sedona after the Lee Ranch party? Did he stay behind to press Whittaker about the land trade? I pictured again the wrapped packet he held out to Barbara. Information? Cash? Little blue and red pills?

A chorus of gasps pulled my attention back. We'd arrived at Buddha Beach, a clearing popular for sunbathing (and skinny-dipping) for as long as I could remember. The shallows here were placid and crystalline. Toward the opposite bank, large flat-topped boulders hid deeper pools, shaded by sycamores. A few hikers perched atop the boulders, relaxing in the riparian oasis. Farther downstream, a family picnicked and kept watch as their kids played on a rope swing. Behind them, a lush mix of willows and alders screened the reddish cliffs that formed the base of Cathedral Rock.

But it wasn't the idyllic scene that made our passengers gasp. Fanciful, gravity-defying rock stacks teetered along fallen trees and rose from the creek. Large and small, smooth and rough, gray and tan and red—hundreds of rocks balanced on the slickrock and gravel "beach," blending into the background like an illusion. Both couples scattered, looking for loose cobbles to build their own.

Though he'd lost his audience, Evan intoned, "The ages have been at work on it . . ."

". . . and man can only mar it," I finished, joining him in the dappled shade beneath a pale-trunked sycamore. Teddy Roosevelt's 1903 speech referred to the Grand Canyon, but the words transcended time and place.

Evan nodded toward the rock stacks. "The first big monsoon thunderstorm and Mother Nature will wipe that slate clean."

"My money's on July fifth. Yours?" I referred to our office pool.

"The eighteenth."

"Wow. And I thought Teejay was the pessimist."

"Realist. The dew point isn't anywhere near monsoon levels yet."

"Sure feels like it." I watched enviously as the two women abandoned their shoes and their husbands—now competitively engineering elaborate rock stacks—to wade into the creek. I itched to join them but knew without being told doing so would be un-guide-like. Besides, a twisted ankle or bashed knee might sideline me—though I suspected Chase-like-the-bank would be only too happy to step into my hiking boots.

As though reading my mind, Evan called out a warning about the hazards of slippery rocks and hidden drop-offs, telling the women to stick to the shallows. Then he lowered his voice so only I could hear. "Sometimes you gotta let 'em get their ya-yas out."

Knowing Evan wouldn't leave them to their own devices for very long, I took advantage of the pause. "Has Teejay shared any theories with you about how Franklin ended up in the box canyon?"

"Nope." Evan fixed his attention on our passengers, all four in the water now. Yet I suspected his reluctance to meet my gaze went beyond solicitude for their safety.

"You were a Forest Service lifer. Based on experience—" I hesitated, knowing our conversation would get back to Teejay. "Do you think Franklin was trying to block the land trade?"

"My role during exchanges was to help preserve habitat or identify rare species. Neither is an issue for Lee Ranch or The Flats." He turned to face me, his expression neutral. "The trade's within the guidelines established for the Red Rock District. Don't see how Franklin could have prevented it, or why someone would kill him for trying."

So Teejay *had* confided in Evan. "A lot of locals fought for a national scenic area designation. Jack Lyman's development for The Flats *will* impact the viewshed entering Sedona." He looked unconvinced, so I added, "We took people to the signing party, and this morning our Jeeps were plastered with anti-growth bumper stickers. Coincidence?"

"Teejay's got some ideas about that."

"He didn't say anything to me."

"Maybe he's not sure yet where your loyalties lie."

Before I could ask what he meant, an ear-splitting shriek interrupted. We looked toward the creek. One of the women had stepped off a boulder into a deep channel. Submerged to her shoulders, the ends of her dark hair dripping, she was holding her phone high in the air. "Don't worry," she called. "It didn't go in."

"Ah, hell." Evan hurried to fish her out, though one of the hikers had already plunged in to help, and a couple of the picnickers were wading upstream to lend a hand. The woman's husband beat them to it, but in his haste, he lost his footing and went under.

Soon, everyone was soaked except me. We sloshed back to the Jeep, and I handed out blankets to ward off the evaporative chill that would set in as soon as we started driving through the desert air. Evan offered hot coffee from his thermos, and when the scent of hazelnut wafted toward me, I was relieved no one took him up on it. I drove while Evan huddled in the back with our bedraggled passengers. Judging by the smiles and laughter, the shared dunking had forged new friendships.

After dropping them off, I helped to dry the Jeep and restock it with clean blankets for the next tour. Evan was about to leave when I stopped him. "Is Teejay questioning my friendship with Ryan?"

He parried with a question of his own. "Driscoll ever tell you why he keeps getting passed over for promotion?" I waited, a lump forming in my stomach. "Word gets around. While he was stationed at Kootenai, he got a little too friendly with a suspect during an investigation. Nearly wrecked the case."

"I see." All too well—Ryan's sin sounded a lot like my own.

* * *

I watched Evan pull away for his next tour. Arnulfo was off on Sundays. Megan wouldn't finish her history excursion for another half hour, and Sam was late returning from Schnebly Hill. I took advantage of the lull, heading for Steve's office, stopping short on finding the door closed. I tapped and waited.

Teejay used the office when he wasn't in the garage or leading a tour. Gina went in and out to access the filing cabinets or to work on the computer. On hot afternoons, Arnulfo would come inside to cool off with a soda, his chair tipped back below the AC vent. The rest of us popped in to consult the field guides and reference books shelved in the long bookcase. An open door policy, however, wasn't an invitation to snoop. A closed door was probably a warning not to.

I swallowed a bubble of anxiety. Gina and Harmony's voices carried from the reception area. Hoping they hadn't heard the garage door chime, I turned the knob, Evan's words echoing in my ears.

Maybe he's not sure where your loyalties lie.

I crossed to the desk. The computer screen was dark, the password a mystery. Next to the monitor I saw a couple of sticky notes with Teejay's angular scrawl, a stack of mail that looked like bills, and a blackened sage bundle resting on a palm-sized flake of reddish shale.

Bending to slide open a file drawer, I thumbed over the tabs until I spotted the incident reports Evan and Teejay had been studying earlier. I flipped through older reports about road conditions, missing trail signs, trash dumping, graffiti . . . Gina would have logged each incident and forwarded it to the appropriate contact at the ranger district or county. I was scanning over Evan's encounter with the naked UFO spotter when a noise from the doorway caught my attention.

"There you are, Del."

I whirled to see Gina, headset around her neck. Hoping I didn't look as guilty as I felt, I closed the file behind my back, my fingers still gripping the report. "Teejay said he was going to dig up a USGS map for me."

She shrugged. "He left for a meeting in Flag. He told me to slot you in. There's a last-minute cancellation for Sam's Soldiers Pass tour, but you'll need to hurry."

"On my way." I stuffed the report into my waistband underneath the tail of my shirt and followed her out the doorway.

I'd been on the Soldiers Pass route a couple of times with Teejay, who taught passengers about geology while I avoided breathing in the dust that marked it as one of Sedona's busiest 4WD trails. Sure enough, a bright red Jeep was already parked at the base of the Sphinx, a pyramid-shaped monolith that loomed over Soldier Wash about a half mile north of my aunt's house. Sam pulled up beside it, and our passengers— six middle-aged women who'd traveled to Sedona for an astrology workshop—scrambled out to follow him around a gaping maw as large as my loft.

The sinkhole was deep and shadowed. A jumble of appliance-sized rocks marked where its ceiling collapsed, once in the 1880s, then twice more when I was a kid. Sam herded our group to one side, pointing out the joints and fractures crisscrossing the sandstone beneath our feet. When a third Jeep pulled up, and more people clustered to peer over the edge of the sinkhole, I stepped back to make room.

While Sam talked geology, I puzzled over who Teejay might be meeting on a Sunday afternoon. One of our guests abandoned Sam's geology lesson to ask if she and her friends could hike to the arch from here. It took a few beats, but then it dawned on me what she meant. "Devils Bridge?"

She nodded. Popular trails led to Devils Kitchen (where we were standing), Devils Dining Room (another sinkhole), and Devils Bridge (a rock arch). Despite the similarly creepy nicknames, the trailheads were miles apart. The slim brunette held out a hiking map. "Would you show me how to get there?"

"Sure." I knelt to spread out the map on sandstone. "The trail to the arch starts west of town. We're here, and this is your hotel." I stopped, my finger on the map. "Does your vehicle have high clearance?"

"No, we rented a minivan."

Reassured by her fit appearance and sensible gear—wide-brimmed hat, hydration pack, and sturdy, broken-in hiking shoes—I said, "In that case, use this connector trail. It's a two-hour hike, but there's good shade most of the way."

I started to fold the map, then changed my mind. "May I borrow this for a few minutes?"

She nodded and returned to her friends. I flipped the map over. At this scale, the box canyon was smaller than my little fingernail, but as I suspected, only a single ridge separated it from Lee Canyon. The ridge was so steep the contour lines were a solid blur of ink. I needed more detail—the USGS quadrangle Teejay had promised me—to gauge whether the ridge might be negotiable.

We piled back into the Jeep, heading for Seven Sacred Pools, a chain of tinajas that usually offered a reliable water source for wildlife. The sandstone basins had dried to dust about three weeks ago, leaving coyotes and bobcats to prowl neighborhoods for water. Sam grinned as he described how a local, standing in his kitchen making breakfast, had glanced outside to find a black bear napping on his deck. The women were thrilled, and our drive back to their hotel was punctuated with growls and laughter.

Teejay still hadn't returned, so I led our rescheduled Schnebly Hill tour under Megan's benevolent supervision. "You'll be fine tomorrow," she assured me, after helping the fishhook family document their adventure with a video. She'd included a close-up of the tidy Steri-Strips covering dad's earlobe—a Sedona memento he wouldn't live down for a while.

When we got back to headquarters, it was after five. Megan sped off for a sunset excursion in Gramps Cherokee; Sam and Evan had already set out on their last tours. After hours of road noise and loud conversations, I savored the relative quiet while I rinsed dust from the Wrangler. Evan had rigged a system to reuse the water on the landscape plants in front of the building, desert willows and sages blooming in pinks and lavenders. The sound of running water always attracted birds, and I was listening to a pair of ravens chuckling from the roof edge when the trill of a cedar flute interrupted.

It was a ringtone I'd downloaded from an app and assigned to Teejay, and usually when I heard it, I'd smile at my private joke. Now my muscles tensed, the purloined incident report burning a hole in my pocket. Had Gina ratted me out?

"Delilah, we need to talk."

*   *   *

Thirty minutes later, I fidgeted at The Market's deli counter while the gaggle of tourists in front of me ordered wheatgrass shots and veggie vortex wraps. I was running late. I'd waited until Gina drove off before slipping the report back into its file, its mysteries safe from me. Evan's naked guy had been wandering near the Vultee Arch turnoff, an area where people often reported seeing strange lights to the west. An unsurprising destination for a UFO watcher—though I suspected the hovering alien ships were actually cars traveling to Jerome, a former mining town perched on the side of Mingus Mountain.

As I waited to order, my gaze landed on a table of women in yoga wear, reminding me of the day four months ago when I'd first met Teejay. On that drizzly February morning, a few of my yoga classmates had gathered at The Market for tea and sisterhood. Our conversation swung from the difficulty of finding a decent job in Sedona to the impossibility of finding a decent man. I was only half-listening, aware I had nothing relevant to offer, when my friend Leah muttered, "Speak of the devil."

Everyone turned to see a lean man with raven-black hair and skin the color of honey waiting at the counter for his coffee order.

"Didn't you two go out a few times?" the woman next to Leah whispered.

"Me too," said a third, and my companions all looked at each other with varying expressions of merriment and dismay.

"Hey, Teejay," Leah called. He'd approached our table with a half smile that might have been self-mocking or wary. "Is Blue Sky hiring? Asking for a friend." Her blue eyes sparkled with amusement as she slid her chair over, making room for him to sit next to me. "Say hello to Delilah Cooper. Del, meet Teejay."

Though my cheeks burned at Leah's obviousness, I forgot my embarrassment once Teejay and I started comparing notes about our favorite trails and the waterfalls that had sprouted in Oak Creek Canyon after the unusually wet winter.

"We should go hiking sometime," he said as the others began to stand and gather their things.

"Sure," I'd agreed, acutely aware that although my friends appeared busy with yoga bags and purses and drink cups, they'd fallen silent to listen. After Teejay departed, Leah looked at me, eyes bright, and said, "Don't overthink it, Del. Sedona is a small town, and dating is like driving around looking for a space at the post office. We've all parked in that spot."

I heard their laughter again in my mind, but this time I was the butt of the joke. The young man working behind the deli counter had tried unsuccessfully to get my attention, and now the gaggle of tourists, hyped up on wheatgrass, were chuckling at the spaced-out local.

I ordered food for two and, with the sack of takeout on the seat next to me, threaded through traffic toward Teejay's. I'd nixed his suggestion to meet at my place. It would have been closer, but I'd never invited anyone inside the loft, preferring to keep it my retreat from the world outside.

Besides, ever since Gina had mentioned Jack Lyman was Teejay's landlord, I'd been curious about the RV park off Schnebly Hill Road. I spotted his aging silver Toyota pickup waiting near the trading post at the intersection. We turned up the road, and I followed him through the maze of RVs and travel trailers, a ten-acre oasis screened by tall trees and lush with ivy and periwinkle.

We rounded an overgrown photinia that had all but swallowed a graying lattice fence. Behind it, a small Airstream trailer was tucked beneath the sycamores like a modern version of a fairy-tale cottage. I squeezed in next to Teejay's pickup and got out. Oak Creek burbled from the other side of a grassy berm. A picnic table sat on a concrete pad, and beyond it, a hammock stretched between low limbs. A light breeze, carrying the scent of moisture, rustled the leaves overhead.

I nodded my approval. "Peaceful."

"Most RVers stay only a day or two, and everyone's pretty good about sticking to curfew. Some nights I sit out here in the dark and listen to the creek." He took the sack I was carrying and led the way to the Airstream. "Be it ever so humble . . ."

He unlocked the door and gestured me in. Far smaller than my loft and, I had to admit, much neater, the Airstream was as spare as a monk's cell. The severity was softened by a reclaimed wood floor, a small photo gallery, and a Pendleton blanket in blues and tans tucked tightly over the pull-out sofa. After being closed up all day, the interior was hot and stuffy, but next to the sink, a pint jar of Cleveland sage added a crisp, resinous scent. Except for the aluminum walls curving up to the ceiling, the effect was more like a stylish micro apartment than a travel trailer.

"Wow. You're organized."

"Two tours with the army." I hid my surprise as he set the sack of food down on the counter and reached under the sink for a rag. "It's cooler outside. Give me a minute to clean off the picnic table."

"I can do that."

"Thanks. I'll bring out plates."

Fuzzy cottonwood seeds stuck to the wooden table. Wiping them away gave me a few moments to recover from an unexpected bout of shyness. I'd taken Teejay at face value, but as Megan had pointed out, he wasn't just a pretty face. In Sedona, a "past life" could mean anything from a day trader who'd dropped out to a reincarnated Egyptian priestess. I had no interest in swapping stories about how I'd deep-sixed my career, or why I dreamed of ancient villages and a dark-haired man in woven yucca flip-flops. Yet when Teejay joined me outdoors, I said, "I didn't know you served in the military."

"After 9/11, I dropped out of college and joined. Thought I'd be using my hydrology background to build roads and bridges, but I ended up with a combat unit in the mountains."

"You don't talk about it."

"I don't."

He finished setting out plates and silverware, his expression closed. I was the least likely person on earth to press someone about a personal past. But now that I'd gone there, changing the subject felt awkward, and thanking him for his service felt even more awkward. I focused on dividing up a container of pasta salad.

He saved me by speaking first. "When I got back, it was rough. Nightmares, insomnia. Stuff would trigger me—the sight of blood, loud noises, helicopters. Maybe you know what that's like."

I froze, a forkful of salad halfway to my mouth. Though the planes of his face revealed nothing, his amber-brown eyes were soft with sympathy. Chewing was a good excuse to keep my mouth shut. Teejay was right. Discovering Franklin's body had cracked open dark memories. I was pretty sure Claire hadn't talked to anyone about what happened to me in Boston, but the murders had made national news, and a few people must have pieced together the story. Like Ryan. And, it seemed, Teejay.

Somewhere nearby, a dog barked wildly, breaking the spell.

"Raccoons. Every night around dinner time," he said. I'd managed to swallow past the tightness in my throat when he continued, "Been doing okay since Friday?"

"Mostly." I deflected. "You told Evan that Franklin was murdered."

He shrugged. "He figured something was up when the sheriff closed the canyon. I thought it was better to tell him than to have him interrogating his Forest Service friends."

His tone was mild, but I got the point. "I'm not running around looking for a story. The last thing I want to do is call attention to myself while Franklin's killer is still out there."

He studied my face, then nodded in acknowledgment. Though he'd barely touched his food, he shoved his plate aside and leaned his forearms on the table. "Word is, when the Lee Ranch trade is finalized, public access to the canyon will be limited. Small groups with approved outfitter guides."

"That's great." Then I noted Teejay's somber expression. "Isn't it?"

"Sure. If Blue Sky is one of the outfitters. We need an edge. Operating expenses keep going up, and if we don't modernize and expand, we'll keep losing ground to the competition."

I thought of Pink Jeep and the others, all of us vying for a limited number of commercial permits on national forest routes. Small, focused tours to Lee Canyon would dovetail neatly with Blue Sky's interpretive approach, but Teejay was right—we'd be short on drivers, and our fleet was old. "What does Steve think?"

He shrugged. "He's happy as long as we make enough money to keep him in beer and boards. Our permit's up in a couple months, and it'll be tough to convince him we need to reinvest."

"Want me to talk to him?" I assumed that was why Teejay had wanted to meet with me tonight, so I was surprised when he shook his head.

"We might have more leverage with the Forest Service if one of our drivers was already familiar with Lee Canyon. Someone who knows the history of the ranch and has an interest in archaeology."

"*Me?*" I was the lowest driver in the rotation, with little hope of advancement unless the company expanded or one of the other drivers quit. The problem was, I was nearly as ambivalent as Steve. "Is this why I got the job instead of Chase?"

He laughed shortly. "Chase is in his last year at NAU, and he's majoring in computer engineering. Think he's going to be driving Jeeps next year?"

I didn't respond, thinking I might not be driving Jeeps next year either. Staying on would mean accepting my career as a journalist was over. And though I'd yet to come up with an alternative plan, I couldn't afford to hide away in Sedona forever.

"The forest archaeologist, Ronnie Jackson, is briefing volunteers on Lee Canyon tomorrow night. You and Megan are our history buffs. Ronnie agreed to let you sit in." When

I hesitated, he upped the ante. "You're not on the schedule till nine tomorrow. You can sleep in, knock off after your second tour, then come back in Wednesday. After that, we'll be heading into the Fourth of July weekend, and we'll need every driver."

A day and a half off—maybe I could wangle an invitation from Barbara and Whittaker Lee, have a look around the canyon myself. "Okay. I'm in." He looked relieved, so I reminded him, "That topo map would be helpful."

"I sent a link to your email hours ago." He grinned at my blank stare. "Welcome to the digital age, Delilah. USGS quads are online now."

"Oh. Right." I thought wistfully of the pile of maps my aunt had kept in her studio. She'd given away most of her supplies to her friends and donated the rest to the community art center, but before renting the house, I'd stored boxes of her things in the horse barn. I'd take a look later, I decided.

Teejay picked up his fork again, and while we finished eating, I entertained him with the afternoon's highlights— Evan's unexpected swim, Sam's bear tale, the family who'd rescheduled after the fishhook mishap. Across the creek, the cliffs turned copper, then pink as the sun sank behind the horizon. When the colors cooled to twilight tones, I carried our dishes inside to wash them in the doll-sized sink.

Teejay joined me in the cramped space to dry plates, and I retreated to the other end of the counter to put away silverware. The photo gallery caught my eye, a tidy arrangement on a sheet of cork curved to accommodate the wall. Sedona scenes were interspersed with a few people shots, including one of Teejay and Steve, seated in an older version of our blue Wranglers, and an informal portrait of a half-dozen young men in dusty camouflage and heavy tactical vests.

"Is this your unit? Which one is you?"

"That's my squad, yeah. Bottom row center."

"Wow. I never would have guessed." The picture showed him kneeling with his rifle across his knee, wearing a grin that didn't quite convince me. His cheekbones were blade-sharp, his black hair so short I could see his scalp.

"What can I say? I was a skinny kid."

I leaned in for a closer look in the dimming light, spotting a familiar wolfish smile. "Is that Jack Lyman?"

"Yep. He was our staff sergeant."

Everything clicked into place. How Teejay had landed a long-term spot in this RV park. How Blue Sky got picked to taxi partygoers. Why Teejay was on board with the land trade. And why I needed to keep my suspicions about Lyman to myself. *Brothers in arms.*

He switched on a lamp, then stood so close behind me I could feel the warmth radiating from his skin. I resisted the urge to step away, fixing my attention on the photographs, now easier to see in the lamplight. I knew a little about photography, another thing Henry Grisom had taught me while he was living in my aunt's horse barn. With Teejay's geology bent, the artful shots of rock formations were a given, but I was more interested in the cliff dwellings and pictographs. "These are good. Evocative, mysterious."

"Thanks."

I felt the tension leave him and realized with surprise my opinion had mattered.

"I took some photography classes after I returned stateside, then traveled a bit before ending up here. I liked being outdoors more than I liked being a starving artist, so I started driving for Steve. The rest, as they say, is history."

I searched the rock art photos more closely, able to link a few to their locations, including the snake pictograph Teejay had shown me in the box canyon. Had he photographed the spiral that kept eluding me?

"You have others?"

"Not here. Lately I've been using a digital camera. When I have time, that is. My prints and negatives are in a storage unit, along with most of my gear."

No wonder he could keep the tiny Airstream so neat. "Ever shoot a spiral petroglyph?"

"A few, sure. Tell me where, and I might be able to dig it up. I keep an index by location."

"I wish I could remember. I haven't seen it since I was a kid." I turned around. His face was inches from mine, and my breath hitched. The tiredness I'd noted earlier was even more apparent in the lines around his eyes. "You've got the sunrise tour tomorrow. I should get going."

"Stay a while. I've got a bottle of white wine in the fridge."

"I don't drink." The invitation had caught me off guard. I wasn't sure if he was offering more than wine, and the thought of asking him to spell it out made my knees weak.

"Tea then. Or water." He waited while I wrestled for an answer. For a moment, I was tempted. Then common sense won. He must have recognized the resolve in my expression because he stepped back.

"Thanks anyway." I made what I hoped was a dignified retreat to the door. "I'll see you tomorrow."

"Sweet dreams, Delilah."

CHAPTER

7

MONDAY AFTERNOON, I hobbled up the stairs to the loft like an old woman, convinced the rough roads had shortened my spine by an inch. I wanted a yoga class and a nap, not necessarily in that order, but Megan was picking me up in a couple of hours, so I doctored my leftover breakfast coffee with milk and ice and headed downstairs to the barn to pick up where I'd left off.

After returning from Teejay's last night, digging through storage boxes was a welcome distraction. Though I didn't find a map, I landed an even bigger prize: Claire's leather-bound address book, the Lees' unlisted phone number noted in her looping flourish. Since it was late, I set it aside, a vague hunch spurring me to keep searching. I found snapshots of art receptions, painting references scrawled with notes, and more than a few pictures of me. Henry teaching me how to make a pinhole camera, me holding my first (and last) 4-H ribbon, and (shudder) the horrible perm I had at fourteen. Some photos helped me sharpen hazy recollections. Others threatened to send me wandering aimlessly down memory lane. I worked under the tack room's dim overhead bulb until my nervous energy finally drained away.

Now, in the bright light of day, I sighed at the Herculean task before me. I'd done a lousy job of packing up my aunt's house, dragging my feet until it became obvious it wasn't healthy, financially or otherwise, to live there on my own. The loft was short on space, so I'd crammed furniture and household goods into the two horse stalls, throwing tarps over the top—a less-than-ideal situation that required constant vigilance for pack rats. The semi-underground tack room, more defensible thanks to a concrete floor and block walls, housed Claire's artwork, papers, and photographs.

I propped the door open, cracked the window for cross-ventilation, and scrolled through my phone for an upbeat Motown playlist. This afternoon I needed the reward of quick progress, so I stepped over boxes and started on the canvases propped against the wall. When I turned over the first painting, a small oil of Coffee Pot Rock, an appreciative chuckle bubbled up. According to Claire, she'd painted it *en plein air* from the driveway while the house was under construction. From this angle, the iconic rock formation looked more like a perched raptor than a percolator. She'd kept it in the kitchen, between a window with a view of the rock itself and—because she had a sense of humor—her coffee maker. Liberated from the chunky beveled frame, it would tuck into the space next to my favorite chair.

The next canvases looked like work from teachers or students at the local art center. I set them aside, promising myself I'd make the effort to return them to the artists or their families if they were still in town. I sorted through the remaining art, hesitating over a large oil landscape that once hung in Claire's bedroom. The bold palette and angular forms suggested it wasn't her work, though I didn't see a signature. The scene reminded me of the smooth sandstone canyons on the Navajo reservation. Even if I removed the frame, it was too large for the loft, but I hated to part with it. Before I could change my mind, I leaned it near the door.

I switched off the music and started to lock up, momentarily distracted by a snapshot lying on the floor—Henry Grisom leading one of the Lees' horses. Long before teaching me how to drive, Henry had taught me how to ride, starting with an elderly chestnut mare that had once been Barbara's. After my aunt had converted the barn's hayloft into an apartment, Henry moved in. I must have been around eleven or twelve, increasingly oblivious to the adults in my life. If I'd given it any thought at all, I'm sure I assumed he and Claire were being discreet for my benefit.

A drop of perspiration rolled down the back of my neck, snapping me back to the present. I grabbed a box of photos, piled a couple of my aunt's journals on top, and went upstairs. I cleared space on the small table, but before I could dig in, my phone chirped. I snatched it out of my pocket, hoping Barbara Lee had responded to the message I'd left earlier.

Ryan's number flashed on the screen. "Have you seen Jane?"

My breath constricted at the urgency in his voice. "I thought I'd call the justice center tomorrow to arrange a visit."

"Don't bother. She's gone."

"Gone?" I echoed. "Where?"

"That's the million-dollar question." I didn't take the sarcasm personally. He sounded as astonished as I was. "The sheriff released her this morning. No charges."

"Released? That's great." He was silent, and then it hit me. I'd been pacing around the loft, but now I sat on the edge of the bed. "Unless whoever killed Franklin thinks she might know something."

"*Exactly.* Franklin's been in and out of trouble for years. Mostly small-time stuff, but the detectives think Franklin tried to horn in on someone else's action and got killed for it."

"So now the killer could be looking for Jane?"

"Yep. One of the department's volunteers dropped her off at Walmart in Cottonwood. Jane told him she had to use the bathroom. When she didn't come out, he looked for her, but since she was free to come and go . . ."

I groaned. "They can't be using her as bait, not without her consent. Can they?" Ryan didn't answer, maybe because he wouldn't criticize another branch of law enforcement. Or maybe, if what Evan said was true, the sheriff's office elected not to confide in him. "It'd be easy to slip under the radar in that huge store. Find a ride to Sedona."

"No one's seen her." Ryan's words were clipped. "I asked at the homeless camps earlier, but, Franklin excepted, she's always kept to herself." I thought about Jane wandering around, unaware she might be in danger.

"We'll find her." I wished I felt as confident as I sounded. The town spread over nineteen square miles, and the surrounding ranger district encompassed more than a half million acres, most of it waterless and rugged high desert. Arizona had the dubious distinction of being one of the leading states for missing persons.

"Come with me. We've got a few hours before sunset. She's probably camped somewhere nearby."

"Can't. Megan Ramirez is picking me up in a few minutes. We're heading to the supervisor's office in Flag for an archaeology talk."

His tone changed to persuasion. "I'll teach you everything you want to know about local archaeology. We can start tonight."

"It's my job. Anyway, I'm looking forward to meeting Ronnie Jackson."

"Yeah, so she's the senior forest archaeologist. She may have the anthropology degree, but I've been hiking around these canyons since I could walk."

I laughed at his exaggerated affront. We kidded around a couple of minutes longer, until I said I needed to get ready to leave. The meeting started at six, and the winding twenty-five-mile drive could take an hour or more, depending on traffic in Oak Creek Canyon.

I showered off the cobwebs, then dressed in jeans for Flagstaff's chilly evening temperatures. I grabbed a paisley shawl to throw over my sleeveless shirt later. Almost everything else was in the laundry basket. I could use my time off tomorrow to catch up with everyday chores . . . but already I felt the familiar laser-like buzz that alerted me whenever I was onto a big story.

* * *

Megan arrived minutes later, brimming with apologies. She'd driven past the narrow driveway—twice—before catching a glimpse of my aunt's house through the thick screen of sugar bush and juniper.

"Aren't you nervous living here all by yourself?"

I chuckled at her look of dismay as I ducked into the small Honda's passenger seat. Megan lived in a rollicking multigenerational household that included her parents, grandmother, and younger brothers, plus an older sister who'd moved back home, kids in tow. Not long after I started at Blue Sky, she'd invited me for dinner, and her family had folded me into their cheerful chaos.

"I like how quiet it is. *After* the traffic settles down," I added as we met a convoy of sherbet pink Jeeps turning up Soldiers Pass Road on their way to the trailhead. "Wow. I thought business was slow this afternoon."

"Yeah, but we'll be booked solid over the Fourth." Somehow, she'd found time to drive home and change into a blouse and tan chinos, freeing her hair to fall sleek and dark around her shoulders. She nodded toward a paper bag in the back seat. "For you. My *abue* says you're too skinny."

I reached back and opened it, inhaling the delicious aroma of freshly baked empanadas. "What about you?" I asked around a mouthful of flaky pastry, moaning with appreciation for the filling of roasted green chiles and cotija cheese.

"Don't tempt me. I ate a half-dozen straight out of the oven."

I felt virtuous for leaving a few in the bag before folding it closed, taking care not to scatter crumbs in the elderly but meticulously tidy Honda.

As we crawled behind the line of cars snaking through Uptown, I described the ups and downs—mostly literal—of my first day soloing. When I confessed to nearly unseating a five-year-old while going over a rut, Megan was sympathetic. "It was a month before Teejay turned me loose. I still get sweaty palms when I have to take one of the Wranglers. And his geology fixation—"

"Yeah." We shared a commiserative groan.

We neared Indian Gardens, where Oak Creek Canyon's first settler had found plots of corn and squash, abandoned by Yavapai farmers when soldiers came to march them to the reservation. Megan told me about the canyon's one-room school, how children would sometimes see bear tracks on their way to class. As I listened, it occurred to me each of Blue Sky's employees brought something personal to the company. Megan's connection to local pioneers, Evan's botany background, Sam's ease with kids. Though she'd started the same week as I did, Harmony could chat easily with callers about the best place to shop for crystals or who to book for a qigong session. I wasn't sure yet where I fit in, though it seemed Teejay had my future mapped out at Lee Ranch.

Megan's thoughts may have been traveling in a similar line because she said, "I wish we offered more history tours."

"Isn't that why Teejay pulled strings to get us invited tonight? To learn more about Lee Canyon's archaeology?"

"I'd rather hear about the ranch and its Hollywood angle. He said you'd know something about that." Her tone was curious.

"Not as much as I thought. My aunt took me to the ranch to ride or picnic. But that was ages ago." The conversation at the history museum underlined how my knowledge was limited to tales suited for children. Gossip about Barbara's pregnancy was hardly relevant, but what other tidbits had I missed or forgotten?

Belatedly, I realized Megan might be able to fill in some gaps. "You grew up here. Did you know Franklin?"

"Not really. He turned up when I was a kid, but I was still in middle school when we moved to Cottonwood to live with my *abuela*."

I calculated. "So Franklin's been around at least fifteen years? That's a long time to be homeless."

"Homeless? Mm, I don't think so. Well, maybe he never had his own place, but it's not like he camped in the forest every night. People took him in for a few weeks or even months at a time."

"Anyone in particular?" I asked.

"Women mostly. He was a ladies' man, I guess."

Again, I thought of Franklin's intense green-eyed stare as he reached to lift my hair from my jaw: *Do you think that hiding that scar will keep people from seeing the scars inside?* I must have made a sound of dismay because, even focused on driving, Megan picked up my automatic revulsion.

"I didn't figure you for a prude, Del." Her tone was amused.

"I'm not, but . . . *Franklin?* A ladies' man? I'm trying to picture it. Scratch that. I'm trying *not* to picture it." Other than Jane, I hadn't seen him in a relationship. Whenever I'd spotted him holding court at The Market, his acolytes were mostly young men, though one or two might have had girlfriends in tow. I itched to ask Megan if she could think of anyone who might resent Franklin, an angry husband maybe, but the cause and manner of his death weren't public knowledge yet, and I didn't want to earn another warning from Teejay.

I let the subject drop and tipped my head back to look at the soaring canyon walls, searching among the shadows and streaks of desert varnish for the break where West Fork flowed into Oak Creek. Back in March, snowmelt had plummeted down the Coconino sandstone in a misty waterfall. Today the cliffs were dry and pale as bone above the tall conifers. The beauty made me ache, and I wished we had time to get out and splash along the shallow tributary. The longing vanished when we drove by the packed parking lot, cars spilling out to line the narrow roadway.

"You could ask Sam," Megan said, startling me with the abrupt return to the conversation.

"Our Sam? But he's from San Diego."

Megan squeezed between an oncoming RV and a family loading their parked hatchback with dripping shoes and daypacks. "This isn't his first Sedona rodeo. Before he started at San Diego State, he was a Rainbow Family kid."

"Like an indigo child?"

She snickered. "Teejay should have you boning up on Sedona 101 instead of geology. The Rainbow Family is sort of a mashup between Druids and Deadheads."

Which didn't enlighten me, but I didn't want to sidetrack her now, especially since she was concentrating on avoiding the pedestrians along the curving roadway.

"A few years back," she continued, "there was a big Rainbow Gathering on the reservation. It got rowdy, and when the cops came in to bust it up, some of the younger ones drifted down to Sedona. They looked pretty rough around the edges, and a few people were ready to run them out of town. I mean, my Grammy Murphy was freaking, and she used to be a hippie."

"Sam was one of the kids?"

"Yeah, I remember him hanging around The Market, busking for donations. Back then, he had long bleached-blond dreadlocks. With that café au lait skin . . . *wellll*."

I turned to stare. Megan and *Sam*? Though they were close in age, I couldn't imagine two people more different. Her cheeks pinked, and she kept her gaze on the road as it curved over Pumphouse Wash. The concrete bridge marked the beginning of the switchbacks that climbed from the canyon to the plateau, nearly a thousand feet up in a couple of miles. Near but far—like Megan and Sam?

While I had a hard time picturing Megan with Sam, I had no problem picturing Sam as one of the starry-eyed young men in Franklin's orbit. "You think he knew Franklin from hanging around The Market?"

"Maybe. But the Rainbow Family was just a rebellious phase. He's starting grad school in environmental science this fall."

Her defensive tone warned me I'd probably asked enough about Sam, at least for now. Did I even remember what it was like to nurture a crush? I felt bad about pumping her for information. And even worse for what I was about to do, cover my tracks by making it seem like I was indulging in idle curiosity for the sake of conversation.

"Okay, that's Sam. Tell me about the rest of the crew."

"Hmm . . . Arnulfo is an amazing dancer. He and his wife travel all over the Southwest for ballroom competitions."

"Huh." I nodded, only mildly surprised since Arnulfo and his vintage boombox were inseparable.

"You know Evan was a botanist for the Forest Service. But I bet you didn't know there's an endemic wildflower named after him in Texas. And he paints. Imagine a cross between Audubon and Georgia O'Keefe."

"Seriously? And Gina?"

"One of Steve's first hires after he took over the company from his grandparents. Moved to Sedona after her divorce."

"Guessed that."

"Her *third*."

"Yikes. What about Teejay?" Carefully nonchalant.

"Man of mystery."

"Come on."

"He *never* talks about himself. It's all about Blue Sky for him. He started when Gina did. I know he's not technically the boss, but he might as well be. He asked everyone to weigh in on hiring you. He told us you were a strong hiker, you were interested in archaeology, and"—she glanced over, eyebrow lifted—"being a reporter meant you'd be good at drawing people out."

Busted. Heat rose to my cheeks, and I rolled down my window. Megan switched off the AC. We'd topped out on the plateau, home to the world's largest ponderosa forest. The tall pines bordered the roadway, and I breathed in their subtle butterscotch scent until I recovered from my embarrassment.

"I'm guessing I had Arnulfo in my corner when he saw me drive up in the Willys."

She laughed, as I'd hoped, but then turned serious again. "I know driving Jeeps isn't exactly what Harmony would call a soul mission. But Del—" She switched to a persuasive tone. "Finding a good-paying job in a tourist town isn't easy. The hours suck, but it beats waiting tables or selling postcards."

She finished in a rush. "It's been great having another female driver. I hope you're going to stick it out."

I sighed. "No promises, but I'll give it my best shot."

* * *

The supervisor's office, a large metal-roofed building tucked into the ponderosas on Flagstaff's west side, served as headquarters for all three districts of the 1.8-million-acre Coconino National Forest. The front office staff had gone for the day, but Megan and I followed the sound of voices down a hallway to a small conference room, where a couple dozen people had filled the first rows of seats or staked claims with notebooks or hats.

Judging by the archaeology-themed polos and tees, this wasn't a novice crowd. The room buzzed with chatter about projects and field trips. I recognized a few faces, including a diminutive brunette who volunteered as a docent at Palatki, the cliff dwelling a few miles from Lee Ranch. Megan and I were the youngest in the room and the only commercial tour guides. Teejay must have worked his charm to get us here, I thought, as Ronnie Jackson entered.

Despite the Forest Service's frumpy khaki-and-sage uniform, the middle-aged woman was stunning, her dark hair pulled back with a colorful clasp made of tiny seed beads. I recognized her from the party at Lee Ranch, where she'd spent most of the evening leading tours of the canyon, giving partygoers a closer look at some of the archaeology that would be protected under the auspices of the USDA Forest Service.

While she was busy connecting her laptop to the projector, I checked my phone again for a message from the Lees, then switched it off, disappointed. People were settling into their seats when the docent asked, "Will Lee Canyon be a sacrifice site like Palatki or Honanki?"

Before Jackson could answer, a shocked exclamation drew people's attention to the front row. A large, balding man spun around in his seat, wearing an incredulous expression and a T-shirt that proclaimed his life was in ruins. "The Anasazi performed human sacrifices?"

Megan's eyeballs nearly rolled out of her head, and her mouth worked with a suppressed giggle. I elbowed her to be quiet. Others weren't as polite, and chuckles exploded through the room.

Jackson's expression stayed impressively neutral as she explained to Ruins Man that "sacrifice sites" referred to places the Forest Service had offered up to visitor traffic despite the resulting wear and tear, in the belief that educating people and satisfying their desire to explore helped prevent damage to unprotected backcountry sites.

She continued by addressing the group. "We haven't finalized plans for Lee Canyon, but we're leaning toward small tours so visitors can enjoy the natural soundscape and experience a sense of discovery. First, we'll need Dana's team of rock art recorders to help survey the site"—she nodded toward the Palatki docent—"and a few site stewards who can add another location to their patrols. Here's what's at stake."

She launched into a brief overview, using PowerPoint to illustrate a continuous human presence in Red Rock Country, from the Pleistocene to the present. Most of the area's cliff dwellings dated to the two-hundred-year period beginning AD 1150 and were associated with the Ancestral Puebloan culture anthropologists referred to as Southern Sinagua. I waited for Ruins Man to ask about the "mysteriously van-ished" Anasazi, but he was busy writing. I scanned the crowd to see most had pens in hand.

I contemplated powering on my phone for notes, but then Jackson zeroed in on the system of canyons that encom-passed Palatki, Honanki, and Lee Ranch, and I didn't want to look away. She flashed an aerial photo, and I felt a fizz of excitement as I recognized the outlines of the box can-yon. The ridge separating it from Lee Canyon looked like slickrock—easy hiking if the layers of sandstone had eroded into a natural staircase.

I swallowed an involuntary protest when she advanced to the next slide, a black-and-white photo of picnickers dressed in late nineteenth-century clothing, horses tethered nearby. A bewhiskered man posed comically with a whiskey bottle, as though dividing the contents among a half dozen ancient pots arrayed on the picnic blanket.

"When the Lees, a Flagstaff cattle-ranching family, acquired the property from the original homesteader in the 1940s, locals had already been visiting the canyon for decades, collecting pottery and arrowheads from its small cliff dwelling."

Over *tsks* and groans, Jackson reminded us archaeo-logical protection measures beginning in 1979 covered only public lands at first. I remembered the pottery and arrow-heads displayed throughout the ranch house. With a flush of guilty embarrassment, I also remembered how the Jack-aloons scrambled over the crumbling cliff dwelling, trading potsherds like baseball cards and using them for a game like checkers with our own made-up rules.

The game triggered another hazy memory that grew fainter the harder I tried to recall it. The moment it evapo-rated, I realized I'd also lost the thread of Jackson's lecture.

". . . and about twenty years ago, as a sort of commune or retreat center."

"*What?*" Faces turned to look at me, and I realized I'd spoken aloud.

"The goddess cult," someone said behind me.

"You mean the prostitution ring," from across the room.

"I heard it was drugs."

"Both."

"Pothunting."

"Pot *growing*," another piped in.

"In any case . . ." Ronnie Jackson forged on, but not before I heard a nearby whisper.

"*Didn't someone die?*"

Shocked, I twisted around to see who'd spoken, but everyone was focused on Jackson.

". . . group members used the alcove for ceremonial fires and rearranged some of the masonry into a small amphitheater. So, from an archaeological point of view, the site's value is lost. Except"—she switched to another slide—"for the rock art."

The screen filled with an image of the long cliff face adjacent to the ruins, a veritable gallery of painted forms. An awed silence descended over the group as she clicked through closer views.

"Though some have been damaged by smoke or spalling, more than five hundred pictographic elements remain. Most are white, made from a kaolin clay mixture brushed onto the stone, but a few incorporate other pigments, including hematite, limonite, and what appears to be ground malachite."

Hushed *oohs* and *ahhs* swept through the group as she switched to a flute player surrounded by animals, most painted rusty red with a notable exception—a large ocher-colored mountain lion with remarkable green eyes. A meandering spiral connected the animals and flute player. Though it was painted on, and not pecked into the stone, the scene reminded me of the spiral in my visions. I felt a vertigo-like sensation, as though the floor had dropped away beneath my feet.

"Is it a calendar? Like the sun dagger in Chaco Canyon?" someone asked, and the room stopped moving.

"Maybe, or it could be a map suggesting migration." She smiled, drawing out the suspense, using a laser pointer to trace a path back to the flute. "Or maybe the lines represent sound, life force . . . or something else, depending on the viewer. This scene might have meant one thing to children or outsiders, for example, and something entirely different to an initiated adult, if we assume the Ancestral Puebloans organized in societies or clans, as today's Hopi do."

She let that sink in before using the laser to highlight charcoal zigzags and starbursts that outlined figures on the periphery of the spiral. "Most of the rock art in Lee Canyon was made by the Sinagua, but these marks came later. See how the charcoal lines are superimposed over older pigment?"

"Graffiti?" Ruins Man sounded affronted.

"No, they were added by Yavapai groups who camped here seasonally to hunt or gather plants. My mother's grandmother told her about harvesting agaves in these red rock canyons. Families gathered here and stayed for days, tending to agave roasting pits, catching up on news and stories, ending with a feast."

Ruins Man pointed toward the image. "If I picked up a piece of charcoal and drew around that flute player, you'd call it graffiti."

"I'd call it vandalism." She sighed. "Here's what I believe: Rock art was made by someone invested with authority from the community. Graffiti is an impulse of ego."

"But what do the charcoal markings *mean*?" he persisted. "Why aren't they graffiti?"

"Okay, most of you already know how often I warn docents—and Jeep guides—not to interpret rock art. But I'm the archaeologist," she joked, then turned serious. "Based on research and oral history, I think the charcoal lines were intended to emphasize or reanimate. And here's something else—"

She changed the slide, deftly changing the subject as well. "If you need more evidence that rock markings aren't mere decoration, look at these made during the archaic period that predated the Sinagua." She pointed to a group of geometric forms high on the cliffs. "The upside-down figure might imply death or diving into the unknown. The zigzags and clusters of dots may indicate a trancelike state, perhaps induced by hallucinogenics or fasting."

"Hallucinogenics? *Get out.*" Ruins Man again.

Jackson fought a smile. "Anthropologists worldwide have found evidence suggesting psychoactive substances were used to induce mystical experiences. Peyote, sacred datura, fermented beverages—but that's a topic for another day."

She finished her presentation by reminding us the labels we used to distinguish cultural groups were a twentieth-century invention, one that emphasized artifacts rather than a continuous population who adapted to change with different tools and strategies. My brain whirled with information, yet "my" spiral petroglyph was still a mystery.

The Q and A continued for a few minutes longer, then Jackson's audience began to gather up their belongings. I overheard Ruins Man suggesting a few of them might seek out fermented beverages at one of Flag's local breweries. I told Megan I'd follow her outside. The archaeologist was closing the laptop she'd used for her presentation.

"Ms. Jackson?"

"Ronnie, please." She smiled and held out her hand for a brief clasp. "You're Blue Sky's new guide."

I introduced myself and told her I'd been a frequent visitor to Lee Ranch as a child.

"You're related to Claire Cooper, the artist?"

"My aunt. She and Whittaker knew each other from Hollywood. She started out painting backgrounds for movies."

"I have one of her later pieces, a small watercolor of a blackware jar. I met her a few years back, during a retrospective of her work at the art center. She mentioned then she had some old photographs of Lee Canyon, but . . ."

She trailed off, and I understood. No one liked to talk about cancer. I knew the painting she referred to, or at least I knew its subject, a cracked and chipped piece of Santa Clara pottery Claire had kept next to the kitchen's rotary phone and used to store pens. I was still using it for the same purpose. "I have her photos in storage, if you're interested."

"Definitely." Her dark eyes flashed. "Photographs give us a better idea of how sites change over time. In this case, I can't tell you how helpful that would be."

I thought of our incident reports and wondered if Franklin had been stealing artifacts from Lee Canyon. I had the feeling Ronnie was about to say something more, but she excused herself as a trio of volunteers approached—site stewards, according to their name badges. As I was leaving, I heard her ask if they had anything more to report.

8

I STEPPED OUTSIDE, THE air cool against my bare arms. Above the treetops, the Milky Way arched across an inky sky, the stars only slightly blurred by haze. Earlier today, the Antelope Fire had grown to six thousand acres and crossed into the national park, but here, eighty miles south, the night was quiet.

The blue glow of Megan's phone led me to the Honda and reminded me to check mine for messages. I powered it on, my pulse accelerating when I saw a voice mail from Barbara Lee. I listened standing next to the car in the dark. Her tone was polite but perfunctory as she extended an invitation to the ranch. The lack of welcome didn't matter. I was certain I'd find answers there.

As Megan turned onto the highway, we traded our impressions of the meeting, and I asked if her grandmother Murphy knew the Lees. She shook her head, her attention on driving. "Those two are hermits. They keep to themselves."

Her description caught me off guard—so different from my memories of how Barbara and Whittaker had been part of a social network that intersected Hollywood and Sedona.

Earlier Ronnie Jackson told us how rock art might mean different things to different people, and I thought the same was true of Sedona, with its own small tribes of insiders and outsiders.

"Most of those people tonight were newbies," Megan said, unaware she'd confirmed my theory. "They don't know what they don't know."

Megan's Sedona wasn't mine. The truth was, even my Sedona wasn't mine. The poolside barbecues, the horseback rides—these were Claire's Sedona, or more accurately, hers filtered through the eyes of my child self. The Lees, once the center of the town's social life, were now that odd old couple who lived in the backcountry. Change had left them behind. Change or—what had that person called it?—*the goddess circle.*

"Anyway," Megan was saying, "we'll find out more when we start leading tours to the ranch."

"*If* the trade is approved and *if* Blue Sky lands a permit."

"Right." She was quiet for a few moments, then said, "No one asked me, but Lee Ranch doesn't need protecting from development. Who'd want to live all the way out there? An eccentric millionaire with a helipad?"

"Huh." She had a point.

"It's The Flats we should worry about. The Chamber likes to brag about Sedona's small-town charm, but if we don't draw a line, we'll end up with strip malls and resorts from Sedona to Camp Verde. Once the charm is gone, people will stop coming."

"You're right." And yet I couldn't dismiss Teejay's concern for Blue Sky's future. Unease stirred in the pit of my stomach. The forest's deep shadows pressed in on either side of the road, the older car's headlights too weak to penetrate the gloom.

Megan's voice rose. "I can't afford to live where I work, so I never meet anyone new, except tourists, and the traffic—"

A female elk stepped onto the road. Megan hit the brakes hard, and the screech of tires split the night. We sat there, speechless and shaking, as two more cows followed her across, then a bull sporting a rack that looked almost as wide as the car. He turned to look at us before disappearing into the dark forest.

"Whoa." Megan's eyes were white, and my heart was doing double time.

"Traffic, huh?"

She met my weak attempt at humor with a nervous giggle.

After the close call, we fell into a tense silence, both of us straining to spot movement in the trees as she drove—slowly—toward the switchbacks. I relaxed when the forest opened, and we started descending, the familiar turns and sways eventually lulling me into a reflective state as we entered Oak Creek Canyon.

Megan switched on the radio and lowered her window. With Taylor Swift singing softly in the background, and the waters of the creek scenting the air, I closed my eyes and wondered if the Sedona I longed for had ever really existed.

* * *

When the sun woke me, I felt a moment of panic, thinking I'd overslept again before remembering it was my day off. It was still too early to leave for the ranch, so I went outside and practiced sun salutations on the edge of Soldier Wash until the sandstone got too hot for my bare feet. After breakfast and a shower, I was about to pull on a pair of shorts when the image of Barbara, youthful and elegant in her flowing white party clothes, popped into my thoughts. I traded the shorts for a stretchy coral athletic dress that struck the right note between feminine and practical, and found a pair of hiking sandals still new enough to be respectable.

I stuffed a day pack with water, snacks, and gear, setting it by the door while I went back to the closet for a thin cotton shirt to cover my arms, digging through the laundry basket for one that wasn't too wrinkled. While I checked the shirt in the small bathroom mirror, my phone chirped with a text. I found it on the floor next to the pile of laundry.

Jane still MIA, read Ryan's message. I felt my heart sink.

Talk later? I texted, then noticed the time. Now I *was* running late. I grabbed my hat and dashed down the stairs.

Five miles along No Trees Road I realized I'd forgotten the pack by the door. Fortunately, I'd left an almost-full bottle of water in the wagon after work yesterday. It was nearly ten and already hot when I pulled up to the ranch's metal gate. I left the Willys' engine running and was relieved to find the gate dummy-locked, just as Barbara's message had detailed, the open padlock hidden behind a crossbar and the chain looped around a few times to look convincing.

In years past, the ranch road had been surfaced with gravel, but most of it had eroded away, leaving a narrow strip of sand and rock with a high crown in the center, cut by channels where water flowed across during rains. The rough road was why Jack Lyman had paid Jeep companies to shuttle partygoers to the ranch. It was also an effective deterrent to any curious joyriders unconvinced by the faded sign hanging from the gate: TRESPASSERS WILL BE SHOT ON SIGHT.

Reddish sandstone cliffs rose on my left as I neared the homestead, a collection of wood and adobe buildings surrounded by a grayed fence. With the livestock long gone, the fence had fallen into disrepair, but masses of cow's tongue prickly pear still stood guard. I continued past the bunk-house and pulled behind a late-model Land Rover parked in the carport attached to the house.

Last week's signing party was only surface glamour, gilded by the rosy glow of golden hour. In the harsh light of day, nothing suggested the Lees had received an infusion of cash from the proposed trade. According to Ryan, the trans-fer of ownership wouldn't be official until environmental reviews and surveys were complete, a process that could take a few months . . . or a few years.

The Lees had expanded the original stone-and-adobe cabin over the decades, and yet the house looked smaller than I remembered, worn by the elements and dwarfed by the backdrop of cliffs that climbed toward Bear Mountain. Flagstones led to the front door through a neglected cactus garden. I paused halfway, remembering Whittaker telling how his newlywed mother, homesick for Santa Barbara, had planted the prickly pear and cholla for their deep-pink and yellow blooms. Now the prickly pear pads were shriv-eled and pockmarked with fungus. The cholla had died, leaving heaps of fallen branches that looked like bleached bones.

After a decade of dry farming and ranching, Whittaker's parents retrenched to Flagstaff, using the old house infre-quently. Then Whitaker had discovered something more profitable than ranching. He started pitching the homestead to filming companies, renting riding stock, working as a wrangler or stunt double, eventually taking on small acting roles. Flush with movie money, he'd enlarged the house and added a swimming pool, an outrageous use of water, con-sidering how deep into the rocky earth he must have drilled for a well. As kids, we'd splashed in the pool until the adults claimed it, then played until dark in the sagging cowshed, which had appeared in several westerns, including Whittaker's ill-fated television series.

As I continued up the path, the front door swung open. The scent of Barbara's Shalimar perfume drifted toward me before I saw her standing in the shadowed entry. At sixty-something, she was tanned and slim, her blond hair in a deliberately casual updo. But when she stepped into the sunlight, the carefully applied makeup couldn't quite conceal the fine lines that had settled around her mouth, now stretched into an unconvincing smile.

"Del Cooper. So good to see you. Please come in out of that hot sun."

She'd dressed in all white again, this time an elegant linen tunic and slacks, the simple lines setting off a wire-wrapped amethyst pendant. I couldn't help being impressed. I'd owned a pair of white jeans when I first moved back to Sedona. After a few wearings, red rock dust had permanently stained the hems.

I returned her smile and air kiss before stepping into the hush of thick adobe walls and removing my sunglasses. Part of the original homestead, the entry was dimly illuminated by a narrow, deep-silled window. A tiled hallway stretched toward the new addition. In the shadows to the left, I could make out the arched doorway that opened into Whittaker's office.

"Whitt, come say hello to Claire Cooper's niece Del." Barbara's voice echoed down the hall, and after a few moments, Whittaker peered from the doorway. "Remember her?" She turned back to me, her tone confiding. "What am I saying? He won't remember what he had for breakfast an hour ago."

I'd seen Whittaker the night of the party. Even so, I was shocked when he shuffled toward me, slightly stooped, wearing a plaid western shirt, his faded Wranglers hanging loosely from a tooled leather belt. His hair was thick, but in the two years since Claire's memorial, it had gone completely white. Never had the twelve-year age difference between him and Barbara seemed so vast. His blue eyes flickered briefly as he reached to shake my hand, his fingers dry and cool.

"Claire Cooper, you say?"

"No, Whitt, this is Del, her niece."

With a flash of the testiness I remembered, he said, "I know it's not Claire." Slowly, he released my hand. "You sure liked that little paint."

"Zorro." The colt's name came to me out of nowhere. I'd called him that because of the black splotch across his eyes, and even before I'd learned to ride, I'd fallen in love with him. I'd been heartbroken when I learned Whittaker had sold him to an actor friend.

He grinned and shook his head, as though reading my thoughts. "He mighta busted your leg, or worse. Wild streak, that one. Mebbe why you wanted him."

I laughed. "Maybe so. But I learned to appreciate that gentle old mare you and Henry picked out for me."

His blue eyes grew distant. He looked at Barbara, bushy eyebrows drawing together in a frown. "Is dinner ready yet?"

"You just had breakfast, Whitt. Marisol is making some coffee." A round-faced woman dressed in a fuchsia scrub set appeared, her thick-soled clogs soundless on the tile floor. She was sturdy but petite, her dark hair piled into a bun atop her head. She smiled shyly at me before leading Whittaker away, one hand under his elbow.

Barbara turned to me. "Never get old, Del."

She'd put those words into practice. Her face wore the slightly flat affect of someone who'd spent thousands on surgery or Botox or both. I followed her through to the newer part of the house, filled with light from the wide glass sliders that opened onto the pool. A tray with iced tea and cookies sat on the coffee table between a pair of facing sofas upholstered in restful tones of cream, mauve, and peach.

I sat opposite Barbara, who paused in the act of pouring. "Unless you'd rather have coffee, like Whitt?"

"No, thank you, tea is perfect." I set the glass on a coaster after a small sip. *Too much lemon.* I bit into a cookie to chase away the sourness. "How long has he been . . ."

"Addled? Confused?" She waved away my concern. "He got lost driving home from town one day about three years ago. Imagine, after living here for over fifty years. I took away his keys and hired Marisol." She sipped tea, then reached for a napkin to dab at her lipstick. "The changes aren't all bad. Whitt is a better husband now than he ever was."

At the oddly intimate disclosure, my memories stirred. The filmmaking business had brought glamour to the ranch, but also the kind of dysfunctional drama that sometimes trickled down to us kids. "Has the prospect of moving been hard for him?"

"You've seen how it is. One minute he's the old Whitt, and the next he's like a child." Her gaze slipped from mine to look toward the swimming pool. "There's a room opening up in a memory care facility in the Village of Oak Creek. It's for the best."

I felt my awareness kick up a notch. Though I understood Barbara's dilemma, I got the feeling Whittaker wasn't on board with the plan. "I have wonderful memories of coming here with Claire—picnics, horseback rides, stargazing . . ."

"You were just a dumb kid. What did you know?" She scooped several heaping spoons of sugar into her tea and stirred so vigorously I thought the glass would shatter. "*Stargazing.* Whittaker's old friends thought they were too good for movie people, but they sure liked to come out here and gawk. The men couldn't keep their eyes off the latest starlet, and the women . . . If they weren't mooning over Jim Garner or Clint Walker, they were making eyes at my husband."

She rolled her shoulders, as though shaking off unhappy memories. "I guess I was just a kid too. Crazy with jealousy. I was so sure Claire was after Whittaker." Her laugh was brittle. "It finally dawned on me your aunt had no romantic interest in him, or any other man."

Eyes narrowing, she gauged my surprise.

"You didn't know." She laughed again. "Claire came here to hide. Or to heal. Sedona—the land of broken dreams and broken hearts."

"But Claire and Henry—"

"Henry Grisom was a drunk and a thief, a washed-up stuntman who followed Whitt out here when no one else would hire him. Claire took pity on him and put a roof over his head. That stopped anyone from speculating about her own romantic preferences."

Something didn't ring true, but I was too taken aback to sort it out. I drained my tea, letting the sour taste ground me as I thought back to those days at the ranch. Even as a *dumb kid* I'd sensed Barbara's neediness, the ingenue trying to stay in the spotlight.

"I've heard that *you* helped people, too. Or did you start the goddess circle to save the ranch?"

She bent to refill my glass, but not before I caught her calculating expression. When she looked up again, I glimpsed a ghost of vulnerability through her carefully applied makeup. I reminded myself she'd been an actress.

"You think it was a scam, don't you?" Tears sparkled on her eyelashes—as improbably dark and thick as I remembered—but her aquamarine eyes were clear. "It wasn't about money. I wanted Whittaker to look at me the way he used to. Before I gave up my career to be a wife and mother."

Her words loosened a memory, and I could picture the Lees' daughter, a serious and quiet girl a couple of years older than I was. To my embarrassment, I recalled how the Jackaloons had teased her for being too stuck up to join our rough and tumble adventures. More likely, Barbara didn't want our rowdy ways to rub off on her child. I wondered if she'd fled small-town life the way many of my friends had, but I wasn't about to provide Barbara with an excuse to shift the conversation.

"And so you became a goddess."

In the silence, I could hear the air-conditioner's soft whir. I thought of how similar her story was to my mother's, the ballerina who'd stopped dancing after I was born, blunting her disappointment with pills and alcohol and flirtations. Except in my mother's case, the flirtations hadn't led anywhere.

The corners of Barbara's mouth lifted in a small smile. "I reached out to women like me who needed to reclaim their power. We erased their shame, made them see they were lovable and whole, just as they were. The ranch was a safe space." Then her voice hardened. "Until the jealous, small-minded, small-town gossips stopped us. Henry Grisom finally had his revenge."

"*Henry?*" The gruff old cowboy seemed like the most unlikely candidate for spreading tales. I clenched my teeth together so my mouth wouldn't fall open in shock.

"Of course Claire wouldn't have told you any of this. Henry poisoned her against us long before then. Once the rumors started, I couldn't show my face in town anymore."

My mind raced as I tried to remember when invitations to the ranch were no longer forthcoming, perhaps a couple of years before my last summer, when some of my friends started getting their licenses and my interests turned to boys and cars. Had news of the land trade stirred up old resentments . . . or created new ones?

Barbara reached to rearrange the tea tray. I sensed my time was running out, yet I'd found more questions than answers.

"How well did you know Franklin Johnson?"

She glanced up, her expression shuttered.

"I saw you arguing with him during the party last week."

"That red-haired forest bum?" She waved a hand in dismissal but didn't meet my gaze. "He said he wanted to talk to Whitt. Probably to ask for a handout. I told him so long as he didn't bother anyone, he was welcome to the canapés and champagne."

"Did you see him go?"

"No. He arrived on one of the Jeeps, I think. He probably left that way, too."

"Not with Jack Lyman?"

"Jack?" Her surprise seemed genuine. "No, Jack came with the caterers. His daughter-in-law's company. He helped set everything up and stayed to help clean afterward. He's been a good friend."

I bet. A friendship worth millions. The caterers were likely the first to arrive at the ranch Wednesday, and the last to leave. If Franklin rode with Jack Lyman, his presence would have been noted by several witnesses. Maybe the sheriff had crossed Lyman off his list of suspects, but I wasn't about to let go so easily.

"Did Jack Lyman approach you about the trade? Before the Forest Service did?"

"I wanted to sell the ranch outright. Jack told me—told *us*—that if we were willing to be patient, the land would be worth more in trade. It's all the same in the end, isn't it?

The important thing is to get Whittaker closer to medical care." She set her glass, still almost full, on the tray. "That reminds me—it's time I checked on him. He needs to rest before lunch. You understand."

"Of course." Reluctant but resigned, I stood. "Thank you for the tea. I'd like to use the powder room before I leave—is it still down the front hall?" I started that way before Barbara could object, hoping to run into Whittaker again.

After leaving the small bathroom, I paused in the doorway of the study. Part of the original homestead, this room was as dark and masculine as I remembered, the tall, narrow window shuttered to protect the large Navajo rug from direct sunlight. Whittaker wasn't here, but a hint of old cigar smoke reminded me how he would light up after a meal and launch into funny stories about working with Sam Peckinpah or teaching a famous British actor how to ride western style.

The walnut gun cabinet still stood in the corner, and I was relieved to note a shiny new padlock supplementing the antique latch. But the framed arrowhead collections were gone, and so were the baskets and pots that had crowded the shelves of the lawyer's bookcase, now mostly bare except for a few western novels. A comfortable-looking recliner, incongruously upholstered in a floral fabric, sat next to the carved Spanish-style desk. On top, a neatly folded stack of blankets and pillows suggested this was where Whittaker spent most of his time.

I turned at the sound of footsteps on the tile floor.

"If you're looking for Whitt's old bits and bobs, they're gone. Marisol had enough to do without dusting all that junk." Barbara stepped aside, and I took the hint, leading the way back toward the entry. From somewhere deeper inside the house, Whittaker called, his voice querulous.

Marisol, who'd picked up the tea tray, started to turn back. Barbara stopped her. "I'll see to Whitt, if you'd show Miss Cooper out."

"Yes, ma'am." She set the tray on a nearby console table, and Barbara started toward the living room.

My last chance. I addressed Barbara's back: "Would it be all right if I walked to the ruins? I missed the tours the other night."

She turned, her smile stiff. "I'd be delighted to take you, of course, but I've never cared for hiking. Marisol will go with you. Don't be long," she told the younger woman, then looked at me. "Please lock the gate when you leave."

9

I STEPPED FROM THE shadowy front hall into a blast of sunlight, but I didn't want to waste precious minutes fetching my hat from the wagon. I slipped on sunglasses and followed Marisol around the side of the house to a wide sandy trail. Even after all this time, I remembered the way, but I let her set the pace though the scrubby mix of juniper and mesquite.

As we walked, I asked Marisol how long she'd worked for the Lees, and she confirmed Barbara hired her about three years ago. She'd recently divorced and moving into the bunkhouse had suited her. I asked if the isolation bothered her, but underneath her quick demurral, I detected a note of relief, and guessed she might be avoiding her ex.

"Besides—" She paused to wipe beads of sweat from her forehead. "I drive the Lees to town once or twice a week. I keep an eye on Mr. Lee and use the library's internet while Mrs. Lee visits the salon."

"Is Whittaker difficult?" I hadn't stooped to peering inside the small bathroom's medicine cabinet, but a trio of empty bottles sat next to the faucet, vitamins and two prescriptions—sleeping pills and something I assumed was for dementia.

"We get along fine." Her smile was conspiratorial. "It's Mrs. Lee I need to tiptoe around."

Twenty minutes beyond the homestead, the terrain changed, the path narrowing as we wound through thick undergrowth. I adjusted my pace to accommodate the pink-and-white floral clogs peeping out beneath Marisol's fuchsia scrub pants. Our trail ended at a wide, shallow wash. She nodded toward the opposite cliffs, where a series of masonry rooms perched on a low ledge, sheltered by a broad, south-facing alcove that offered midsummer shade.

I turned to her. "I'd like to get closer. Stay here if you like." Her clogs were no match for the rocks and gravel in the wash.

"As long as you're quick." She cast a nervous glance in the direction of the ranch house.

Before she could change her mind, I scrambled across the wash and up scattered boulders to the alcove. The ruins were less remarkable than I remembered, now bare of pot-sherds and grinding stones, yet I saw no indication of recent vandalism. I continued to the pictograph panel, pausing in front of the spiral from Ronnie Jackson's photos, waiting for a lightning bolt of recognition that didn't come.

I tried softening my gaze and calming my breath before scanning the pictographs again. *Nothing.* Whatever I'd hoped to find wasn't here.

Footsteps heavy with disappointment, I trudged along the base of the cliffs. The rock art petered out, the rusty-colored sandstone becoming rough and mineral-stained. Dampness seeped from the base of the cliff wall. The seam of moisture nourished clumps of ferns, rockmat, even bright green moss. I stepped over a palm-sized puddle, and a long-ago memory surfaced . . . two little girls playing house. We'd collected the precious drops in an old Folgers can, carrying the water to the grinding stones in front of the ruin, where we'd mixed in red dirt to make mudpies, then decorated them with potsherds and wildflower petals.

I smiled, grateful for the memory, though I wouldn't be sharing it with the forest archaeologist. I turned for one last look, wishing I could linger until the sights and sounds and smells gave shape to my hazy recollections . . . but there wasn't time for that today.

The ledge at my feet narrowed to nothing. About to retrace my steps, I remembered the cliff dwellers had chiseled hand- and footholds into the sandstone. I found them and climbed back down into the wash, managing not to scrape my bare knees.

Ephemeral flows had dumped a thick layer of gravel here, where the canyon curved sharply right, but as I crossed to the sandy bank on the other side, I saw dozens of prints where Ronnie Jackson must have ended her tours. When the monsoon arrived—next week? next month?—all signs of last week's visit would be wiped away.

About to head back toward Marisol, I spotted a single set of large bootprints continuing faintly down the wash, then disappearing into the gravel. I knelt for a closer look, but the boots hadn't left a detailed impression, maybe because the tread was worn down. *Franklin was a big man, and he'd had on an old pair of boots the night of the party.*

Lightness spread through my limbs, goading me to follow. Then, remembering Marisol's wariness of Barbara, I rock-hopped back up the wash. When she saw me, her expression cleared. As she led the way back, I asked about recent visitors. Marisol said she'd seen Franklin around town a few times before he turned up at the party, but that was all. Jack Lyman had been to the ranch several times, and a few months ago Ronnie Jackson had stopped by to inquire about the Lees' collection.

"What happened to it?"

"Mrs. Lee sold it, I think. She sent me into town with Whittaker and a long list of errands. When we came back, everything was gone."

"Was he upset?

Her face clouded, her gaze darting toward the house. I saw Barbara step behind a window frame, and I knew Marisol wouldn't say another word.

After thanking her, I drove back out the ranch road, closed the gate behind me, and snapped the lock shut. I turned to stare at the cliffs, thinking about the bootprints as the wagon's engine idled. I got back behind the wheel, but instead of turning toward town, I headed farther down the forest road, pulling over as soon as I could park without disturbing the high desert soil.

Dispersed camping was illegal along most of the roads around Boynton Pass, but I'd passed erosion scars suggesting boondockers had flouted the rules. Maybe one gave Franklin a ride to the box canyon.

Still, I was reluctant to give up my theory that he'd fallen from the cliffs above. Urgency tightened my ribcage. Whoever killed Franklin was still out there somewhere, and so was Jane.

I grabbed my hat and water bottle and started walking, telling myself I'd turn back as soon as I found Franklin's trail. I spotted a section of fence where the rusted barbed wire sagged like loose guitar strings. Beyond it, the wide mouth of Lee Canyon beckoned. I glanced around in the unlikely event someone was watching, mostly because I was trespassing, but also because it's hard to look graceful climbing over barbed wire in a short dress.

The rangeland displayed meager signs of life—churned-up dirt where a javelina had gnawed on the pads of a prickly pear, the undulating impression of a snake near a pack rat nest of juniper twigs and duff. Decades had passed since Whittaker Lee ran cattle here, but the land was still recovering. The scattered junipers were browning and ragged. Steep-sided arroyos cut deeply into the valley floor. Clumps of snakeweed, leached of color, waited for the monsoon. I checked the sky for nonexistent clouds, then entered the canyon's main channel, where the walking was easier.

On my left, the canyon wall rose in a staircase of rocky ledges. As the raven flew, the ruins were maybe a mile away, but I didn't know how many bends and twists the canyon would take as it climbed. The Forest Service boundary was somewhere on that cliffside. Right now, I was not only trespassing but also entering an emotional twilight zone, caught between present and past, the girl I was and the grown-up who still hadn't quite figured where she was headed.

About a half mile in, I started seeing potsherds mixed with the broken shale and gravel. The plainware was the same reddish color as the earth, probably washed down from the cliff dwelling's trash midden. Most were smaller than my thumbnail, but when a larger piece caught my eye, I knelt and rubbed the edge to free it from the compacted soil. I recognized the smooth curve of a rim, shaped by another's hand eight hundred years ago. Gently, I returned the sherd to its resting place. Just as I was about to straighten up, my gaze landed on a shallow half circle in the sand.

A heel mark? Where the forefoot would have landed, the surface changed to bedrock. I continued up a low pourover, then another, searching for pockets of sand in the eroded stone. My progress ended at an eight-foot-high pourover that might become an impressive waterfall next spring. Below it, past flows had carved a basin in the bedrock, depositing gravel and banks of pinkish sand.

I blinked. The sand was crisscrossed by bootprints that appeared to go nowhere. On my left, the canyon wall was nearly vertical. On my right, erosion had carved a rugged embankment of broken rock and compacted soil.

The midday sun erased shadow and texture. I tried comparing the cliffs to the topographic map I'd saved to my phone, but the small screen made context impossible. I'd have a better chance of orienting myself if I climbed out of the wash.

Something pulled my attention back to a ledge about ten feet up, a shoebox-sized chunk of golden Coconino sandstone resting on top of a dark red flake of shale. I approached the cliff, standing so close I could feel the heat radiating from its surface. I turned my head and . . . *there*. Behind a screen of crucifixion thorn, broken slabs and cobbles made a haphazard staircase. With apologies to my bare legs I scrambled up, one hand on the cliff wall for balance, the other gripping my water bottle. A few yards away, another chunk of Coconino sandstone rested next to a thicket of scrub oak.

I had a few sips of water and considered. My hiking sandals were fine for walking through the wash, but this was a scavenger hunt through brush and along drop-offs. On the plus side, my water bottle was nearly full, and I'd had the iced tea at the ranch. Even so, to climb farther would be the kind of mistake underprepared tourists made when they answered the siren call of a slickrock slope, then needed to be helicoptered down. I knew better—but I walked toward the maybe-trail-marker anyway, promising myself I'd turn around before I got into trouble.

When I saw a third chunk of light stone, and just beyond that a faint bootprint, my good intentions evaporated in the heat.

* * *

My progress was slow. I wandered onto game trails that disappeared into brushy tangles and followed ledges that cliffed out, forcing me to backtrack. At some point, I'd crossed the invisible boundary onto Forest Service land. More than once I wondered if I was on a wild goose chase. Franklin had left the party around sunset. Even with that night's fat moon, it would have been difficult to follow the rudimentary trail—unless he already knew where he was going.

I stopped to rest in the meager shade of a piñon, crowding so close its needles pricked my skin through my shirtsleeves. I sipped water warm enough to brew tea. There was no breeze, and in the afternoon heat, the landscape was eerily silent—no birdsong, no lizards scuffling in the undergrowth. If I strained, I could hear the faint rumble of a vehicle, but I couldn't tell which direction it was traveling.

When I picked up the trail again, the loose rocks and sand underneath my feet shifted from dark orange to gold, marking my progress through geological layers. Now I could see the ranch, its swimming pool gleaming an incongruous turquoise far below. I looked for the Willys, but the long ridge blocked my view of the road.

I pulled my focus back to negotiate a sheer edge, feeling an uncomfortable frisson of vertigo until the drop-off was behind me. Ahead, a long rippling stretch of pale gold stone angled up toward a hip-high forest of manzanita. The twisted branches looked impenetrable. My faint clues had faded to bare rock, and I was almost out of water.

Then I saw *him*.

Across the expanse of stone, the cliff dweller stood watching me. For a moment, he seemed perfectly real, and my breath stopped. I blinked, and he was gone. In his place stood a low cairn.

Heart pounding, I aimed for the cairn of stones, and soon afterward spotted Franklin's boot tracks. I followed his footsteps through the manzanita, almost shocked to glance up and see I was mere yards from the saddle ridge high above Lee Canyon. The boot tracks made a hard right, disappearing behind a stony monolith that seemed familiar. I thought about following, but after glancing at my diminished water supply, I continued up to the saddle instead, hoping it might give me a view of Franklin's destination.

When I topped out and looked down, I recognized the monolith next to me—the Giant's Claw, the hook-shaped spire that towered over the small box canyon. I was standing on an overhanging cliff that hid the back of the canyon, but I had a hawk's eye view of the mushroom rock, and I could just make out the narrow trail leading toward the glossy green cottonwoods at the canyon's mouth. The trees screened the earth tank, but a patch of bright blue caught my gaze—a Blue Sky tour Jeep, the color unmistakable even at this distance.

I looked at the ledge where I'd spotted Franklin's body, then up to the rim. A clear sight line extended from the box canyon trail to the rim, though the shot would have been impossible in the dark. That meant someone had waited below until sunrise. Someone who knew the canyon and guessed where Franklin was headed.

Movement drew my gaze downward. Two figures were making their way toward the back of the box canyon. Even from this distance, I recognized Teejay's loose walk, the dark braid falling between his shoulders. Though the woman with him was hatless, layers of blond hair and enormous dark sunglasses hid her features. Teejay reached out to help her across a section of jumbled stones, and they disappeared below the overhang, their destination the snake pictograph and ruin hidden at the back of the canyon.

Reflexively, I knelt to lower my profile, even though the cliffs shielded me. I bit back an exasperated laugh at Teejay's come-see-my-etchings routine, familiar from our visit months back, my so-called job interview. The Jeep implied a paying client. I could find a reason to ask Gina about it tomorrow. Or I could just ask Teejay, at the risk of sounding like a jealous girlfriend, even though I was neither.

Then the sound of a cedar flute floated from below, piercing and sweet, and something inside me shattered—so delicate and brittle I hadn't even realized it was there. I closed my eyes, imagining Teejay serenading his audience of one, the snake pictograph and crumbling granary behind him. Pure southwestern schtick, except Teejay's performance never held any hint of phoniness.

Or maybe I was just easily fooled.

Before the last echo faded, I retreated down the slickrock saddle. I hesitated at the spot where Franklin's trail intersected but resisted the temptation to follow it around to the rim of the canyon where he'd fallen. Teejay and his companion might see me, and I was already courting heat exhaustion.

I threaded my way through the maze of manzanita. The sheer drop-off wasn't as terrifying this time, yet I paused a few moments to breathe, slowly, in and out. The dry air burned my throat, so I drank half my remaining water, counting each swallow—*one, two, three, four.* I started downward again, noting a line of clouds on the southeastern horizon. Had they been there earlier today? Or was that yesterday?

Before tackling the steepest section of the trail, I knelt to tighten the Velcro straps of my sandals, fighting back a wave of dizziness when I stood. Far below, the ranch looked deserted in the hot afternoon sun, like a mirage that rippled and blurred at the corners of my visual field. It seemed an apt metaphor for my childhood memories—hazy, imperfect, unreliable. That Sedona was mostly gone, hollowed out by timeshares and vacation rentals, tarted up with amusements like helicopter rides and ATV rentals. Selling their piece of the red rocks would give the Lees enough money to live comfortably. It would be hypocritical of me—a newly minted Jeep guide—to begrudge them a chance to benefit from their hard-earned investment.

I drank the rest of my water and told myself to stop thinking, to focus all my energy into putting one foot in front of the other. Finally, I reached the lip of the wash. Relief rushed through me, followed by a sharp edge of panic when I didn't see the stones that marked my route. Somewhere farther back, I must have wandered onto another game trail.

I paced back and forth along the cliff edge, searching. When I spotted my sandal print, laughter rose to my throat, then died as realized I'd stepped there moments ago to bypass a fallen branch. Maybe there was another way down, but cramps had begun to gnaw at my calves, and I was beginning to fantasize about the pack I'd forgotten by the door.

Time stretched while the ten-foot cliff continued to defeat me. Finally, I recognized the chunk of tan sandstone that marked the start of my route. I was out of water, but relief was just as sweet when I set my foot onto the bed of the wash and headed back toward the road.

Somehow, I found myself behind the wheel of the Willys, wanting a shower, a glass of cool water, a nap—maybe even all three simultaneously. The old wagon apparently had other ideas. The engine caught, then sputtered and died, and I rolled to a stop on the forest road.

CHAPTER

10

I WAS STANDING NEXT to the wagon's open hood, steeling myself for a long trudge back to the ranch where I could refill my water bottle and use the Lees' landline, when I heard a vehicle approach. As the white pickup got closer, I recognized Ryan at the wheel. He pulled over behind the wagon and got out.

"Tell me you didn't break the Willys."

I managed a dry laugh, even though the heat had made me irritable and, for once, I didn't appreciate his easy humor. "I don't know what's wrong. It stalled barely a minute after I started it. I checked the hoses and plugs. Everything looks fine."

"Gas?"

I sent him a withering look.

"Okay, okay." He laughed and held up his hands in surrender. "If we can't figure it out, I'll give you a ride back to town." He looked at the empty Nalgene bottle gripped in my hand. "Come on. I've got some water in back. First order of business is getting you rehydrated. You know better than to drive anywhere without an extra gallon or two."

"My spare jug was leaking. I haven't gotten around to replacing it." He gave me a look. I wouldn't make excuses, and I wasn't in the mood for a lecture. "Yeah, I know."

I followed him to the back of the pickup. An insulated ten-gallon container was strapped behind the wheel well, but first he unlocked the large chest below the rear window. I caught a glimpse of climbing rope and carabiners, along with a fire rake and other tools. He reached around the hardware for a red stuff sack marked FIRST AID and pulled out a packet of electrolyte powder. He shook the powder into my bottle, then filled it with water before handing it back.

The cool liquid was almost painful against my dry throat. I resisted the urge to drain the bottle and took slow sips instead, rolling the salty, citrus-flavored water around in my mouth before swallowing, leaning against the side of the pickup where at least my legs were shaded.

"We have to keep meeting like this." He paused expectantly, wearing his trademark crooked smile, but I didn't have the energy for a flirty comeback. "What brings you out here, Boston? You been poking around Lee Canyon for your glyph? Or just poking around?"

He hadn't come right out and accused me of trespassing, but I could feel my tired muscles tense. "I wanted to see how the Lees were doing. I didn't get a chance to visit with them during the party last week." His smile cooled a few degrees, so I added a partial truth. "Barbara said I could have a look around."

I managed to keep from glancing toward the ridge. Now that I knew about it, the trail leading up to the saddle seemed as obvious as a billboard. Let him think I was referring to the canyon's ruins and rock art. I was reluctant to tell him more

until my sunbaked brain had a chance to recover and sort
things out. I owed Teejay that much, at least.

I redirected the conversation. "I asked Barbara about the
land trade. Have you spoken to her about it?"

He shook his head slowly. "My folks lost touch with the
old crowd after we moved to Texas. Barbara and Whitt are
getting on—must be inconvenient living so far from doctors
and whatnot."

"The trade's a good solution for them." The admission
was hard for me. "The ranch is beautiful but too remote for
development. No internet or cell service."

"I could live with that." He joined me to lean against the
truck. "Besides, there's always satellite. Works great for me."
Ryan owned a mobile near Beaver Creek, a rural area that
appealed to Forest Service employees, artists, and others priced
out of Sedona's real estate market. "Hey"—he elbowed me—
"does this mean you're giving up on Jack Lyman? Because I'd
like to stop worrying about you getting in trouble."

"Maybe." With half a bottle of water inside me, I could
feel my thoughts sharpening. Ryan had transferred back to
Sedona only six years ago. How much had he heard about
Barbara's goddess circle? I shifted, scanning his profile.

He nodded toward the ranch. "Imagine what it was like
when the first homesteader got here. Grass for cattle, no roads
or fences. Paradise on earth."

"Uh-huh. No well, no electricity. A four-day wagon ride
to Flagstaff."

"Ah, but the pottery and arrowheads—"

Ryan stopped when he saw my eyebrows lift. He colored and fixed his attention on his boots, a pair of worn
hikers reddish with trail dust. Who was I to judge, the girl
who played house in the ruins, making mud pies in grinding

stones and decorating them with the prettiest potsherds I could find?

I took pity on him. "Whittaker's collection is gone. Sold to a dealer two years ago."

"Yeah?" He turned to look at me, his gray eyes speculative. "Man, I loved those arrowheads, the way Whitt arranged them in patterns before framing them."

At Ryan's description, another memory surfaced. "He chased you out of his study once when we were kids. Didn't he make you turn out your pockets?"

"Yep. He was using this big spearpoint for a paperweight. Lucky for me, I put it back after I'd picked it up to admire it. Two, three inches long, beautifully flaked chert. Might have been Clovis. I think Whittaker still holds a grudge." His sheepish grin faded.

I straightened, testing my legs—not as rubbery as before. Long-term care was expensive. "The other night, you said Whitt was throwing good money after bad. You think they sold his collection because they needed cash?"

Ryan shrugged. "Probably. Whittaker sold off the summer ranch in Flagstaff to fund that TV show. Later he tried breeding some designer cattle."

"Longhorn crosses, wasn't it?" I'd overheard Henry telling my aunt about the venture, predicting Lee Ranch couldn't provide enough graze for the lean and ornery beasts.

"Yeah. He lost a bundle on 'em. And then there was that other business . . ." He handed me the water bottle, his gaze sharp.

My skin prickled, and not only from sunburn making itself known. "You mean Barbara's goddess circle?"

"*Goddesses?* Is that what she called them?" He snorted. "All I know is, she started some sort of retreat center that went south."

He straightened and led the way back to the Willys. I hovered nearby as he opened the hood. "Didn't some people identify it as a cult?"

"Hey, this is Sedona. One person's cult is another's spiritual awakening or whatever." He didn't look up from checking the spark plugs and cables, something I'd already done. My irritation returned. "I wasn't around when it all went to hell, but word is, somebody died, or almost died. Like that sweat lodge incident a few years back."

I felt a chill creep up my neck. "Claire never said anything to me."

"Your aunt never struck me as someone who'd turn on her friends."

"She wasn't." Ryan's words of support were like a balm after Barbara's catty remarks. I suspected even after all these years she still resented Claire's friendship with Whittaker. "Do you think there's a connection?"

He looked up, eyebrows lifted. "Between Franklin's death and something that might or might not have happened almost twenty years ago? You're making it too complicated. Could be I'm just a lowly Forest Service cop," he said, drawing out the words, "but my theory's pretty basic. Franklin was a small-time dealer who got in over his head. Once I find his lab, I'll figure out who killed him."

"What about ballistics?"

"State crime lab's got a two-week backlog, and no one seems to think this is a high-priority case. Except me." He lowered the hood, faced me. "Keep it to yourself, but the shooter used a .300 rifle. Common enough for elk hunters. Or ex-military types." My thoughts skipped around, refusing to settle. "I can see the wheels turning, Boston. Something you want to tell me?"

I should let him know what I'd found, the route up to the saddle and a clear shot from the box canyon for someone with a powerful rifle and sharpshooter skills. But I thought again of Teejay, and the words didn't come. I shook my head, and he walked around to the back of the wagon.

"There's your problem." He nodded toward the exhaust. I didn't see it at first, but then he reached down and tugged at the corner of a rag, releasing a small rock that landed on the road with a muffled thud. "Someone wrapped a wet rag around it and shoved it in to seal the tailpipe." He ran the cloth through his hand. "Still damp."

I recognized the old terry dishtowel I used to stop the spare tire mount from rattling. I could feel Ryan's gaze as I checked the liftgate window, which I'd neglected to lock, and looked inside. The towel was gone. "It's mine."

"Anything else missing?"

"No. I don't keep anything inside except the spare, a tool kit, and—*usually*—a jug of water for emergencies."

I thought back to the engine I'd heard earlier, the seemingly deserted ranch. I couldn't picture Whittaker Lee kneeling to block the wagon's exhaust. Well, maybe twenty years ago, but he seemed a broken-down version of the man I remembered. And why would he want me stranded . . . unless it was to keep me here while he called the sheriff to bust me for trespassing?

Or would he call someone closer? *Like a ranger district LEO?*

I looked at Ryan, Evan's warning ringing in my ears. Though the water had restored me, I wasn't up to verbal sparring, nor did I want to alienate Ryan with a direct accusation. Instead, I turned my doubts into a question. "Why would anyone want to prank me?"

"Maybe it wasn't a prank. At the risk of casting suspicion on yours truly, maybe someone wanted the Willys. Make it so you'd abandon it, then they'd come back toward evening and tow it. Or hot-wire it and drive away in the dark."

I thought about Ryan's theory. A little internet research had informed me the old wagon was worth a shocking amount to enthusiasts and collectors. Even so, I found it doubtful anyone would attempt to steal such an obvious vehicle. I managed a tight smile. "Then I'm lucky you just happened to be passing by."

He crossed his arms over his chest. "I was headed for Palatki. Sometimes people park down the road and try to sneak in over the fence."

"They'd be pretty foolish to strike out cross-country on a summer afternoon."

"Must have been a long walk to the ruin," he returned, nodding toward my legs, scratched by scrub oak and pink from sunburn.

"Being a redhead sucks sometimes."

"Yeah, we'd better get you out of the sun. I'll follow you back to No Trees Road."

I see-sawed the Willys around and headed toward town, Ryan behind me until I reached the fork. He waved before making a U-turn and heading back, presumably toward Palatki.

You're making it too complicated.

Maybe Ryan was right. Or maybe he was trying to get me out of the way so he could be the hero. Heart sinking, I realized Teejay and Ryan weren't so different after all. Both knew more than they were saying, and I couldn't trust either of them.

*   *   *

The alarm jolted me from sleep, and I woke feeling the world had slipped off its axis. Dull orange light seeped through the loft's windows. The usual cacophony of quail and towhees was muted, and the air carried an odd metallic scent tinged with a hint of smoke. I got out of bed, my muscles complaining, and the previous day's events rolled back through my mind.

After my Lee Ranch misadventure, I'd stumbled through my evening routine like an automaton and fallen into bed early, only to startle awake at one AM, heart pounding, chilly with sweat. I got up to switch off the swamp cooler and heard wind beating against the stable doors below. The wind howled all night, entering my dreams and spinning a sense of dread that still clung to me like the haze dimming the view outside my window.

The heaviness of my limbs had to be the aftereffects of heat exhaustion. The heaviness in my heart wasn't as easy to explain. I was tempted to crawl back into bed, but I'd set the alarm for a reason. I was going to crash Teejay's sunrise tour.

I listened to a news podcast as I got ready. A massive dust storm had plowed through Phoenix, snarling rush hour traffic and downing power lines before moving north overnight. At the Grand Canyon, firefighters struggled to hold the containment lines on the Antelope Fire. Meanwhile, the winds had whipped up two new fires in the Tonto National Forest, with crews scrambling to respond.

I switched off the grim report. Though the storm had blown away some of yesterday's oppressive humidity, we'd top a hundred degrees by afternoon. Even so, I swapped my usual shorts for hiking pants to hide my scratched legs. I drank a glass of water to ease the headache throbbing behind my temples, then took a quick tour around the house and barn to check for damage. A peek into the tack room—no messier than before—reminded me to load the painting into the wagon.

When I pulled into Blue Sky's driveway, I discovered the gate's padlock and chain had been replaced with heavier versions. My key was useless. The upgrade was likely in response to the bumper-sticker incident, though if anyone wanted to get to the Jeeps parked behind the building, it would be easy enough to find a cooperative juniper to help scale the cyclone fence. I tried to remember if all the Jeeps had been stickered, or only the ones parked outside, but then I heard Teejay's truck coming up Airport Road, and I got back in the wagon to wait. If he was surprised to see me, he didn't show it, sweeping his arm to usher me through with mock gallantry.

Despite the morning chill, the sleeves of his chambray shirt were rolled up past his biceps. He was wearing a leather cuff with a rectangle of stamped silver—a *ketoh* or Navajo-style bow guard. For some reason, it reminded me of his private tour in the box canyon and underlined why I was here.

"Got room for one more?"

He nodded curtly and unlocked the bay doors with his shiny new key. Lucky for us, one Wrangler had spent the night in the garage bay next to Gramps Cherokee. The dust storm had coated the Jeeps outside with a layer of grit. Sedona's two car washes would be busy today. Thinking coffee might chase away my lingering headache, I headed down the hallway for the break area while Teejay added a list of storm-related maintenance to the garage's whiteboard.

When I came out, he'd finished the pre-tour check and was waiting in the bright blue Jeep, engine idling. I handed him his mug. Maybe coffee would improve his mood. Until then, confronting him could wait.

Our passengers—Dean and Diane Spade, a twenty-something couple from Henderson, Nevada—stood next to their dark gray compact in The Market's empty parking lot. Teejay got out to help them load their bulky daypacks, then circled around to the passenger seat. "You drive."

I took the wheel, biting my tongue on a comeback about my probation being over. Gradually, as junipers started to outnumber houses, my irritation faded. Suspended dust refracted the early morning light, turning broken clouds into shades of mango and peach. The Spades appeared unimpressed, though they nodded politely at Teejay's backcountry introduction. As we passed the shimmering grasslands below Bear Mountain, Dean removed his hat to wipe his forehead, his blond hair already darkened by sweat.

The box canyon was still in shadow when I pulled up to park below the cottonwoods. The Giant's Claw rose above like a guardian, shielding the saddle and the secret trail from view. Preoccupied by the sight, I nearly missed the warning signs.

The Spades had seemed unremarkable, despite their identical black jeans and polos, odd garb for a pair of desert dwellers. When Dean reached to help his wife from the back seat, I noticed matching tattoos on their inner wrists, a single playing card. The Ace of Spades. *Got it—ha-ha.*

My amusement vanished when they started rifling through their packs, moving aside rolls of crime scene tape and evidence markers to pull out a set of black windbreakers emblazoned with the letters CSI. As Diane shrugged into hers, I read the smaller script below: *Conspiracy Spies of the Internet.*

I placed a hand over Teejay's arm to warn him. He stopped fiddling with the intercom and looked up just as Spade fished out a small drone camera. "Whoa, hold up, Dean. Got a permit for that?"

While Teejay explained we were obliged to act on the Forest Service's behalf to enforce commercial filming fees and permits, I walked over to block the canyon path, happy to put more distance between myself and a red-faced guy with a crime fetish and a death card tattoo. The thwarted vloggers opted for a refund.

As I drove back to town, I tried to convince myself the incident was just another one of those wacky things that happened with regularity in Sedona, like being late for work because a hot air balloon landed on the highway and blocked traffic, or being hailed, like Evan, by a naked and lost UFO spotter. Still, I puzzled over how the Spades heard about Franklin's death. They weren't locals, yet it looked like they'd come to Sedona prepared.

After we'd delivered the Spades safely back to The Market, Teejay took the wheel and headed for the nearest gas station. While he was filling the Jeep, I pulled out my cell to search for the Spades' videos. I froze as the dispatch radio squawked. Teejay grabbed it before I could, but I heard the panicked note in Gina's voice, the phones ringing in the background.

"The Forest Service just announced they're closing all campgrounds and trails in Oak Creek Canyon. *Tomorrow*. Because of the fire danger. When it rains, it pours, and when it doesn't rain—" She stopped, out of breath or aphorisms.

* * *

By the time we walked in, Harmony, Gina, and Chase were all fielding calls, patiently explaining that Blue Sky's tours traveled outside the closure boundaries. Chase hung up and told Teejay, "We've had a lot of cancellations anyway, mostly folks who had campsites or rooms in Oak Creek Canyon."

"Did you offer to reschedule?"

"Yeah, but first they want to know when the closure order will be lifted."

"Tell them to ask Mother Nature," Gina muttered between calls.

I followed Teejay to his office and closed the door behind us. "I found Dean and Diane Spade's channel on YouTube. They did a story on Evan's naked guy."

He spun around to face me, a frown creasing his forehead. "*What?*"

"The Spades have a thing for Sedona mysteries—UFOs, black helicopters, interdimensional portals." I played the teaser for an upcoming episode, Dean Spade promising to reveal how someone, presumably Franklin, had been silenced after stumbling onto a UFO crash site the feds and county sheriff were covering up. "No wonder he was upset. You ruined his scoop."

"Yeah, well, we don't need that kind of publicity right now."

"Haven't you heard? There's no such thing as bad publicity."

"I happen to know that's bullshit. And the timing couldn't be worse."

"Because of the closure?"

"Yes." He glanced toward the computer. "If Gina works her magic and converts some of the cancellations, we can get by for three, maybe four weeks." He ran a hand through his hair, forgetting the braid and dislodging a few dark strands. "You've got a Schnebly Hill tour at ten. In the meantime . . ." He handed me a pair of keys. "Go to the hardware store, get these copied."

CHAPTER

11

THE HARDWARE STORE was one of those rare Sedona institutions that hadn't changed much since I was a kid, calibrated to meet the needs of locals instead of chasing tourist dollars. I circled around to park in back where a few junipers offered shade, passing stacks of lumber, garden soil, and livestock feed on my way to the side entrance.

Inside, the shelves were stocked almost to the ceiling, and the combined scent of machine oil, house paint, and cleaning supplies filled me with nostalgia. The five-and-dime, the Flicker Shack movie theater, even Claire's favorite art supply store—all were long gone now. Sedona boasted dozens of shops selling crystals and tarot decks, but the hardware store remained a shrine to the practical, whether you were seeking a hex bolt, a coffee maker, or a bale of hay.

I tracked down a clerk to cut keys, the metallic screech following me as I threaded through the pet food aisle to housewares. I nearly collided with Ryan Driscoll, who'd beaten me to a display of water containers.

"Hey, Boston. You heard the news?" His uniform was still morning-crisp, while I could already feel the dust and sweat gathering under the loose twist of hair at the nape of my neck.

"That last-minute announcement from the ranger district?" Annoyance prickled my skin as he steered me away from the gallon jugs to a heavy-duty three-gallon container. "You could have warned me yesterday. We're losing bookings."

"Not that." He leaned toward me. "Barbara Lee is missing."

"*What?*" I almost dropped the container he'd chosen for me. "When?"

"Sometime last night. Her bed wasn't slept in, according to their caregiver. She called the sheriff early this morning."

"Her name's Marisol," I said absently, my mind busy working the timeline. I'd left the ranch house before noon and returned to my loft after five. My breath caught. I might have been the last person Barbara had spoken to outside of Marisol or Whittaker.

"She *claims* Barbara gave her the evening off." He lifted an eyebrow. "Says she didn't hear anything. Neither did Whitt, not that he's a reliable witness."

"Marisol lives in the bunkhouse. I think Whittaker's been sleeping in the study." The key cutter stopped abruptly, my words loud in the sudden silence. "Besides, it was pretty wild last night when that storm blew through."

"Yeah, campgrounds were a mess this morning— collapsed tents, broken branches. Lucky no one got hurt." His gaze went past my shoulder. I turned to see a gray-haired man wearing the store's red work vest, idly polishing an already sparkling cold case. Ryan nodded toward the door. "Meet you outside."

I got in line to pay, adding the latest *Sedona News* from the stack at the end of the counter. I walked out with my purchases, blinking at the bright sunshine. A white Forest Service pickup was parked beside the Willys.

I opened the hatch, and Ryan took the water container to strap it in with a bungee cord. He tipped his head toward the landscape. "Nice painting. Claire's?"

I nodded, then thanked him again for helping me the day before.

"Next time, call me before you go haring off. I'll bring the volunteer paperwork, you can sign off, and it'll be an official patrol."

"Speaking of patrols . . ." I told him about the incident with Dean and Diane Spade. Now that they knew the way to the box canyon, only their compact car and Teejay's warning would keep them from returning on their own. Ryan pointed out that watching for the Spades was far down on his list compared to an unsolved murder and a missing person case.

"*Two* missing persons," I reminded him. "Any word about Jane?"

"Jane isn't missing. She's hiding." He closed the hatch, his jaw tightening. "She can spot a uniform a mile away. Thing is, she'd better off talking to me than to the feds. "

"You *are* the feds." I nodded toward his gold USDA badge, and he flushed. Ryan might be right about Jane, but I'd been wise to that tic in his jaw ever since he was a pig-headed ten-year-old. Was he hoping to boost his career prospects by solving the case on his own? I wasn't about to offer unwelcome advice. Instead, I asked, "Did Barbara leave a note?"

"Caregiver says no, and the Land Rover is still there. But here's the thing, Boston. The sheriff found out the caregiver's ex is a bad dude, belongs to a gang in Phoenix. That's why the feds are getting involved."

My thoughts raced. Federal agents wouldn't take on a small-time drug deal or a straightforward missing persons case. "They must suspect foul play."

"What did you two talk about, anyway?"

For a moment, I thought he was referring to my encounter with Jane outside The Market. Then I realized he meant my conversation with Barbara. Stalling, I went around to the driver's door and opened it to let the heat escape. Had I said something to frighten Barbara or put her in danger? She'd all but sent me packing, and maybe she'd gone looking for the Willys to make sure I'd left. Had she tampered with the exhaust out of spite? Yesterday Ryan had dismissed my theories as *too complicated*, but maybe I could change his mind.

"I asked her about Jack Lyman."

He tipped back his head back and huffed out his exasperation.

"What if Jack and Barbara were having an affair and Franklin found out, threatened to tell Whittaker?"

"She's a dozen years older than Lyman."

"So?" I stared until he slipped his Ray-Bans out of his pocket and put them on.

"You think Barbara and Whitt were having marriage problems?"

Had I told Ryan that yesterday? I'd been half out of my mind with heat exhaustion and trying hard not to over-share, but I remembered talking with him about the goddess circle. Only I was pretty sure he'd brought it up first. "Money problems. Isn't that what you thought?"

"Sometimes it's the same thing," he pointed out. The radio on his belt squawked. "Gotta go. The patrol captain's organizing search teams to back up the sheriff's posse. I'll be in and out of cell range all day. Text me if you see Jane."

After he drove off, leaving a puff of reddish dust in his wake, it occurred to me that Ryan knew I'd talked to Barbara yesterday. Maybe he'd already tipped off the sheriff that I'd been to the ranch. Would he have described me as a harmless but nosy ex-reporter who got in the way?

Or did I just become what cops liked to refer to as a "person of interest"?

* * *

I looked around headquarters for Teejay, then handed the new keys to Gina when I couldn't find him.

"He had a couple of meetings. He won't be back till late." She consulted the schedule on her screen. "It's been a juggling act today. Lots of cancellations, but since we're one driver short . . ." She peered at me over her readers. "Can you take his eleven o'clock?"

"Sure." I'd passed Chase in the hallway, and Harmony wore the dispatch headphones over her streaked locks, seafoam green today. I leaned across the counter, my voice low. "I saw him hiking with someone yesterday. Is he taking some time off, or . . . ?"

Gina didn't take the bait. Then Chase returned, carrying a can of soda, and the moment was gone.

I was returning from my last tour when I remembered Claire's painting still waited in the wagon's hatch. The office was eerily quiet as I carried the landscape down the hallway to the reception area. Chase-like-the-bank had apparently gone home early, leaving Harmony to stare at the dispatch radio, her expression bored.

I held up the landscape to get Gina's attention. "I thought we might be able to hang this somewhere. I don't have room for it."

Her face brightened. "That sky is the same blue as our Jeeps."

Harmony unplugged and walked around the institutional gray reception counter for a closer look. "Let's hang it now. We could use some happy vibes."

We turned to Gina. She shrugged. "Why not? The phones aren't ringing, and many hands make light work."

The three of us managed to slide a display rack of water bottles out of the way to make room for the large frame. Gina found a hammer while Harmony and I measured and marked the space. We'd just finished when a soft electronic chime signaled the door to the garage had opened. Moments later, Evan strolled in, coffee in hand.

"Nice," he said, eyeing the painting. "Looks like Canyon de Chelly. One of your aunt's?"

I shook my head. "Not her painting style, but she was an avid collector. Unfortunately, I don't have wall space for this one."

"Del loaned it to us. I think it's stunning, but it makes everything else look dingy." Gina frowned at the pinky-tan walls, a color that someone—*Steve? Teejay?*—must have thought looked like sandstone. "If it's slow after the holiday weekend, we'll use the time to repaint."

"Sounds like a good job for Sam." Evan winked. "Let's vote on it before he gets here."

Like magic, the garage door chimed again. A split second later, one of the phones buzzed and Harmony dashed to answer. While Evan consulted with Gina about tomorrow's schedule, I left to find Sam. He was fiddling with the coffee maker, his back toward me.

"Hey, Sam. I've been wanting to talk to you."

He whirled around and leaned back against the counter, blocking my view. Was Sam our resident prankster? It wasn't a stretch to imagine him plastering the Jeeps with an anti-growth message. His idea, or had he been acting on orders from someone else? I aimed for a casual note. "Megan mentioned you were hanging around The Market with Franklin a few years back."

"She remembers that?" He straightened his lanky frame.

Though I wasn't inclined to play matchmaker, if Megan's interest made Sam talkative, I could work with that. "She was still in high school then, but I think you caught her eye."

Sam reached up to smooth his gold-brown curls, his gaze unfocused, as though he might be reminiscing about the dreadlocks. I brought him back to earth. "Did Franklin ever tell you anything about his personal life? His family?"

"Um, an ex-wife? LA maybe? Her lawyer went after him, so he quit his job, gave away his stuff, and hit the road, because you can't get money from a rolling stone." His shoulders relaxed as the clichés rolled off his tongue. "Franklin wasn't a slave to the system, you know?"

I leaned one hip against the counter next to him, mirroring his posture while keeping an eye on the entry to the reception area. Any minute now, Harmony would leave for the day. "I ran into him a few times around town, but I never got to know him. What else did you two talk about?"

"Philosophers, poetry, astronomy . . . That dude was smart. He was really into Tibetan Buddhism, said they were related to the Navajo, right? And he knew a lot about stars. I think he was some kind of scientist before." Then his hazel eyes narrowed. "Is it true? Someone shot him?"

"Who told you that?" Between tours I'd flipped through the *Snooze*. A few lines squeezed below a recap of last week's planning and zoning meeting referred to Franklin's death as a hiking accident "under investigation."

Sam read the truth on my face and swallowed hard. "*Jesus.* I heard about it from a buddy. Maybe he had a couple of run-ins with cops, but Franklin was a good guy."

The clamor of conversation and ringing phones washed down the hallway, muffling our voices. Even so, I pitched my words lower. "A good guy who was dealing drugs?"

He started to shake his head, then stopped. "Maybe some pot now and then."

"How about Oxy, stuff like that?"

His mouth twisted. Sam was loquacious by nature, and I could tell he wanted to keep talking. He looked at the scuffed hallway tile. Finally, he said, "Okay. You didn't hear this from me, right? A while back, some of the local kids were raiding the family medicine cabinets and trading with Franklin for pot. Nothing hard-core. Just stuff people needed, prescriptions, like."

Now Franklin's arrest made sense. I'd heard about similar schemes: Rich kids steal their parents' drugs, but the details get swept under a rug once daddy has a word with a police chief, a council member, someone with connections. *Whatever.* That didn't interest me. The scratch marks I'd seen on Jane's arms did. "Not meth?"

"*No way.* No street drugs." I outstared him, and he started to fidget. "Maybe some X now and then. And he used to bring mushrooms to the drumming circles out in the forest. Sometimes a tea he made, like ayahuasca or something, for visions."

"You gave Franklin a ride to the party at Lee Ranch."

His eyes widened at this new tack. "Um, no?"

I waited. Most people were uncomfortable with silence. My patience was rewarded.

"He rode out to the pass with me on the sunset tour last Tuesday. I dropped him off near the fork. He told me he was going to camp someplace, said he'd see me in a couple of days. I didn't know he was going to crash the party."

Sam looked past my shoulder and snapped to attention. "Teejay—I was just heading out."

"Yeah? Change of plans. Evan's leading your sunset tour today. You're coming with me." Visibly struggling to hold back a protest, Sam turned toward the garage. Teejay shifted his attention. "You, too, Delilah."

"Where?"

"Lee Ranch." Teejay's gaze didn't leave mine. "Barbara Lee's missing. We volunteered to help with the search. We'll take one of the Jeeps. Make sure the water jug is full," he called to Sam as the door chimed.

I turned to follow, but Teejay reached out to stop me, his fingers cool through my shirt sleeve. "You don't seem surprised."

"Ryan Driscoll told me. I ran into him at the hardware store. I meant to say something earlier, but . . ." I swallowed my excuses. Teejay must have been working in Steve's office. How much of my conversation with Sam had he overheard?

He released my arm. "Be ready in five minutes. I'll let Gina know we're going."

* * *

Coppery afternoon light struck the layered sandstones of Lee Canyon as Teejay turned the Jeep onto the ranch road. A tall gray-haired woman waved us through the gate, gesturing with her clipboard toward an open spot in the line of vehicles parked along the road. Below the cliffs, a string of volunteers in fluorescent orange vests slowly crossed the rangeland toward the wash, heads bent.

"Stay here," he told us. "I'll check in."

He jogged back toward the barrier of traffic cones and caution tape. We'd made the drive in tense silence, Teejay's jaw hard as stone, Sam still sulking at having to relinquish the sunset hike to Evan. I figured I had a couple of minutes before Teejay returned, so I tried to coax more information out of Sam. His responses were short and distracted. I gave up and got out of the Jeep.

The *chuff-chuff-chuff* of a helicopter echoed between the sides of the canyon, and I looked up at the saddle where I'd hiked the day before. A gray and yellow chopper hovered against a faded blue sky. The day's heat was only beginning to loosen its grip, upping the stakes for the searchers, who radiated intense purpose. Besides the ground and air teams working the canyon, we'd also passed a few 4×4s bearing the star-shaped logos of the YCSO Jeep posse, trained volunteers who assisted the sheriff's office during search-and-rescue operations.

Behind me, Sam scrambled out and I spotted Teejay making his way back. He'd donned a safety vest, a radio clipped to the pocket. We kept up with his long strides as he filled us in. "Search teams started a couple of hours ago. There's a lot of ground to cover before dark."

We cut toward the cliffs on a diagonal, the sandy soil already traversed by bootprints. Teejay kept to a straight-line march, deviating only to bypass an occasional one-seed juniper or piñon. As we descended toward the wash, the patchy undergrowth thickened. When I realized what his objective was, I felt unease spread around my ribcage.

"We'll drop in here." He gestured toward the dry waterfall where I'd stopped yesterday.

The short downclimb was easy enough to negotiate with hands and feet, and soon Teejay and Sam were across the wash. I lagged behind, unsurprised when Teejay headed directly for the staircase of loose rock that had taken me so long to find.

I watched from a safe distance while Sam climbed. Teejay waited on the ledge, his legs wide, and for a moment I saw the cliff dweller standing in his place, staring back at me. I shook my head to clear my vision and started up the rocks, my limbs heavy.

"Can't see the ranch from here." Sam's voice floated down. "But the searchers will be at the fence line soon."

I didn't catch Teejay's reply, something about another search team on the opposite side of the road. Then he gripped my arm to steady me as I stepped up beside him.

"You okay?"

"I'm fine." I blamed my breathlessness on the aftereffects of yesterday's heat exhaustion.

"Hey, guys?" Sam had already spotted the second trail marker and was on his way through the brush. "I see a couple of prints over here where the scrub oak protected them from the wind. They're small, maybe a woman's size."

"They're mine."

Teejay whirled around to stare at me. I stared back.

"Guys?"

I reminded myself we were there to look for Barbara and confessed. "I came out to visit the Lees yesterday. I was wearing Tevas. Is that what you see, Sam?"

"Yep. I recognize the tread." He shot me a surprised look over the brush. "Didn't know you were so hard-core, Del."

"Delilah has many hidden talents." Teejay's voice held an edge.

"Oo-kay." Sam drew out the word. "You two work it out. I'm gonna see where this path leads."

"We'll catch up," Teejay told him, his gaze still locked on mine, golden-brown irises steady as a cougar's.

I could hear Sam scrabbling over loose rock. I waited until the sounds faded and he was out of earshot. "I talked to Barbara about the party. She said Franklin came looking for a handout. Unlikely, don't you think?"

He crossed his arms over his chest, and I changed direction. "You know there's limited enforcement on public lands. Isn't that one of the reasons we share incident reports with the Forest Service? We're their eyes and ears."

He nodded shortly. "And?"

"Ryan thinks Franklin hid a meth lab somewhere."

"And you decided to look for it." His arms dropped to his sides as he stepped closer. "Are you kidding me?"

I was going about this all wrong. I shook my head. "That's not why I was here. I asked Barbara if I could walk to the ruins because—" *Slow down.* "Something felt off. Then I saw footprints heading this way. Franklin's."

His jaw clenched. "You could have mentioned that earlier."

"I could have." I decided to stop circling around. I watched his face as I lobbed the grenade. "But I think you already knew where he was headed."

His private tour, the rifle shot, his army experience. What else was he hiding? A rock clattered from the slope far above us—Sam. I wanted answers, but now—standing on a ledge next to someone I wasn't sure I could trust—wasn't the time or place.

Teejay nodded in the direction of the ranch. "Might be a good idea to talk to the investigators so they can eliminate your footprints."

"Of course." After years of reporting from crime scenes, I knew better. Or was he trying to get rid of me? I looked up toward the saddle, hoping my hat brim shielded my expression. "Aren't you going to follow Sam?"

"In a minute. Did Barbara say anything else?"

I swallowed. It was one thing to discuss the Lees' troubles with Ryan, who shared my childhood experiences of the ranch. It was another to tell Teejay, who still hadn't volunteered how he knew about this route to the saddle.

"Just some old gossip about my aunt. Nothing relevant."

His shoulders relaxed. "Sam's half mountain goat. Shouldn't take us long to search the ridge. We'll meet you back at the Jeep before sunset."

* * *

The homestead had transformed into a hive of activity, its hub the sheriff's boxy-looking remote command vehicle parked next to the bunkhouse. I headed that way, my feet leaden. A uniformed deputy intercepted, ushering me up the veranda of the bunkhouse and inside, where a burly detective in a gray crewcut had commandeered Marisol's quarters.

Detective Haberman debriefed me about my visit the day before, focusing most of his questions on Barbara's state of mind. Mouth dry, I leashed my responses, wary of sounding like a raving conspiracist (hello, Dean Spade). He let me go after a not-so-subtle warning about steering clear of an active investigation. Maybe Ryan had vouched for me after all.

I stepped outside onto the veranda, relief changing to surprise when I saw him leaning against the rail.

"Hey, Boston. You decide to come clean?"

I gave the weak joke an even weaker smile, though I was glad to see a friendly face. I explained I'd arrived with Teejay and Sam, who were now searching along the route up to the saddle. It was Ryan's turn to look surprised. He turned to stare at the ridge.

"Don't see 'em." Late afternoon sunbeams raked across the cliffs, creating a patchwork effect of violet-blue shadows and glowing sandstone.

"See that spire?" From this perspective, the Giant's Claw resembled a woman's upturned face. "The trail—if you can call it that—leads to it. The lower half is out of sight of the ranch." As soon as I spoke, I realized I'd given myself away.

He spun around, his gray eyes narrowing. "You were there yesterday."

"I saw bootprints heading down from the ruins and decided to take a look." Before he could probe further, I changed the subject, nodding toward the ranch house. "What's *he* doing here?"

A slim, dark-haired man stood near the cactus garden, his eyes closed and palms open. Something familiar about his posture had drawn my attention, and after a few beats, I remembered seeing him in Leah's morning vinyasa class. Male students were rare and tended to slip in and out as though they didn't want to call attention to themselves, which usually had the opposite effect.

Ryan scoffed. "Guy claims to be psychic, says he helped the Phoenix police with a case a while back. Sheriff must be desperate now that the feds are moving in."

"Aren't they working the Phoenix angle?"

"That's what the boss tells me. Says he's glad for the help." The edge to his voice reminded me how badly Ryan wanted to solve this case. I'd met his patrol captain—a former smoke jumper whose knees screamed career change—during a wilderness first aid class at the supervisor's office in Flagstaff.

"Is Lisa here?" Only two law enforcement officers were assigned to the half-million-acre Red Rock Ranger District, Ryan and Lisa Vargas, a young woman who'd transferred from the Cibola National Forest in New Mexico.

"She's setting up a checkpoint in Oak Creek Canyon. Starting tomorrow morning, only residents and through traffic will be allowed past Grasshopper Point. We've got a half dozen volunteers and fire prevention officers visiting campgrounds to persuade people to leave before the closure takes effect."

He glanced toward the command vehicle, and then back at the ridge. "I'll walk you out. My truck's by the gate, and I need to follow up with the search teams. Looks like someone's been parking along the road often enough to leave erosion scars." He clocked my interest and added, "Probably just a boondocker or poacher. Scene techs had a look, but the wind erased any evidence. No sign of Barbara yet, but we've got a lot of boots on the ground."

"How's Whittaker holding up?" I asked as we headed down the ranch road.

"Caregiver moved into the house to keep an eye on him." He sighed and kicked at a loose stone in our path. "The weather service is predicting red flag conditions by Sunday. Meantime, we've got four dozen searchers scouring the back-country, tourists driving around looking for places to camp, all when a tossed cigarette or a bad catalytic converter could spark a wildfire."

Red flag warnings were issued for the trifecta of high winds, high temperatures, and low humidity. I looked across the valley, my focus blurring until everything was the parched beige of tinder. Ryan added, "If it doesn't rain soon, the supervisor will close the rest of the forest, maybe even next week."

My breath hitched. Most of Blue Sky's tours traveled over forest roads. Teejay said he could keep the company afloat three or four weeks, but a forest-wide closure would change the math. We fell into a glum silence broken by our bootsteps and sporadic chatter from Ryan's radio. Our bright blue Jeep stood out among the long string of gray or white SUVs and trucks. I slowed my pace as we approached.

"Will you let me know if—?" I swallowed hard.

"Sure. You got a ride back to town? I'd drive you, but I'll be here for a while yet."

"I'll wait for Teejay and Sam."

Ryan stopped, avoiding my gaze as he removed his hat and wiped a hand across his forehead. "Didn't know how to tell you this before, but some of the other outfitters spotted Franklin in a Blue Sky Jeep."

"Sam gave Franklin a ride a day or two before the party at Lee Canyon."

"Yeah?"

I waited, feeling my throat tighten, while he took his time resettling his hat.

"Come on," he said at last. "I'll see if one of the volunteers can take you."

"I'm leaving now. You're welcome to ride with me." I turned toward the unfamiliar baritone. The psychic had caught up with us. He nodded to Ryan. "Mark Stillman."

Ryan seemed to be struck dumb, so I spoke for both of us. "I'm Del Cooper, and this is Ryan Driscoll."

The men shook hands and eyed each other. This close, I could see Mark Stillman's black hair was threaded with gray, though his skin was smooth and unlined. I guessed he was a couple of years older than Ryan, maybe mid-forties, Hawaiian or Asian descent. His loose cotton shirt and slacks looked expensive, but his hiking books were scuffed and worn.

Something in Ryan's stiff posture told me he was ready to object, but I wasn't about to pass up the opportunity to talk to a crime-solving psychic. I explained that Mark Stillman and I were yoga classmates and flashed my best smile. "A ride would be great. Thank you."

I followed him toward a white Tesla X parked a few car lengths from the Jeep, turning to send Ryan a wave, trying—and mostly succeeding—not to enjoy his nonplussed expression.

12

M ARK STILLMAN'S TESLA was an SUV only in theory,
 inches lower to the ground than the Willys and infi-
nitely more luxurious. It still had that new car smell, mixed
with a hint of sandalwood that I realized was him. I tried
to slow my racing thoughts and enjoy the AC, but I winced
every time I heard a chunk of gravel smack against the
panels.

He seemed unruffled, his long fingers resting easily on
the steering wheel. "I haven't seen you in Leah's class lately."

New job, new schedule, I explained. We talked about
yoga classes for a few minutes, and I learned he'd moved to
Sedona from LA almost three years ago. I hoped the small
talk would transition naturally to his appearance at Lee
Ranch, but when it didn't, I addressed the elephant in the
room.

"Ryan mentioned you were helping the sheriff. How does
that work? Did he call you or . . . ?"

"Like dial-a-psychic?" He laughed. "Fair question. It's
not like there's a Chamber of Commerce for mediums and
healers."

"Um, actually, there is."

"Seriously?" The corner of his mouth lifted in a smile. "I've worked with law enforcement before, but I don't seek out clients. I'll take a referral now and then."

"Who referred you this time?"

He shrugged. "No one. I offered."

I shifted to search his profile. "Why? Do you know Barbara Lee?"

"Never met her. I read the story about Lee Ranch in Friday's paper and remembered seeing her around town a couple of times. She struck me as a tragic figure. I thought I could help."

A tragic figure? I hadn't thought of Barbara that way, yet even as a child I'd sensed something awkward about the Lees. My skepticism about Mark eased a notch. I explained I'd spent summers with my aunt, who visited the ranch often. "If you read the article, then you know Lee Ranch was a magnet for movie people. The parties were legendary. I was too young to understand then, but in retrospect, I think Whittaker treated Barbara like a child. He was indulgent, dismissive. Sometimes she'd act out to get his attention. She was so jealous—"

A light bulb flicked on. Barbara was so jealous that the Lees' marriage had no room for anyone else, not even their child. *Like my parents.* Mark turned to glance at me, and I continued in a rush. "Anyway, I drove out to see them yesterday. Whittaker's health is declining. The land trade will give them the chance to move into town." I was talking too much. *Some interviewer.*

I started again. "How does it work? Do you get visions?"

"The best explanation is I can identify patterns and follow them to their most likely outcome." He sent me a measuring side glance before slowing to steer around a swath of loose gravel. "You seem underwhelmed."

"I thought psychics could sense what someone's thinking or feeling. Or"—I chose my words carefully—"see the past or future."

"I don't really think of myself as a psychic. I'm an architect. Space—what's *not* there—is as important, maybe even more important, than what *is* there. Sometimes I can extrapolate based on impressions or qualities." He frowned briefly, as though the explanation didn't satisfy him. "I knew I was different when I was around twelve. My grandparents practiced Shinto. I guess some of it rubbed off. They looked for the essence of things—trees, rocks, animals. People, too."

I thought of the rock art Ronnie Jackson showed us during her slide presentation. "Shinto's a type of shamanism, right?"

"Most belief systems have shamanic elements. Shinto also has a tradition of what you might call channeling. As my grandmother aged, she began hearing the spirits speak to her." He grinned again. "Of course, some people thought she was crazy."

Was "crazy" just differently wired? Was Whittaker losing his mind or letting the past speak to him? Was Jane drug addled or a wise fool? Were my dreams and visions simply my traumatized nervous system misfiring? I was curious, but I wanted facts, not philosophy. "Did you know Franklin Johnson?"

"That guy who fell off a cliff last week?" He glanced over quickly. "Ah. *You* found him."

"He didn't fall by accident. He was shot."

We'd arrived at the fork, but instead of turning, Mark rolled to a stop and closed his eyes. Reflexively, I reached for the door handle, half convinced I'd see his eyelashes flutter and hear him start speaking in someone else's voice.

"It happened near the ranch." His tone was matter of fact, and my hand relaxed.

"That news story about the land trade—the one with the photo of Barbara? Franklin was at that party." I searched his face for a sign that, behind closed eyelids, Mark was seeing something.

He exhaled loudly. "It's all connected. The land trade, his death, Barbara's disappearance."

At last, a man who listens. Maybe that was the secret to Mark's heightened perception. "Franklin and Barbara argued at the party on Wednesday evening. We found his body in the next canyon on Friday. I spoke to his ex-girlfriend later that afternoon, and she vanished without a trace a few days afterward. She might know why he was killed."

His eyes blinked open. He turned to me, his gaze curious.

I shrugged. "Sketchy, I know. But my gut tells me there's a link somewhere."

A car horn blared behind us. I hadn't even heard the pickup pulling closer. The driver wore an orange safety vest, identifying him as a member of the sheriff's volunteer posse. Mark restarted the Tesla and turned right. The pickup hooked left toward Palatki.

"Nothing wrong with gut instinct. We spend our lives reading subtle cues, but because we process them unconsciously, we tend to dismiss them. We're taught to value facts instead."

"Mm." I murmured in agreement, thinking of my experience as a reporter, how facts validated my hunches. In this case, however, facts were elusive. Though it'd been one week since the night of the party, I felt no closer to learning who'd killed Franklin or why. Ryan seemed to think it was a drug deal gone bad. Ronnie Jackson had mentioned pothunting, and I'd seen Teejay heading for the ruin in the box canyon. Jane was hiding, Barbara missing. Or had the killer targeted them as well?

The harder I tried to fit the pieces together, the less sense the puzzle made. I sighed, made myself relax back into the seat to gaze out the window. The road snaked over a savanna-like expanse of desert grassland, with long views west to Mingus Mountain, the sun sinking behind. A herd of prong-horns occasionally grazed here, though recently, packs of crust-busting UTVs were a more common sight. The air was hazy from dust or smoke or both, but Jerome's streetlights twinkled from the mountainside's purple-blue shadows.

"Beautiful sunset. You said you spent summers here?"

I decided not to spoil Mark's enjoyment by attributing the dramatic colors to wildfire smoke or last night's dust storm. "Until I was fifteen. I grew up back east, moved here a couple of years ago, when my aunt got sick. She and Whittaker Lee were old friends, though they drifted apart."

I shifted the subject to the Lees' string of business failures, from the ill-fated TV series to the retreat center.

"Ah. The goddess circle."

My pulse jumped. "It's been almost twenty years."

"A few people still talk about it. A cautionary tale about the negative consequences of acting out of alignment. Like misusing one's gifts or disregarding spiritual principles."

I tried to read him, gave up. "You think Barbara Lee's goddess circle was a scam?"

"You brought it up. What's your instinct saying? Is the goddess circle relevant to her disappearance?"

"Maybe." I frowned. "It's like I have all the pieces, yet something's keeping me from putting them together."

Mark turned onto the highway, the Tesla suddenly quiet as we made the gradual climb to town. The silence didn't bother me. I settled deeper in my seat and regarded him surreptitiously. He was serious and thoughtful, yet attractive in a slow burn kind of way.

He didn't speak until we stopped for the first red light, shifting in his seat to look at me. "You thought you'd be safe here." The light changed, and he returned his attention to the cars in front of us. "Don't look so worried. I'm not a mind reader."

Thank goodness for that. Fortunately, twilight camouflaged my burning cheeks.

"You think of Sedona as your safe space, and it is, but not in the way you expected. You have a deep connection to the natural world. That's healing for you, but it may also break you open . . . when you're ready."

Boom. Just like that, Mark Stillman sounded like every stereotype I'd ever held about Sedona's mystics and healers. Feeling wariness creep back in, I coolly directed him to Blue Sky's headquarters, where I'd left my vehicle. He pulled up to the gate, and I thanked him for the ride.

"If you'd like to talk more . . ." His words trailed off, maybe because he already knew I was going to say no.

I reconsidered. If the sheriff was open-minded enough to consult a psychic, then so was I. "How about after work tomorrow?"

We made the arrangements, and I waved him off with a smile at least two parts self-amused. My ulterior motives probably meant I was out of alignment with spiritual principles, but I could live with that.

* * *

The next morning I looked for Mark as I unrolled my mat in the back of the yoga studio. The class was entirely female, a mix of regulars and drop-ins. I tried to lose myself in the flow of poses, but my monkey mind swung from thought to thought. At last, during Shavasana, an image of the spiral petroglyph floated peacefully behind my eyelids, dissolving when Leah struck the brass bowl she used to signal the end of class.

As the others filed out of the studio, I talked her into joining me at The Market. While I downed a breakfast smoothie, she told me everything she knew about Mark, then reached across the table, her fingers cold on mine. "Is it true? Is something out there preying on people?"

I felt the last of my yoga high vanishing like a raindrop in the desert as I assured her she had nothing to fear. By the time I walked into Blue Sky's reception area, I was braced for bad news, and Gina's morose expression made my shoulders tighten another notch. Most days, she was quick with a compliment or a word of support, even if only an inspirational trope. This morning, she swiped a hand over her face and sniffled.

I didn't have the heart to tell her she'd smudged her mascara. "What's wrong?"

"Sorry"—she reached for a tissue—"just catching up on the overnight messages. Mostly cancellations."

I waited for her to finish dabbing at her nose, but she didn't remind me to look on the bright side. Or assure me Blue Sky might be small, but we were scrappy, and we'd get through this by working together. I leaned my elbows on the counter. "Teejay once told me we didn't need new reservations software because your power of persuasion was our best marketing tool."

She attempted a smile, but it didn't reach her eyes. "I just talked to him. He and Sam spent the night in Lee Canyon. Barbara Lee's still missing. The rumors . . ." She *tsked*.

I'd heard rumors too. Whispers before my yoga class. Gossip at The Market, while Leah and I waited at the juice bar. Barbara had—*take your pick*—left Whittaker for a younger man, wandered into an interdimensional portal, been abducted by aliens . . . or encountered Franklin's killer.

The garage door chimed and Megan entered, eyes wide, explaining she'd overheard something crazy while filling up at a gas station on her way into town. Before she could elaborate, Harmony swept in, a swirl of purple gauze. "One of my roommates told me that satanists kidnapped Barbara Lee."

"Oh, for crying out loud." Gina slammed her pen onto the desk.

The door chimed again, Evan this time, smelling of hazelnut and the outdoors. "Did you hear—"

"Yes," we chorused. Through the front window I saw Teejay and Sam pull in.

Gina saw them too. She waved us toward the hall. "Team meeting *now*. Steve's office."

I rolled a chair down the hallway and parked it next to Evan's. He whispered that he'd guided guests into the box canyon as a helicopter hovered above them. We scooted over to make room for Megan. When I raised my eyebrows at her joggers and T-shirt, she told us she'd spent the night in the hospital with her grandmother. Before I could ask for details, Teejay entered, Sam at his heels, and the room went silent.

Sam glanced around, then folded his long legs to sit on the floor, leaning back against the wall. "Where's Chase-like-the-bank?"

"He's not coming. Arnulfo's at the tire store. He'll be in later." Gina perched on the edge of the low bookcase. She wore a dispatch headset around her neck, though at the moment, all our drivers were here.

Harmony hovered near the doorway, ready to dash for the phones, assuming they'd start ringing. I took in the somber faces and felt lucky to have my own little corner of Sedona, thanks to my aunt. Even if you could find a guest house or apartment that hadn't been converted into a vacation rental, rent was out of reach for most workers. Our drivers could swing it by saving cash from busy months, but it was still a stretch. Harmony had three roommates. Megan lived with her family in Cottonwood. I was pretty sure Sam spent his summers camping and couch-surfing.

Teejay moved the chair from behind the desk to face the rest of the room. "Looks like the rest of the ranger district will close after the holiday weekend."

Groans led to the usual debate. The tall conifers growing in backcountry canyons posed the greatest threat of catastrophic fire, not the open piñon-juniper woodlands surrounding the town of Sedona. On the other hand, only three routes led in and out of town, and crowding more people into a smaller space seemed unwise.

Teejay raised his palm to stop the back-and-forth. "Either way, we'll focus on our sightseeing excursions in town. Any ideas for filling seats?"

I sat back and listened as the others chimed in. When Harmony pointed out we didn't have a vortex tour, the drivers groaned again. Megan wanted to team up with local artists for studio visits. Gina suggested trips to Verde Valley vineyards.

Sam straightened. "How about a true crime tour?" Teejay shot him an exasperated look, but he pressed. "You know people would dig it, especially now."

"Sam, that's just gross." At Megan's disapproval, he slumped back against the wall. The sad thing was, Sam was right. I'd been monitoring comments on the Spades' videos, and this morning an alarming number of new messages linked Franklin's death and Barbara's disappearance. Everyone wanted to be a detective, including me.

Sam closed his eyes, his mouth a stubborn line. My reporter's instincts buzzed. *Something happened after I left him and Teejay in Lee Canyon.*

A ringing phone ended the meeting. Gina and Harmony scurried away, and the rest of us stood to gather cups and chairs.

Relief crossed Teejay's face. "Gina and I will adjust the rotation as fairly as we can. We're booked over the Fourth, but if you're thinking of taking time off, next week would be good. Megan—"

She paused in front of Teejay, her gaze aimed at the floor. "Why don't you take some time today? Sam can lead your ten o'clock."

Megan shot Sam a small smile, and his stubborn expression softened. He followed Evan out the doorway. I squeezed Megan's hand and started to walk out behind her, but Teejay stopped me.

"Delilah—" He leaned back against the desk, his hands gripping the edge. This close, I could see he hadn't shaved. "I'm sorry, but you're lowest on the rotation. Sam may need help covering Megan's routes today, and you might pick up a couple extra tours over the weekend."

I felt a flicker of panic but pushed it aside. Time was freedom, and I wanted to find Jane and Barbara before Franklin's killer did. With the monthly check from my renters, I'd get by without tips for a while, as long as the Willys kept running and I didn't replace the loft's swamp cooler.

"Chase quit to drive for Pink Jeep. He says they plan to use the closure to train more drivers and focus on their Grand Canyon runs."

I nodded, only half surprised. "Good opportunity for him."

"Frankly, I'm glad to be rid of him. Our friend Dean Spade? His cousin."

"The bumper stickers?"

"Chase denied it." He hesitated, as though weighing his words. "Look, I'd understand if you want to jump ship, too.

But with Chase out, Gina and Harmony could use some help fielding calls."

"Okay." I held back a sigh. He stood, but I wasn't ready to be dismissed. I went to the door and closed it. "You and Sam found something on the ridge."

He nodded shortly. "There's an alcove on the other side of the Giant's Claw. Franklin's tracks led there."

I'd been minutes from discovering Franklin's hideout myself. Instead, I'd followed my imaginary Sinaguan friend to the saddle and spotted Teejay in the box canyon below. Something dawned on me. "Sam told me he dropped Franklin off a couple of miles down the road. He was staying in the alcove, wasn't he?"

"We saw his gear. Empty water jugs. Clothing. I think he spent a night or two there."

"Barbara?"

"Afraid not. There's a small granary, some pictographs." He pegged my interest. "Not your spiral. I'm still looking."

"Thanks." Considering the circumstances, I was surprised he remembered.

He leaned against the desk to continue his narrative. After finding Franklin's things, he'd sent Sam back down the trail to bring up a deputy to secure the scene. By then it was dark, so the three waited until morning for an evidence team. After the scene techs finished in the alcove, Teejay guided them farther along the rim.

"You were right. He fell after he was shot." His voice hushed. "We found something else. I took a photo to show Ronnie." He reached into the back pocket of his jeans for his phone, and I walked over to perch next to him on the desk. The photo showed a necklace coiled on the sandstone, its pendant almost half the length of the pen laid next to it.

"May I?" He handed over the phone, and I enlarged the photo to zoom in on the shell pendant, shaped into a bird and inlaid with tiny squares of turquoise. Though a few stones were missing, the exquisite inlay took my breath away. My thoughts scattered. *The plastic-wrapped object I'd seen Franklin trying to hand to Barbara. Ronnie's looter. Our incident reports.*

I handed the phone back, trying to gather the pieces. The photo didn't rule out Teejay planting the necklace before the others arrived—but he would never disgrace something so ancient and beautiful. "The silver chain obviously isn't original. Someone found this artifact, and then altered it to make a necklace. Who would do that?"

He shrugged. "Ronnie might have some ideas."

"The incident report?"

He nodded. "She asked me to contact her about anything odd."

"Did you tell her about Sam? Ryan said someone's been parking near Lee Ranch often enough to damage the soils."

"Sam?" Teejay lifted an eyebrow. "The guy who stops traffic to guide a tarantula off the road? Who badgered Gina until she got a compost bin for the break area?"

"Okay, *not* Sam." But Sam wasn't the only acolyte in Franklin's orbit, and he wasn't the only person with access to our Jeeps. Something else nagged at me, and then I remembered. "How did you know about the trail to the alcove?"

A sharp rap on the door drowned out the end of my question. Gina opened it and peered inside, nodding toward the office phone on the desk next to us. A red light blinked on and off. "Teejay—Steve's on hold for you."

She opened the door wider, addressing me. "This would be a good time to practice with the radio, while Evan and Sam are still on their way to pick up passengers."

The dispatch lesson was followed by an hour-long blur of disappointed callers who'd planned their Fourth of July vacations around camping in Oak Creek Canyon. When it was time to get in the Jeep and grind my way up Schnebly Hill, a family of five in tow, I felt like a prisoner whose sentence had been commuted.

I scarfed down a burrito on my way back to headquarters. By this time, Gina seemed confident enough in my dispatch skills to let me take over the radio while she and Harmony alternated lunch breaks.

During a lull, Harmony lowered her voice, though we were the only two in the office. "I didn't want to say this while Gina was around, but something creepy is going on. Something *dark*. That's why the sheriff can't find your friend. Barbara's trapped by evil energies, and only a lightworker can release her."

"Who told you that?"

She waved her hand vaguely. "Everyone was talking about it at The Market. There's a ceremony tomorrow night. A group of people are joining together to amplify their vibration so they can push back the negative forces and make contact with her."

My mouth turned to dust, and I reached for my water bottle. Before I could tell Harmony the story had been whipped up by Chase-like-the-bank and his disgruntled cousin, Gina's white Lexus pulled into the driveway.

"Please don't tell Gina. You know how cynical she is about anything New Age-y."

"I won't say a word." Not to Gina, anyway. I had a pretty good idea who might help me find out more about tomorrow night's gathering.

During my last tour of the day, distant thunderclouds lined up like soldiers above Schnebly Hill, seeming to look over our shoulders as I pointed the Jeep back toward town. I settled into Chase's empty chair to help with the phones, but they were ringing less frequently, the tone of the calls shifting. Most people canceling reservations were concerned the entire forest would shut down, limiting their hiking options. But a few wondered if it was safe to travel in Sedona at all.

Gina caught my frown after I hung up from reassuring yet another caller. "Go home, Del. It's almost time to switch over to voice mail, and the guys have the tours covered. Tomorrow is another day."

I was idling at the stoplight at the bottom of Airport Road when something occurred to me. Earlier, when Gina said Steve was calling, it was only three AM in Hawaii.

13

M Y APPOINTMENT WITH Mark Stillman wasn't until seven, so I had a couple of hours to kill. I remembered I'd last picked up my mail the day before I found Franklin's body, exactly one week ago. I turned east toward the post office and the army of slate gray clouds camped above Munds Mountain.

According to local lore, Sedona's PO was built atop a vortex—perhaps explaining the nearby roundabout's discombobulating effect on drivers. I gritted my teeth and managed to squeeze in front of a lumbering RV, then sailed into the parking lot just as a red hatchback pulled out of my favorite parking spot.

My luck held. The Lees' silver Land Rover was parked at the building's entrance, next to a hulking white Tahoe with the Lyman Construction logo on its side panel. As Harmony would say, *there's no such thing as coincidence*—though she probably didn't mean it in quite the way I was thinking.

The lobby, with its aisles of PO boxes, was open twenty-four hours. A long line of customers waited to enter the service area, separated from the outer lobby by a glass partition. It was closing time, and a postal clerk began herding the waiting customers inside, his key ring jangling. The half dozen who'd arrived on my heels groaned and grumbled, but he shook his head.

"Line ends here. We open again at nine tomorrow." He locked the door.

Those who'd made the cut crammed into a snaking queue in front of the service counter. Peering through the glass partition, I spotted Marisol's pink-flowered clogs, the rest of her hidden behind taller customers. Jack Lyman stood at the counter, smiling and chatting with one of the agents, the crowd behind him growing restive.

I turned to wait for him outside, pulling up short to see Whittaker Lee lingering at the opposite end of the lobby. He looked like a time traveler who'd lost his way, dressed in a western-style shirt with a white silk scarf tied around his neck and a dove-gray felt Stetson atop his head. The full weight of Barbara's disappearance settled over me. I wanted to offer my sympathies, yet I had no idea what to say.

"Mr. Lee? Whittaker?" He squinted at me as I approached, his once-bright blue eyes now faded. I heard the metallic rattle of keys, the door opening and closing, and I didn't need to glance behind me to know Jack Lyman was slipping away.

"Claire?"

It was kinder not to correct him, or at least that's what I told myself as I joined him to lean my elbows on the lobby's counter. "How are you, Whittaker?"

"How do you think I am?" The flash of temper faded quickly, and the lines around his mouth sagged. "I knew she'd leave someday."

I glanced toward the service area to see Marisol had moved up to the front of the line. She'd emerge through the glass doors any moment and spot me with Whittaker. *Nothing wrong with that, unless—*

"Was Barbara having an affair?" The words blurted out before I could stop them.

His mouth worked. "You warned me about her, Claire. That scheming bitch married me for my money. She drove away our little girl. She took everything that mattered."

His voice echoed around the lobby, catching the attention of several curious onlookers. I heard the clerk's keys again and glanced over my shoulder. Relief washed through me when I saw Marisol heading our way.

"Look, here comes Marisol."

He grabbed my wrist, his bony fingers trembling but shockingly strong. "Did that lousy thief give it to you?" His hand dropped away as Marisol joined us, and he turned to her, his tone petulant, almost childlike. "Are we going home now?"

"Yes, Mr. Lee, as soon as we pick up a few groceries."

He grumbled something about wanting supper, and then started shuffling toward the lobby's double doors. Marisol smiled at me, though her brown eyes were troubled. "Thanks for keeping an eye on him. I couldn't let him sit outside in the car in this heat. He's been so agitated since . . ." She cleared her throat.

"Does he understand what happened?"

"He has his moments." She nodded toward the doorway. Whittaker had reached the double doors and gallantly swept one side open for a middle-aged woman, his demeanor so transformed I wasn't a bit surprised when he tipped his hat and flashed his dentures.

"If you need help—" I halted, thinking how insubstantial the offer was. "I could bring groceries or mail," I finished lamely as Whittaker started making his way to the Land Rover. The space next to it was empty. So much for my suspicions about a not-so-clandestine meeting of conspirators at the town's busy post office.

."Thank you." Her attention was fixed on Whittaker. "I'd better go. A couple months back, he found Mrs. Lee's key fob and went for a joyride. It's like having a toddler. You can't let down your guard."

Marisol scurried to catch up, and I turned for my PO box. I extracted a fistful of mail, mostly flyers and junk that I tossed into the nearest recycling bin. I slid the bills to the back, to be worried over later, and allowed myself a moment of relief when I recognized my renters' return address on the next envelope. I opened it, grateful to see they'd sent July's check, confused because the amount was twice what I expected. I scanned the enclosed letter. The gist was their first child was on the way, and their priorities had shifted. They were canceling their contract and wished me luck finding new tenants.

I groaned. My father, a real estate lawyer, had helped word the contract so I wouldn't be locked into an arrangement in case my circumstances changed, but the flexibility worked both ways. Our agreement allowed them to exit the lease so long as I could find another renter. That wouldn't be a problem, but I'd gotten spoiled at having the property to myself most of the time.

My phone chirped as I got into the Willys, and I glanced at it. *Ryan*. I didn't feel like talking to anyone, so I merged back into the roundabout. I heard the voice mail alert and played his message after parking around the corner from the newspaper office. He urged me to join him later to search for Jane. With the holiday weekend, he warned, we might not get another chance.

I hesitated, then sent a brief text saying I had plans for the evening, adding a plea to keep me posted. After hitting SEND, I noticed I'd missed an earlier message from Teejay.

Dinner tonight?

My heart skipped. My finances might be in a wreck, but it looked like murder and mayhem were good for my social life. I responded with a text almost identical to the one I'd sent Ryan.

Even with the windows down, the wagon was stifling, so I got out and sat on a low masonry wall shaded by a leafy mulberry tree, scrolling through the rest of my messages while I waited. At five PM every Thursday afternoon, the next day's edition of the *Sedona News* became available over the counter or in the coin-operated box outside. If you were an enterprising job hunter or dedicated garage saler, you could get a twelve-hour jump on everyone else.

I wanted to see what the local paper had to say about Barbara's disappearance, but if Blue Sky's business continued to plunge, I'd be joining the job seekers. My fifteen minutes of infamy had disqualified me from serious journalism. Not long after my fall from grace, a publisher had tried to tempt me with an advance for a tell-all true crime book, but no amount of money could make me rehash my horror story for anyone else's titillation. Even if the forest closed, I'd be okay for a while, though I wouldn't be settling my account at the hardware store anytime soon.

A muffled thump signaled the arrival of the latest *Snooze*. I went to drop my quarters into the box, scanning headlines as I walked back to my shady perch. In a town that relied entirely on tourist dollars, visitors were treated like easily startled deer, so I wasn't expecting a splashy headline like *Most Beautiful Place in America Rocked by Crime Spree!* I was surprised, however, to see Barbara's disappearance rated only a brief article on page three, closing with a plea to call the sheriff's tip line. I reread the paragraphs. Not one word about Jane or Franklin, reminding me how easily Sedona's unhoused population slipped under the official radar.

As for the *un*official radar . . . I checked my phone, and gasped. The latest update to the Conspiracy Spies' video channel pitched a new theory: Blue Sky's tours had activated a curse left by a Sinaguan shaman, meant for those who violated the peace of their ancient villages. Anywhere else, that scenario might earn a hearty chuckle.

But this was Sedona.

* * *

Two hours later, I pulled up outside an iron gate. Beyond it, a contemporary-style house clung to the side of Airport Mesa. Discreet and impressive, it stood in stark contrast to the faux-dobe McMansions nearby. Definitely an architect's house.

Though Leah had sworn Mark Stillman was the real deal, I'd googled him anyway, verifying that "Stillman" wasn't a Sedona concoction like Ravenstrong or Starkeeper, reassured by links to photos and stories on projects he'd completed in Los Angeles. I leaned out to press the call button, and the gate rolled to one side, revealing an entry courtyard with a swale of light-foliaged plants that suggested water flowing through the desert.

When Mark opened the door to greet me, I was glad I'd taken the time to change into loose cotton pants and a peasant-style top. He was dressed similarly, though his slacks were more tailored than bohemian, and his sleeveless black shirt looked like silk knit. His feet were bare, and I paused to slip off my sandals. I left them next to a wooden bench before stepping down the broad travertine stairs that led into the living area.

Across from me, a wall of windows offered a breath-stealing panorama of West Sedona's buttes and spires. Clouds cast deep blue shadows as they gathered above the fiery cliffs. I tore my gaze from the spectacle to scan the wide room, simply furnished with an old kilim rug on a pale maple floor, a low sofa angling toward the window, and two deep chairs near a suspended metal fireplace.

"Have a seat." Mark's tone was casual. He continued toward a compact kitchen, set off from the rest of the room by a black granite countertop. A pendant light of small glass globes hovered above it like a constellation. "I started some tea."

I sank into one of the chairs, noticing another flight of stairs twisting downward out of sight. Opposite the sweep of windows, a single abstract painting hung over a bench-high bookcase. Atop the bookcase, a bronze raven perched on a large hoop, a skeleton key in its beak. I smiled to see the sculpture—I knew the artist, who'd been a friend of my aunt's.

"Your home is beautiful. Did you design it?"

He nodded his thanks. "I'm not licensed in Arizona, so I still spend a lot of time in LA. But I'm always glad to get back here."

"Sedona's a magnet for Californians escaping city life." On weekends, it seemed like half the cars cruising through my neighborhood bore California plates, slowing to a crawl as they approached real estate signs.

"I loved the city—the work, the weather, the ocean." He talked while deftly filtering tea into two pottery mugs. "Then three years ago my girlfriend persuaded me to come to Sedona to relax for a few days—hot stone massages, aura cleanses, the whole scene. I went along with it, but I couldn't wait to get back to LA. On our last morning, she dragged me to the Airport Saddle vortex. While she was realigning her chakras or whatever, I followed a raven. He'd fly ahead a few yards, then sit in a tree and squawk."

He carried the mugs over, handing one to me. "But quietly, like words, you know?"

I nodded. "Quorking, some people call it."

"Quorking? I like that." He smiled and perched on the edge of the sofa, setting his tea on the low coffee table so he could use his hands to continue his story. "So, this raven. I'd catch up, and then he'd fly a few trees away, same thing, over and over, like a conversation or a game. By now, I'm a half mile from the car. Lost in the trees. Then I walk around a big juniper, and *bam*, there he is, sitting on a For Sale sign in an empty lot. That afternoon, I signed a contract at the realty office, while my soon-to-be-ex-girlfriend was on the plane back to LA."

"Not your typical case of Red Rock Fever."

He chuckled. "No, more like a cosmic shove."

"You must have hired a contractor—Jack Lyman's company, maybe?"

Surprise chased across his features. "I don't think Lyman bothers to accept one-offs. I acted as my own contractor. Subbed out most of the work, spent as much time on site as I could."

"You probably heard some things about the local building scene."

"Yeah, those guys gossiped like teenagers during homeroom. Relished enlightening the newbie."

"Maybe they told you a few stories about Lyman?"

His expression shuttered. "Why do you ask?"

"You don't like him." Maybe I was pretty good at the psychic stuff after all. I smiled behind the mug of tea—jasmine, brewed at just the right temperature to bring out the floral notes.

"I don't know him."

"*But.*"

"Okay." A corner of his mouth lifted. "He poached a couple of my subs. A plumber and the best tile guy in northern

Arizona, just when we were starting on the bathrooms. It wasn't personal, Del."

I quirked an eyebrow. He shook his head, his smile widening. "Well, not for him anyway. From what I heard, he's, ah—what's the word?"

"Transactional?"

"*Exactly.*" He reached for his tea. "Maybe I still hold a bit of a grudge when I look at the uneven tiles in the hall bath, but Jack Lyman isn't your killer. That's why you're asking about him, isn't it?" He looked at me over the rim of his mug. "Emotion, violence—they're not what drives him."

"The gateway development is a multimillion-dollar *transaction.* Franklin could have been just another obstacle, like a tree in the wrong place, or an inconvenient building code."

Mark took his time, sipping tea, returning the mug to the table. The massing clouds had swallowed the sun while we were talking. Though the kitchen pendant glowed softly, the stormy green light entering the windows made me feel like I was in an aquarium, the watery effect heightened as lightning rippled through the clouds' dark bellies. At last he spoke. "Money's only part of it. I sense revenge, hunger. An emptiness that can't be filled. That's the real danger. Be careful, Del."

I told him about the wild rumors, Leah's concern, the Spades' conspiracies. I tried to spin away the growing hysteria as silly gossip, but my humor landed awkwardly. "What do you think? Have we unleashed a curse?"

"I don't believe in curses. We create our own misfortune."

His gaze was pointed, and I sank deeper into the low chair. "I'm not sure what you're getting at."

"*You* found Franklin's body. *You* spoke to his girlfriend before she disappeared. *You* visited Barbara Lee the day she went missing."

I leaned forward to set my cup on the low coffee table, hoping the fall of my hair shielded my expression. Foolish of me to think I was the only one to see the common denominator. "Are you saying I make bad things happen?"

"You make choices that endanger yourself. It's as though you're"—he closed his eyes briefly—"*punishing* yourself. Why?"

"Because I killed someone." Too late, I clamped my lips shut.

"You didn't intend to."

My throat felt too thick to respond. Gently, he said, "I'm not a mind reader, remember? Leah mentioned you were a journalist. I followed up, read a couple of things on the internet. I'm sorry. I didn't want to open a newspaper and see a story about the crime-solving psychic."

An objection rose to my lips, but I recognized the hypocrisy in time. "Then you know I was reporting on a series of murders when the killer started sending me messages. *Fan mail.*"

His dark eyes held no judgment, and I found myself telling him the rest, a secret shame I'd never repeated to anyone in Sedona, not even my aunt, because it still made me shrink with self-loathing. Grateful for the deepening shadows, I explained that when the lead detective on the case warned me to butt out, I'd only pretended to step aside. Instead, I reached out to one of his subordinates. Joe Bradley and I made a good team, poring over the killer's messages to me, studying his victimology . . . and falling in love.

Too late, I'd learned Joe was married. Apparently, he'd been willing to do anything to boost his career. Like me. *Like Ryan?*

Distracted by the insight, I finished quickly. "We went over and over every piece of evidence until we were sure we'd figured out the killer's next move. We knew he liked to torture and kill petite blond coeds. What we didn't know was he also liked to play games with foolish reporters and rookie detectives. He ambushed us, used me as a shield to lure Joe closer. Joe died to save me. He became the hero cop, and I was the reporter who seduced him into risking his life for my scoop."

Mark's gaze flicked over my jawline, then locked with mine. "Cops protect their own. Why did you go along with their version of the story?"

The scar along my jaw burned. For someone who claimed not to read minds, Mark seemed to be pretty good at it. I said simply, "Letting him be a hero seemed like the one thing I could do for his family." Before Mark could weigh in, I said, "I know Joe made his own choices. Understanding that doesn't stop me from reliving those moments over and over, hoping for a different ending."

"Most people would need help working through something like that. Otherwise, there's a danger of internalizing the trauma."

"Like PTSD?" He nodded, and I explained the newspaper had paid for therapy sessions. "But the nightmares and panic attacks continued, and now . . ." Knowing Mark of all people might understand, I told him about my hallucinations, how I'd "seen" a cliff dweller where Franklin died. "Am I losing my grip on reality?"

"Maybe that's not a bad thing." He spared me a small smile before continuing. "Talk therapy isn't for everyone. Sometimes you need to lose your mind, metaphorically speaking, dive into the dark places in order to tap your inner wisdom. Maybe that's what this ancient guide represents."

I risked another stab at humor. "Are you going to take me through a past life regression next?"

"Do you want me to?" His lips quirked, and I knew he'd picked up on my need to lighten the conversation. I shook my head. "Good, because I don't do that kind of thing, though I could ask around, get you a referral."

I laughed uneasily. "No thanks. But if you want to help . . ." I told him about tomorrow night's gathering to connect with Barbara.

"I'll see what I can find out, maybe get myself invited." He leaned forward. "In return, I'd like you to try something for me."

My breath hitched. I nodded for him to continue.

"Take a step back, watch your dreams and visions unfolding like a story. Remember Persephone, the Greek goddess who brought treasures from the darkness?"

His dark eyes were kind, but my gaze slid away. I'd wrestled with shadows, then tried drowning them instead. Moving in with Claire had anchored me, but now she was gone. I'd fought hard for my peace of mind, and I didn't want to drift again.

"Thanks, but I think I'll leave the psychic stuff to you." I smiled to show I wasn't being a smart-ass, then stood. I saw my reflection, ghost-like, in the windows. The sky had darkened, but I felt oddly reluctant to leave. "If you learn anything about Barbara . . ."

"I'll let you know." He walked me to the door, and I thanked him for the tea. I was halfway across the courtyard, the river of plants glowing in the dusk, when he called after me. "Be careful, Del."

I turned. He was silhouetted in the doorway, his face shadowed. "Is that a friendly suggestion, or is that the psychic talking?"

"Both. I hope we're friends, and I'm concerned for your safety. You're part of this story now. Whoever set it in motion may be trying to manipulate you."

"Are you suggesting Franklin's killer is someone I know?"

"I'm sure of it."

14

BY THE TIME I turned up Soldiers Pass Road, dusk had deepened to night. A breeze blew through the wagon's open windows, but the increasing humidity held in the heat like a wet blanket. I caught a whiff of rain and then, like a mirage, the promising scent vanished.

The loft was stifling, so I turned on the cooler and opened the slider, hoping to chase out the stale air. If only I could clear my mind as easily. I kept rehashing the conversation with Mark, wondering how I'd let myself get distracted. Instead of drawing him out about Barbara, I'd ended up in the spotlight myself.

Restless, I went downstairs for another cardboard box from the tack room. I needed to finish sorting through my aunt's photos for Ronnie Jackson. I carried the box upstairs and opened the flaps, tears stinging my eyes when I saw the snapshot resting on top—Claire with a group of friends, her head thrown back in laughter. Henry must have taken it on his old Nikon. The photo was black and white, but my memory colored the bright red curls escaping from underneath Claire's straw hat.

The loft felt too small for the emotions surging through me. I dropped the photo on the kitchen table, switched off the lights, and walked into the night.

The black windows of Claire's house reminded me of the letter from my renters—one more problem to add to the messy pile I seemed to be making of my life. I turned away and started toward Soldier Wash, letting habit guide my steps until it occurred to me the temperature was perfect for snakes. I used my phone to light the rest of the way. When I got to the broad sandstone edge, I beamed left and right before switching it off. Then I sat, legs folded, waiting for my eyes to adjust.

The stone still radiated the day's heat. Clouds throbbed with lightning to the east, but the bright pulses faltered, the hope of rain slipping away. Overhead, the cloud layer had thinned to a sheer veil that obscured the stars. I thought of Jane and Barbara, out there somewhere in the night.

A woman's scream cut through the darkness, stopping my breath until I placed the sound. *Mountain lion.* Years ago, sitting with Claire on her patio in the dark, we'd heard that same raspy cry. She'd reassured me then the big cat was far away, the sound reflecting off the cliffs of Grayback, her name for Capitol Butte.

The hairs on the back of my neck lifted. I knew what it felt like to be hunted. Whatever Mark thought, I had no compulsion to re-create my foolhardy attempt to draw a killer into the open. Yes, I *was* the common denominator between Franklin, Jane, and Barbara. But so was someone else. *Who?*

My ears strained, hearing only the dull white noise of distant traffic and an occasional puff of wind stirring the dry grasses. Would confronting the darkness free my intuition? I knew Mark wasn't referring to literal darkness, but right now, this was as far as I was willing to go.

I settled my gaze on the black gash of Soldier Wash and slowed my breath, my palm resting on the sandstone's lightly gritty surface. A faint scent drifted on the night air, something lush that called to moths and other night creatures. Datura? Yucca blossoms? My hearing sharpened. The flutter of a bird as it resettled into its roost in a nearby sugar bush. A juniper branch creaking in the breeze. Then the cougar screamed again, farther away this time. The hoarse cough-meow wasn't frightening at all now, just a lonely creature crying for its mate.

I thought of "my" ancient cliff dweller—and because it seemed harder now to separate the two, Teejay. He'd probably tell me the lion represented courage or hunting prowess. I'd like to think this time I was the hunter, not the hunted.

As the natural world swelled and throbbed around me, the hum of traffic faded. Distant house lights winked out like falling stars. I felt myself dissolving into my surroundings, disappearing into the darkness. Tentatively, I stretched my senses even further. This wasn't the black emptiness that terrorized me in dreams. The night felt like an invisible web, supportive yet responsive to my breath. I rested in that awareness for some time, absorbing the scents and sounds until . . . impatience nudged and poked at me, prompting me to shift my legs. I felt the web around me loosen. Thoughts came pouring back in.

The conversations with Jane and Barbara swirled through my mind. Jane's fear. Barbara's sly comments about the goddess circle, about Henry and my aunt. Whittaker's dementia and the land trade. The stone-and-shell artifact resting where Franklin went over the edge. I sensed a thread, tenuous as spider silk, as circuitous as the spiral I kept seeing in my dreams. Did I know Franklin's killer? Faces flashed like mental snapshots. Jack Lyman, Sam, Gina, Barbara, Whittaker, Ryan, Teejay.

Before the flood of impressions could recede, I hurried back to the loft and fired up my laptop, typing madly, as though a deadline hung over my head. The staccato tap of the keys filled the room as the words flowed through my fingers.

Jack Lyman was the only suspect I didn't have a personal connection with, and I wanted him to be guilty for that very reason. Though Mark said Lyman wasn't a killer, he had the most to gain from the land trade, and he had military training.

Sam? He was a typical college student, dabbling in ideas and probably a few other things. But he was also a Sedona nomad, traveling too lightly across the town's surface to have a stake in the deeper drama I sensed was at play here . . . unless Franklin's messianic pull had drawn him in.

Gina was an unlikely candidate, but she was covering up something, I was sure of it. Journalism was a lot like police work in one sense—people lied. Ryan, Sam, Gina, Teejay, all hiding things. For what it was worth, Barbara Lee was the only one who'd openly addressed her past.

She had motive and access to Whittaker's guns, but I couldn't picture Barbara summoning the grit to kill Franklin. It was far easier to believe she'd persuaded Whittaker to act for her. But was he even capable at this point? I'd felt the tremor in his hand, noticed his frailty as he walked.

Then there was Ryan. Though his connection to Lee Ranch stretched back even further than mine, his boss and the sheriff had shunted him aside. His experience with the Forest Service made him sanguine about the land trade . . . and trained to handle a gun.

So was Teejay. He had the military background. He had the opportunity. And he'd lied to me—at least by omission—about the trail to the saddle. Ryan suspected he'd been helping Franklin. I suspected he was helping Jack Lyman. The rhythm of my typing slowed. I stared at the laptop's screen.

My suspicions had circled back to the beginning, like a dog chasing its own tail.

As a journalist, I'd loved that feeling when a story started coming together. This wasn't it. If I'd lost my reporter's sixth sense that night in Boston, what made me think I could pluck treasure out of the darkness like Persephone? I closed the laptop and shoved it aside. It was late, but maybe I'd have better luck finding answers in my aunt's photographs. I propped the snapshot of her against the wall for luck, and dug into the cardboard box.

*   *   *

Birdsong woke me. I closed my eyes again and let the week's events unroll like a movie trailer, starting with finding Franklin's body and ending with Mark's warning. Resisting the temptation to pull the covers back over my head, I got out of bed to shower and dress. My first tour wasn't until nine, leaving me with a couple of hours to fill. Not enough time to solve a murder or find the missing, but maybe I could make some headway on getting my future in order.

The nearly empty refrigerator yielded nothing more edible than a spotty apple and some peanut butter, but at least I had half a bag of coffee beans. I took my mug outside to the deck. The air was dry, which meant temperatures would soar later, so I allowed myself a few minutes to savor the relative coolness.

Below me, a Gambel's quail perched on a juniper branch, yelling "Chi-ca-go! Chi-CAH-go!" on repeat, his topknot bobbing. I looked for his mate and found her pecking around the weedy undergrowth. A dozen babies rolled out of the brush like fuzzy walnuts on sticks, changing direction in unison when papa flew down to alert them to my presence.

As though yesterday's clouds never existed, unfiltered sunlight started to bake my shins. I went inside to pour more coffee, distracted by the bright beam spotlighting my aunt's photo. I paused to look closer, recognizing Ryan's grandparents seated on a blanket with Claire and Barbara, Whittaker smiling next to her, reddish cliffs behind them. My heart ached. They were picnicking in the alcove among the ruins, good friends laughing and having fun. Most of them, anyway—the petulant set to Barbara's lips reminded me of her aversion to hiking.

A chuckle died on my lips. Nestled in the vee of her blouse was the shell-and-stone artifact.

Buzzing with excitement and caffeine, I used my phone to snap a copy, attached it to a message. About to press the send arrow, I stopped, Ryan's suspicions weaving themselves around my ribcage until I couldn't breathe. Teejay could confirm Barbara's necklace was the artifact Franklin had dropped on the canyon rim. *Or was Teejay the one who planted it?* He'd had plenty of time while Sam hiked back down to bring back the deputy. Tampering with evidence? Creating distraction? Was Blue Sky in that much trouble?

I set the phone down and went to pour another cup of coffee. To send the photo now would grant Teejay the opportunity to consider his response. Though I was already ninety-nine percent certain this was the necklace Franklin had dropped, confirmation would be good. Even better would be seeing Teejay's reaction in real time. I picked up the phone and slowly backspaced over the message. I couldn't trust him. I couldn't trust anyone.

* * *

When I entered the front office my gaze went to the painting of Canyon de Chelly and its soaring blue sky. For a moment my spirits lifted. Then I caught Gina's expression, dark as last night's thunderclouds.

Lids lowering, she reached to pinch the bridge of her nose. "Harmony's running late. Megan's out again today, though maybe that's a blessing in disguise—the scheduling grid has more holes than Swiss cheese. We've lost half our weekend bookings."

"The closure? Or the rumors?"

"This stupid game with Chase's cousin, Dean Spade. Half the people who canceled are afraid. The rest are furious that we've violated sacred space. I can reassure the fearful ones, convince them to reschedule. But the others . . ." She flicked a hand. "This could hurt us."

"It'll blow over eventually."

"Not soon enough." Though Arnulfo was busy in the garage, his radio blaring, Gina spoke in hushed tones. "Our permit with the Forest Service is up in October. We need to get funding in place before we submit a proposal for Lee Canyon tours, but the banks don't want to invest in a company on its way down, and Steve would rather sell than expand."

"Steve is selling?"

Gina pantomimed zipping her mouth, her gaze going past me to the front window. I turned to see Teejay's Jeep pulling in. "Don't tell him I told you."

"I won't." Coffee burning in my stomach, I hurried down the hallway. I knew Blue Sky was in trouble, but I'd been under the impression we had time to turn things around.

Teejay finished sluicing the dust from his Jeep. He glanced up, tossed me a garage towel, and I started drying, keeping my tone casual as I asked, "What did Ronnie say when you showed her the photo of the artifact you found above the box canyon?"

"Nothing, but if it's tied to a case, she wouldn't talk about it." Our gazes met across the Jeep's hood.

"I'm pretty sure the necklace belonged to Barbara. I'm trying to figure out how Franklin ended up with it." After dropping my bombshell, I waited. His eyes widened in genuine surprise. But I saw something else before he turned back to toweling the Jeep. Curiosity? Guilt? Fear?

I explained how I'd been going through my aunt's things, how Ronnie thought Claire's photos might help her inventory Lee Canyon's archaeological resources before the ranger district opened the ranch to tour operators. "Though with everything that's been going on, I wonder if the land trade—"

He pulled the towel from my fingers, his dark brows drawn together.

"Has it occurred to you Barbara went missing after your visit?" He read the answer on my face. "It's good you're helping Ronnie. See if you can manage it without getting into more trouble. I worry about you."

About me? *Or Blue Sky?* I took a deep breath, steadied myself against the Jeep. "Have you heard the latest? That our tours to the box canyon activated an ancient curse?"

"Seriously?" He bit out a laugh. "Let me guess. Dean Spade."

"We're losing bookings. Gina spent yesterday afternoon calling people back, hoping they'd reschedule, but some had already signed on with other outfitters."

"She thinks Chase is poaching them. Maybe Chase and his cousin Dean have been plotting for a while, but once a rumor's out there, it doesn't matter who started it." He tossed the towels into a plastic bucket, leaned back against the Jeep and stretched his legs out, inches from mine. "Megan will be back tomorrow."

He didn't have to tell me what that meant. "Are you firing me?"

"Just asking you to take a few days off. You're a good driver, and we'll need you when things pick up again." His gaze was fixed on the junipers crowding the fence, his profile unreadable. "I don't want to lose you, Delilah."

I felt a deep tug somewhere inside my chest, and my brain locked up like a seized engine. "I saw you taking someone to see the ruins in the box canyon." *Idiot.* I cleared my throat and tried again. "The woman who was hiking with you—was she a guest? Or an investor? Is Steve selling the company?"

"Did he tell you that?"

He didn't move, but I sensed him shift into alertness. I shrugged. Steve was three thousand miles away. Gina was inside and she filled out my paychecks.

"The banks turned us down, but I'm looking at private funding." He pushed away from the Jeep and gave me a strained smile. "Steve's still on the fence, so don't start job-hunting yet, okay?"

* * *

After dropping off my guests, I radioed Gina, who told me I'd be on call until late afternoon. I was on my way home for an early lunch when I thought of the one person I could trust with the photo of Barbara. Twenty minutes and one phone call later, I turned off Brewer Road, the photo zipped into a pocket and a newspaper-wrapped package on the seat next to me.

The lot at the ranger station's entrance was less than half full, but I drove past the empty spaces to tuck into a row of green-and-white trucks shaded by cottonwoods and sycamores. My steps slowed in front of the former residence, a white bungalow-style cottage built in 1917 when the forest ranger's job was to collect grazing fees and manage tree cutting. By the time I started spending summers with my aunt, rangers managed tourists, not cattle, and the "new" headquarters—a nondescript rectangle pasted over by a series of additions—was already old.

Now, with over three million people visiting Sedona each year, a modern visitor center was badly needed. The Lee Ranch trade would make it possible; I wished I could be happier about it.

Muffled voices and static from a dispatch radio reached me through the open doorway. The reception desk was deserted, but before I could press the bell, Ronnie Jackson came out to greet me. I followed her down a narrow hallway, the oily scent of microwave popcorn growing stronger until we arrived at a windowless kitchen-meeting area. Beige metal folding chairs surrounded a scratched and dull Formica table.

Ronnie sat across from me, and I handed her the small bundle cushioned by layers of the *Snooze*. "This is for you."

She pulled away the newsprint, her puzzled expression changing to pleasure. "This is the Santa Clara jar in my painting."

I explained how Claire had found it at a garage sale decades ago, leaned across the table to trace my finger over the lines where the small black-on-black pot had been broken and repaired. "It's not valuable."

"It is to me. Thank you."

I settled back into the uncomfortable chair. "I haven't finished with Claire's photos. We were going to work on them together, but . . ."

"Cancer is cruel." Her voice was gentle. "Have you contacted the museum? They've digitized hundreds of photographs from pioneer families."

"Claire moved here in the seventies."

She smiled. "Ancient history, in Sedona terms. Anyway, your aunt donated several paintings to help fundraise for the exhibits."

"I didn't know that." I swallowed the lump in my throat, slid the old photograph toward her. "This is why I called. Look at the necklace Barbara Lee is wearing—it's the artifact Teejay found, isn't it?"

She pulled a loupe from one of her uniform pockets, slowly moved it over the photo. I heard her quick intake of breath, but when she looked up, her brown eyes were unreadable. "This may link to an ongoing investigation. I can't talk about it."

A wave of relief washed over me. At least Teejay had told the truth about that much. I wouldn't learn more until Ronnie felt comfortable with me. I leaned back in my chair. "Claire's photos bring back memories. Whittaker liked to show off things he'd found on the ranch, especially arrowheads and pottery. Maybe you saw his collection—their caregiver said you'd been to visit a while back."

Ronnie's shoulders relaxed. "So much local prehistory was carted off to museums back east or lost to pothunters. I was hoping Whittaker might show me the pieces his family had found over the years. Unfortunately, they'd sold everything to an antiquities dealer in Scottsdale."

Interesting. I changed direction, asking about her background—a masters in anthropology from the U of A, followed by a stint at a consulting firm, then ten years with Coronado National Forest. "Hohokam territory?"

"That's right." Ronnie's expression brightened as she told me her firm had been retained by developers who'd found signs of a fifteen-hundred-year-old Hohokam village while leveling a shopping mall site. She and her colleagues had worked closely with the Tohono O'Odham tribe to repatriate their ancestors' belongings, including shell artifacts like the one Barbara had worn as a necklace. "We found two inside a cremation jar, exquisite bird mosaics, inlaid with turquoise, jet, argillite . . ."

"Why birds?" Thinking of Ruins Guy, I hastened to add, "I know specifics are lost to time, but I'd like to hear about the possibilities."

"Bird symbolism is common throughout the Southwest, sometimes associated with rain or water sources, very important for desert people." She warmed to the subject. "Additionally, shamanic cultures worldwide considered birds as messengers between earth and sky, or intermediaries between the human and the sacred. At a mortuary site, for example, a bird might guide travel to the spirit world."

Slowly, I released the breath I'd been holding. "Was there a burial in Lee Canyon?"

"I don't think this"—she nodded toward the snapshot—"came from Lee Canyon. Compared to larger villages to the south and the north, these red rock canyons were the frontier, the people who lived here poor cousins. This belonged to someone with high status."

"Whittaker may have dementia, but he wouldn't forget this piece." I tapped the photo. "Have you contacted him?"

Ronnie sighed and shook her head. "Let's just say I've worn out my welcome at the ranch. I got the impression Whittaker didn't part with his collection willingly."

"Barbara's been trying to resolve their financial problems. Jack Lyman helped get the land trade rolling, but it could take months before the Lees see any cash." I told her about Franklin and Barbara's encounter at the party. "Was Franklin acting as a middleman?" Her expression shuttered, but I asked anyway. "Were he and Teejay looting sites?"

"Teejay?" She laughed. Then, catching my expression, she leaned forward, her voice low. "I shouldn't tell you this. Lisa Vargas was tracking down a witness when Oak Creek Canyon closed. Give me a call next week, or whenever you have photos to show me. Maybe I can update you then."

"Deal." I waited for a sense of satisfaction, but it didn't come. Next week might be too late, at least for Barbara and Jane.

Ronnie scraped back her chair. I assumed we'd finished, but when she asked if she could copy the photo, I nodded and followed her past a warren of rooms until we reached our destination, a photocopier that looked like it may have come over on the *Mayflower*. While Ronnie prodded it to life, my attention strayed to the wall above. A half-dozen topographic quads had been trimmed and pieced together to make one large composite map, stuck with hundreds of colored pins and labeled with tiny penciled-in numbers.

As the machine shuddered and groaned, Ronnie noticed my interest. "Mind-blowing, isn't it? Hundreds of sites, from roasting pits to pit houses, and we're still finding more."

"Wow." Goose bumps prickled my arms. Wherever I'd hiked, generations before me had left their footprints in the form of potsherds, masonry, or rock art. Maybe my cliff dweller had been among them. My spiral petroglyph might be on that map, lost in plain sight.

In plain sight. For someone with the right skills and tools, this was a treasure map. I knew someone like that, and he walked by this map every day—Ryan Driscoll.

CHAPTER

15

A FTER MY LAST tour of the day I drove down Airport Road, feeling unmoored. The bright side was I had time for a real life again. Remembering the sorry state of my refrigerator, I stopped at The Market, weaving through a small crowd at the entrance: people waiting for their turn in a massage chair or lined up for a tarot reading, others clustered around a tall man playing a didgeridoo. I eavesdropped shamelessly for any mention of tonight's gathering of light-workers, but murmured conversations faded to silence as I walked past.

I grabbed a cart and pushed it through the aisles, nodding at out-of-towners, greeting people I knew, trading jokes about the "non-soon" weather. A few locals gave me the side-eye. Other than our blue bandannas, Blue Sky's drivers didn't wear uniforms, but I knew I stood out, with my red hair, Tilly hat, and cargo shorts that were more functional than fashionable. Did they think I was cursed along with the canyon?

As I unloaded my selections onto the checkout conveyor, a pair of young women behind me debated their evening plans in fierce whispers, arguing about whether they'd be safe traveling back to their resort after dark. I dismissed their concerns as overly cautious until I turned into the brushy narrow driveway that led to my aunt's.

Suddenly I craved company.

I tossed my keys onto the kitchen counter and called Mark Stillman, leaving a voice message when he didn't answer. *Someone you know*, he'd told me, and I trusted his instincts more than my own. I was too involved, thoughts and emotions clouding my judgment. The solution waited like something I could see out of the corner of my eye, but when I turned to look, it vanished.

After opening the windows and switching on the cooler, I put away groceries, then took a glass of water out to the deck where the air was fresher. A cold beer would be nice. I tested the thought; it didn't trigger me the way it once did. I didn't need the beer because I'd just lost my job and my renters, or because I was feeling anxious or frustrated. I wanted a beer because I was sweaty, dusty, and thirsty.

I settled for the water. I took another sip and conceded Teejay was right about one thing. The law had more resources than I did. The blogosphere was busy inventing links to black helicopters and armies of darkness. The print media soon might connect Franklin's death and Barbara's disappearance. But in the meantime, all the cops, reporters, and conspiracists had overlooked one piece of the puzzle: *Jane.*

With the sun sinking lower, taking the edge off the heat, I picked up my phone. Ryan Driscoll answered on the first ring, his words chopped and distorted, though the gist was clear. I waited for him to drive out of the dead zone, watching the light cooling on the eastern cliffs, wondering if he was combing the backcountry for Barbara . . . or for archaeological treasures. Who would look twice at a parked Forest Service truck?

When Ryan called back ten minutes later, he told me that he was on patrol. "I'll be out a couple more hours. It's easier to spot fireworks and campfires after dark. We've already issued a dozen citations, and it's only Friday."

"What about Barbara? Any news?" She'd been missing forty-eight hours now—too long. He didn't say it, but her chances were fading.

"Sheriff scaled back the search this afternoon. People were dropping like flies from heat exhaustion. One of the volunteers busted a leg, got hauled down Bear Mountain in a Stokes basket."

"I saw Whittaker at the post office yesterday. He thought I was Claire." My voice cracked. "His mind's caught in the past. He seemed agitated, paranoid even."

"Yeah, all those strangers at the ranch, that's gotta be hard on him. Feds are keeping us yokels in the dark, but the sheriff posted a deputy out there, in case."

Ryan sounded sincere, but the conversation with Ronnie had me questioning everything. I realized I was tapping my fingers against my empty glass and stopped. "I still think Barbara's disappearance and Franklin's death are connected. If we could find Jane—"

"I checked the encampments yesterday, but everyone cleared out. A couple of the churches set up cooling centers. She wasn't there, either. Jane's used to living rough. She's probably holed up somewhere. Eventually, she'll need supplies."

"I'll keep an eye out for her." I told him then about the group of people assembling this evening to connect with Barbara on a psychic level. I braced myself for a disparaging comment about woo-woos, but Ryan surprised me.

"Hey, that's good. At least they're not out here playing Sherlock, getting lost or hurt or starting fires. I'll be pulling overtime all weekend."

"Not me. I got furloughed today." I dragged the words past the lump in my throat. Being sidelined, even temporarily, reminded me of getting fired from the newspaper—except then I'd only had myself to blame. I swallowed. "Do you still want to buy the wagon?"

"Seriously? I mean, yeah, sure." His cautious enthusiasm was short-lived. "Wait, does this mean you're moving back east?"

"Thinking about it." I tried to make a joke of it. "You know what people say about becoming a millionaire in Sedona."

"Yeah, come with two million."

"Exactly. Except I didn't have much to begin with."

The obvious solution, I told him, was selling Claire's house. He commiserated with me, then said, "Hey, I know a guy in Williams who runs van tours to the Grand Canyon. I can put in a good word for you. The parkies aren't going to close the gates, not even with the Antelope Fire on their doorstep."

Williams was more than an hour away. My instinct was to say no, but I promised to keep the job in mind, feeling more uncertain than ever about what was keeping me in Sedona.

When we disconnected, twilight had leached the colors from the cliffs, my energy draining with it. I'd been so busy playing detective, I'd neglected the rest of my life, though maybe that was a chicken-or-egg argument. I called my renters and made a plan, then cooked a decent meal for the first time in weeks. I even started a load of laundry before heading downstairs to the tack room and my aunt's photos.

* * *

Saturday morning found me standing in front of Claire's house, keys in hand. During our phone conversation the evening before, my renters had agreed to an early inspection. Despite a short night filled with disturbing dreams, I felt clear-headed, ready to do whatever was needed to move forward. Until I stepped into the front hallway.

A few weeks after Claire's memorial service, some of her friends and students had rallied to help me pack up her studio and furniture. Even after we'd emptied the house, something of her had lingered: echoes of her easy laughter, the scent of oil paints, a stray strand of red hair that must have been floating around for months because after the chemo it had grown back as downy and gray as a baby bird's feathers.

Now, seeing someone else's furniture in the living room, the blank wall in the bedroom where the Canyon de Chelly painting once hung, I felt like I'd lost my aunt all over again. Was I giving up too easily? I didn't want to sell or rent the house . . . but Claire would have wanted me to be comfortable.

No, not comfortable. Claire would have wanted me to *live*, to find whatever filled my days with meaning and purpose.

For her, that was art, a creative breath that animated everything from the meals she cooked to the clothing she wore. She'd tried to get me interested, plying me with sketchbooks and colored pencils, but I'd used them to write with instead. My early scribbles were worthless, but I treasured Claire's visual journals. They told the story of her life in sketches and paints. Sometimes she'd add clippings, pressed plants, or other memorabilia. She'd play with colors and shapes until inspiration took hold. Then she'd move to canvas or clay or whatever medium she was into that week.

Memories walked with me as I went from room to room, making a mental list of things I needed to do once the movers had gone. At the sound of wheels on gravel, I stopped my inventory and went outside to see Gramps Cherokee looping around to the front of the house. Megan hopped out, her usual exuberance dimmed.

"Del, are you okay?" Her gaze took in my cutoffs and washed-thin shirt before she stretched up on tiptoes to hug me. "You're like a block of ice. What have you been doing?"

The hot sun on my arms made me realize I was shivering. The slump-block house held onto the cooler nighttime temperature, but it wasn't *that* cool. I managed a smile. "Keeping busy. You know I got furloughed."

"That's why I'm here. I've got a few minutes before picking up passengers, and I took the chance you'd be home." Her mouth twisted. "I'm so sorry, Del—it's all my fault."

I was at a loss. "*Your* fault?"

"I'm the one who stickered the Jeeps. Teejay was all set to fire me over it, but I played the sick grandma card. And now I feel guilty because my *abue* is better and you're the one without a job. I'm so, *so* sorry," she repeated.

My head spun trying to unpack it all. Megan—sweet, sunny, proper Megan—a neophyte monkey-wrencher?

She'd started to walk backward toward the Jeep. "My sister and her kids are driving up for the Independence Day events. My parents told us to get out and have fun. We're having a picnic later. Come with us?"

I hesitated, and she upped the ante. "Gina's Red Rockin' Grannies are dancing during the concert. Sam and some of his friends will be there too. There's a drum circle after the light show. *Please* say you'll come."

Sam's drumming circle—where Franklin had peddled his mysterious tea. I called to her as she started the engine. "I'll meet you there."

"Text you later." She shot me a wave and a smile through the Jeep's window and spun gravel on her way out. I locked up the house. About to slide open the door of the loft, I felt my phone vibrate.

Mark Stillman skipped the formalities, filling me in on what he'd learned about the gathering on Barbara's behalf. I heard the smile in his voice before he delivered his surprise.

"One of the women was part of the goddess circle."

My pulse picked up.

"She's a shaman. Her name's Lyssa Starbright."

Of course it is. I bit back a sound of exasperation as he spelled it out for me. I had my laptop open even before we disconnected the call. The *shamanka* (her preferred title) had a classy website with red rock photos and a long menu of offerings, even Zoom and Skype options. But I wanted to see her in person, the sooner the better. The phone number listed on her contact page bounced me out of a full voice mail box, so I signed up online for her next available appointment, an hour-long Sunday morning session that serendipitously promised I'd meet my inner guide and awaken to higher purpose.

* * *

When I was a kid, the Fourth of July meant music and fire-works at the old Posse Grounds, now a seventy-acre park at the heart of West Sedona. As summers turned hotter and drier, however, the city council began experimenting with alternatives less likely to spark a wildfire.

Today, July third, Sedona would celebrate the nation's independence with a full slate of events. Megan's sister had driven up earlier for the kid-friendly activities at the park's swimming pool. I was meeting them before the laser light show, in time to watch Gina's dance troupe.

It was nearing six when I turned onto Soldiers Pass Road, a sealed container of sliced watermelon on the seat next to me. Almost immediately, the cars ahead slowed to a crawl, then to a halt. Surprised Sedona's faux Fourth was so popular, I texted Megan to warn her I'd be late. She replied with a string of sad-faced emojis, then hiking boots.

Smart. During my tweens, when I'd sneak out after dark to meet the other Jackaloons, I memorized every secret path to the Posse Grounds. I thought Claire was oblivious . . . until I returned one summer to discover she'd started a garden of agave and prickly pear below my bedroom window. These days, houses and fenced yards blocked most of my clandestine routes.

The wail of gathering sirens chased away my nostalgia. Coyotes answered with yips and howls, and I glanced at the emergency app on my phone. A multi-car accident was the reason for the backup and, as a speck in the sky resolved into the outlines of a DPS helicopter, I knew I was in for a long wait.

The odor of car exhaust drifted in through the wagon's wide-open windows, and I felt my lungs object. The cars in front of me crept forward a few more feet, bunching together like cattle. I couldn't turn the Willys around or pull over on the narrow road, but an escape route popped into my mind. As the margins of the forest had filled in with houses, the city retained easements that connected the "neighborwoods" to hiking trails. One of those easements, unmarked and mostly unused, waited at the end of the next side street.

Horns honked behind me. The cars ahead inched forward enough for me to squeeze by an idling Mini and make the turn. The graveled street climbed past a half dozen scattered houses, then dead-ended at a cluster of unbuilt lots. I parked, grabbed my water bottle, and opened the lift gate. After being caught unprepared at Lee Canyon, I'd started keeping hiking gear in the back. I swapped skate shoes for boots, tied a shirt around my waist, and slung the water bottle around my neck. I left the watermelon on the front seat; my meager contribution wouldn't be missed.

The easement trail was deserted, probably because all of Sedona was locked in traffic. With any luck, I'd reach Posse Grounds before Gina left the stage. Ahead of me, a swath of gray-green mariolas waited limply for rain, when the otherwise inconspicuous plants would burst into white blossoms. Through the foliage an unnatural shade of orange caught my eye, and I halted. A rusted and dented Schwinn lay hidden in the brush. *Jane's*.

A flutter rose in my chest. Jane knew more likely ways in and out of the forest—nearer to places where she could clean up or get something to eat. Did she stash her bike here because it was harder to find? Or because it was closer to her camp? The easement continued west toward the main trail. I turned north instead, aiming for the red and gold cliffs of Capitol Butte.

From a distance, the open space between the dome-shaped mountain and West Sedona's neighborhoods looked like a gently undulating green slope, but appearances were deceiving. Thick growth disguised a network of washes fanning out from the base of the mountain. During dry months, Jane could hole up in one of these tributaries, close to town yet unseen and protected by a defense system of catclaw and mesquite.

I dropped into a wash, where the going was easier—for now. The persistent buzz of cicadas canceled the hum of traffic and the occasional burst of patriotic music. Like most of Sedona's creatures, the insects' cycle was timed around the annual monsoon. A trio of ravens perched near the top of a nearby juniper, quorking and chuckling as they snacked on the emerging nymphs.

The dry channel cut deeper into the reddish Hermit shale as it climbed, littered with rocks and branches carried by past floods. A fallen juniper blocked my way, its roots reaching out like the tentacles of a giant octopus. The moment I stopped, a cloud of cedar gnats zeroed in.

To escape them, I scrambled up to a sandstone outcropping on the lip of the wash. My perch was high enough to catch a breeze, keeping the gnats at bay long enough so I could drink some water and slip on my long-sleeved shirt. A field of catclaw stretched between me and the end of the tree fall. Lush and summer green, its delicate fernlike leaves disguised its barbed armature. Wait-a-minute bush, Henry had called it.

I picked my way through the catclaw, pausing to disengage the curved thorns every time they snagged my pants or shirt, wincing when they caught my skin. Surely Jane didn't come this way. Then I remembered the scratches I'd seen on her arms—perhaps not a side effect of meth addiction after all.

Past the fallen juniper, I climbed back down to the streambed. It curved right, entering the harder orange sandstones at the mountain's base, eventually leading to a broad intersection where three or four channels joined. Past flows had deposited an island of sand, gravel, and duff that supported a few taller trees, including a fat alligator juniper and an enormous cottonwood. Its roots stretched among the boulders, and its rustling leaves made a broad green canopy that reached toward the cliffs, where streaks of desert varnish suggested an ephemeral waterfall.

I halted, so charmed by the Tolkienesque setting it took a few moments for my brain to catch up. The camp blended into the landscape because it was formed from it. Blocks of limestone supported a large flake of sandstone, serving as a table, with rock chairs around it. Nearby, a sofa-sized log faced a firebox built of stone slabs and cobbles. It must have taken Jane and Franklin years to create something so precious and perfect.

Would she return to this sanctuary or avoid it? Wind and time had erased any sign of habitation. Still I hesitated, feeling like an intruder.

"Jane?" I called softly, then again, a little louder. My answer was a scold from a startled scrub jay, the raspy warnings echoing off the cliff walls.

Slowly, senses humming, I circled the camp. Opposite the cliffs, a lichen-splashed slab the size of a VW bus angled up from the ground like a protective wall. Along its bedding planes, the stone had dissolved into a series of niches, creating natural cubbies where Jane had stashed a folded blanket, two hammocks, and a faded T-shirt that might have once been red.

Closer to the ground, baby-food jars crowded a deeper niche, holding colorful chips of stone, dried juniper berries, and glossy dark seeds I hoped weren't datura, though I saw the white trumpet-like flowers blooming in the shade of a juniper nearby. I picked the jars up as I examined them, then I started to resettle the jars inside their cubby. I paused, thinking Evan or Sam would be able to identify the seeds.

Sam. He'd told me the tea Franklin brought to drumming circles induced visions. Sacred datura, beautiful but deadly, was also known as jimsonweed, a reference to Jamestown, where British soldiers suffered for days after accidentally ingesting it. *Mad as a hatter, red as a beet.* ER doctors memorized the phrase. And yet, Ronnie described pictographs suggesting the ancients had developed methods to harness its effects—delirium, hallucinations, fever.

Too late, I remembered fingerprint evidence. Jars clinked together as I hurried to replace them, the cuffs of my shirt pulled down to cover my hands. Though Jane had already been questioned and released, her camp might hold clues about what led to Franklin's death. *If I reported it.* I thought of Ryan, how eager he was to talk to Jane. To solve the case . . . or to stop her from telling the truth?

Then I noticed a small book tucked to the side of the jars. Heart thumping, I carefully slid it from its hiding place. The pages fell open as if by magic, a sense of vertigo rolling over me like an ocean wave. A spiral design, rendered in pencil, crossed two pages. The sketchbook dropped from my hands to land with a soft thump. I picked it up, heedless of fingerprints, as I flipped through the pages.

The spiral, exactly as I remembered it. Animals and humans danced around the edges, a flute player to one side. Fingers shaking, I pulled out my phone to photograph the drawing, wondering if Jane had made it. Was the original nearby? As badly as I wanted to keep the sketchbook, I returned it to the niche and stood to look around.

The main channel dead-ended at the dry waterfall. I searched along the cliff, losing track of time, finding only nature's art—chalky efflorescence and more mineral streaking. I glanced up at the pale sky and reluctantly turned back, guessing I had a half hour until dusk. Enough time, if I hurried.

Then I heard the soft scrape of a rock somewhere above me, followed by the whisper of branches.

CHAPTER

16

I FROZE, AND THE sounds ceased. Hair on the back of my neck lifted. My thoughts flew to the mountain lion I'd heard two nights before, then landed on a half-remembered story about a Canadian hiker who'd scared off a cougar by playing Metallica on her cell phone. I reached for mine, stopped.

Wouldn't a mountain lion stalk soundlessly?

I strained to listen, heartbeat whooshing in my ears. "Jane, is that you?" My voice wobbled. "I want to help."

Help? A hysterical giggle rose, and I pressed my hands to my mouth. I couldn't even help myself. Fear bubbled through my veins, turning my legs to water. *Not again.* Trapped, my back to the wall—stone, not brick this time—powerless to change what came next.

I squeezed my eyes shut, and images flickered through my mind like a scratchy old horror film on high speed. The killer lunging for me, knife raised. Joe running, too far away to stop him, his shots wild. The knife's hot kiss, then me falling, falling, falling as the men crashed together, grunting like animals.

I leaned back against the sandstone cliff and sank to my heels, arms wrapped around my knees, a human speck in an ocean of unfeeling stone. If this was what Mark meant by diving into the dark places, then I hated him. The images in my mind roared to life. Me, scrabbling across the pavement, slipping on blood—mine, Joe's, the killer's. I struggled to reach them, but time shattered like a mirror into sharp pieces I couldn't bear to look at. The killer's face, torn by a bullet, frozen into a death mask. The blade disappearing below Joe's ribcage. My bloody fingers pressed against his chest. His breath stuttered and slowed, then sirens drowned out everything, blue and red lights streaking across the brick wall until my vision blurred and faded.

As twilight settled around me, the memories slowed to a trickle. I opened my eyes, blinked hard. *Nothing to see here.* I pushed myself up and began putting one foot in front of the other, stumbling my way back down the wash. The treefall loomed ahead, but I spotted a route around it to the opposite side of the wash.

I climbed up and saw that I was standing on a faint path. It disappeared then reappeared through the brush like a line of white stitches through dark cloth, angling toward the main hiking trail that circled the base of Sugarloaf. The distant mound of sandstone rose like a guard tower above a West Sedona neighborhood, and I aimed for it instead of going back for the Willys. By the time I stepped out of the forest onto the street, my legs had stopped shaking.

Just as I reached the grassy soccer pitch, the field lights switched on, and the crowd began scattering for their cars. I found Megan and her sister, toting a sleepy toddler in one arm and a folded picnic blanket in the other. I knelt so the four-year-old could show me a unicorn painted on her cheek, feeling the last of my adrenaline drain away as I admired her "tattoo."

After waving goodbye, Megan and I joined a smaller stream of people heading for the nearby amphitheater, following the call of a throbbing tribal beat.

Megan bounced and pointed. "There's Sam."

On stage, a semicircle of men and women pounded, tapped, and shook percussion instruments. It took me a moment to spot Sam, his bony knees wrapped around a narrow wooden drum. He'd traded his neo-safari gear for baggy shorts, a colorful T-shirt, and ropes of juniper-seed beads. The crowd settled onto the grass or swayed near the stage, and the drummers launched into a multi-rhythmic improvisation that rose and fell as it wove an atmosphere of unity between performers and audience.

A group of middle schoolers darted around the periphery like modern-day Jackaloons. Gray-haired seniors watched from lawn chairs in back. My gaze searched the crowd, but I didn't see anything nefarious, only happy people joining together to have a good time. My post-adrenaline fugue left me feeling defenseless, but instead of guarding that soft, open space, I let the intricate rhythms fill it with the joy of being alive. I glanced over, recognized the longing in Megan's upturned gaze.

"He won't see you sitting here in the dark." I bumped my shoulder against hers. "Come on. Let's dance."

* * *

When I swung my legs over the edge of the bed Sunday morning, I laughed to see the bottoms of my feet were green from dancing barefoot in the grass. For a while at least, I'd let myself go, then collapsed on the sidelines, breathing hard, as Megan confessed she'd stickered Blue Sky's Jeeps to impress Sam. I asked who'd supplied them, already guessing the answer—Chase, who'd been angling for my job. Maybe he hoped I'd be blamed, or maybe he'd simply wanted to stir the pot for his cousin Dean Spade's video channel.

It didn't matter. The anti-growth message had nothing to do with Franklin. And yet, much as I hated to sound like Dean Spade, I too believed the land trade had triggered something evil. Long shot or not, Lyssa Starbright might recall a detail that still reverberated after twenty years.

I showered and dressed in shorts, then changed my mind. Thinking of last night's dancers, I dug around my closet for something that looked more . . . *Sedona*. I settled on clay-colored linen pants and a bell-sleeved white blouse that disguised the catclaw scratches on my hands.

The former goddess lived in a modest house in one of West Sedona's older subdivisions, its board-and-batten siding painted a rusty red so popular the hardware store's paint department offered pages of variations. A purple front door distinguished the house from its neighbors. My pockets jangled as I walked up the short driveway. Per Lyssa Starbright's website, in-person fees needed to be made in coins, metal being a more appropriate form of energy exchange. Eager to agree to anything, I hadn't considered the holiday weekend. Every bank was closed, so yesterday afternoon I'd zigzagged all over town, emptying the change machine at the laundry, persuading grocery clerks to let me trade bills for coins in checkout lane donation jars, finally meeting the shamanka's price at the self-serve car wash.

The door swung open just as I reached for the knocker— a dragon with a brass ring in its mouth. Lyssa Starbright wore a flowing caftan the same eggplant shade as the door. Clusters of mirrored stars dangled from her ears, and her lids were so heavily outlined her gray eyes seemed as pale as glass. Behind the theatrical makeup, she looked familiar, and I realized she'd been one of last night's drummers.

Wordlessly, she led me down a hallway to what had probably been the master suite. Now draped in rugs and fabrics, the room felt like the inside of a tent, dimly lit by the warm glow of salt lamps and candles. The scent of roses mixed with sage smoke. A stand next to the door held a candle and a shallow pottery bowl inscribed with runes. She nodded toward it. "You may leave the coins there."

If she was bewildered to see me produce plastic bags holding five pounds of grubby quarters, she didn't show it.

"Shall we begin your journey?" She gestured toward a low circular table surrounded by floor cushions and a pair of ornate wing chairs.

The chair swallowed me in its velvety depths. I leaned forward, hoping to regain a semblance of professionalism. "I'd like to lead off with a few questions. Barbara Lee was a family friend." Hearing myself use the past tense jolted me, but I forged on. "I want to know more about her goddess circle."

She nodded, her earrings reflecting the candle flames. "We called ourselves the Daughters of Ishtar."

Expecting resistance, I blinked in surprise. "How did it start? Who's Ishtar?"

"We're all Ishtar's children, my dear. She's the Mesopotamian goddess of abundance and love, and she works through us for healing and transformation. Barbara was in her mid-forties, her marriage faltering, when she met an Ishtar devotee."

How easy it would have been to capitalize on Barbara's insecurities. "You?"

"No, not me." Silent laughter set her earrings twinkling again. "I needed Ishtar's teachings even more than Barbara did. I was a nurse, so burnt out I relied on stimulants and sleeping pills to get from one day to the next. Through Ishtar we rediscovered our feminine power, using it as a doorway to step beyond society's limiting expectations."

I managed to suppress an eye roll, relieved when she switched to plain facts. ·

"Barbara wanted to share her freedom with others. She invited the priestess to open a temple of healing at the ranch."

"Whittaker was on board with this?"

"Barbara wanted to relieve some of the financial strain on her marriage. And Whittaker was happy enough to trade his herd of cattle for a harem of women exploring their sexuality."

My mouth fell open. Hers lifted in a smile. "Many, like Barbara, were mourning the loss of their youth. Women damaged by divorce or abuse, and men who ached to be touched by the Divine Feminine. Housewives and veterans, artists and businessmen. Some of us were already healers. For a time, it was magical, a community based on love and acceptance. We were protected, watched over by the goddess in the rocks—Ishtar's Spire."

I guessed she was referring to the Giant's Claw, the column of sandstone that resembled a face when viewed from Lee Ranch.

She sighed, and behind the heavy makeup, I saw a wistful middle-aged woman. "What happened?"

"We fixed up the ranch, turned the old bunkhouse into lodging for paying guests, cleared some space for campsites. Then Barbara's ex turned up." Her voice hardened. "Over Whittaker's objections, she let him get involved. It wasn't long before Frank Johnson became the group's de facto leader. He used the women like bait, drawing people who weren't sincere, who joined the circle for sex, not for transformation."

"Frank Johnson? *Franklin* was Barbara's ex-husband?"

She nodded, smiling again at my shock. "He was still a handsome man then. Brilliant, too. But he couldn't tolerate working for anyone else. He and Barbara were two of a kind—fire and air, both of them. Whittaker was solid as earth, and he was already rich. He provided the security Barbara craved. For a while, at least."

"His movie money. But by this time, the money was running out—"

"—and the happiness with it." She sent me a weighing look. "If you're thinking Barbara was running a scam, you're wrong. She was struggling with the concept of forgiveness, and Frank took advantage. Everyone was an audience for his ego, or a target for his latest schemes. And he was always experimenting, like a mad scientist. We called him Dr. Feelgood."

I thought of the irony, or maybe the inevitability, of a circle of goddesses co-opted by a con man. "He supplied drugs?"

"Most of the women were housewives, suburbanites. Frank convinced them his potions were completely natural and harmless. When Barbara found out it wasn't the teachings sending people into ecstasy, she started to panic. And then"—her voice dropped to a whisper that made my heart skip—"a young woman almost died."

"Overdose?"

"Maybe." She shook her head sadly. "Seekers used to go to an alcove on the mountain for vision quests. Near Ishtar's Spire. When others went there to find her the next day, she was gone. Got scared maybe, or started tripping and wandered off. They tracked her to a ledge where she'd fallen."

The room was stuffy and warm, but goose bumps rose along my arms when I thought of how similar the accident was to the way Franklin died.

"Someone—maybe Whittaker, or even Barbara herself—tipped off the authorities. That was the end of it. People had already started to drift away. When the deputies rolled up, the rest were literally running for the hills."

I looked at her, gauging. Sedona had no shortage of juicy tales about snake-oil peddlers receiving their comeuppance, but this was completely over the top. "No one was arrested?"

She flashed a brief smile. "This happened a few years before people started sharing every grubby detail on the internet. Whittaker kept the story out of the papers, with the help of the girl's family. Even so, the rumor mill churned for months, mostly speculation about the locals who'd been part of it. Some people moved on. The rest of us managed to live it down."

"Or found other lines of work," I said pointedly.

"My work has always been about healing people. Guiding them back to wholeness."

"You and every third or fourth person in Sedona."

"So cynical. Mark Stillman mentioned you were a Jeep guide. You know as well as I do people come here yearning to be transformed, even if they don't see that themselves." She tilted her head, earrings shimmering. "It's why you're here."

"I'm here to find out why Franklin is dead, and why two women are missing."

Her smile turned chilly. "Your anger issues are clouding your energy field, holding you back. Fortunately, you don't have to believe in a system for it to work. Let's begin your session."

"Seriously?"

"You paid for it. Why not?" She bent toward the low table, using a long match to light the contents of an abalone shell. Fragrant smoke lifted and curled, and I thought of Tee-jay's sage bundles. Out of the folds of her gown she produced a small rattle embellished with feathers. "Close your eyes. Allow your breath to become slow and deep."

Reluctantly, I complied. The smoke was earthy and pungent, and the soft chair enveloped me. She waved the rattle, the sound like raindrops spattering against a rooftop. I wanted to protest, to open my eyes, but talking or moving seemed like too much bother.

When she spoke again, her voice sounded far away. "Find yourself traveling inward, diving deep into the well where dreams are born. Embrace the darkness. Recognize it as the place where consciousness begins to take shape, weaving into the universal fabric. What do you see?"

What *did* I see? Nothing. Or to be accurate, darkness, and even though my mind stretched toward it, more darkness beyond. On and on it went, descending and twisting like an underground corridor. Now the burning incense had a foul note, and I wanted to turn around and climb back to the world above, but the black void pressed me downward like an iron hand.

"What do you see?" This time her tone was more insistent.

"Franklin," I whispered. But that was a lie. I saw death. It was shapeless and soundless, but I knew it was there, crouched and waiting the way a killer had once waited for me, knife in hand. My mind probed for a thread, a rope, a way out.

"You have a question. Ask."

I took a ragged breath. "Who killed Franklin?"

"That question is for the sheriff, not for you. Search deeper."

Deeper? I wanted to stand and leave, but my limbs were as heavy as sacks of potatoes, while my thoughts fluttered like a trapped bird. *What did she expect me to ask? If I'd find true love? Whether or not to sell Claire's house? How to contact my aunt's spirit?*

I took another breath to steady myself, and a figure stepped out of the darkness. *The cliff dweller.* He gestured me toward a rock wall covered with images, all of them moving into alignment, leading me away from the shadows. He stepped aside, and I saw the spiral carved into the rock behind him. Something inside me clicked into place.

"I see rock art and a man with dark hair—someone from long ago. Is this place real, somewhere I remember? Or is it just a dream?"

"Nothing is just a dream. The spiral is a map of your journey within. It will lead you back to a place you already know. It may seem unfamiliar, but that's because you've changed. You're a different version of yourself, able to experience things at a deeper level of understanding. The man is your guide."

I frowned. For a moment I'd thought we were getting somewhere. Had I turned back too soon? Or was this part of Lyssa's schtick? Teejay was a guide. So was Evan. Sam. We all were. "And?" I asked, hearing the impatient edge to my voice. "Is the man someone I know?"

"Perhaps. A teacher? A romantic partner?"

"No," I said firmly. I slitted my eyelids open.

Hers were still closed, the lashes thick with mascara, resting on her cheeks. But her lips quirked in a small smile. "Maybe not now. But someday. Trust him."

Trust him? Though I wanted to trust Teejay, I was more inclined to heed Mark, who'd warned me not to trust anyone. Surely that included shamankas. What had she put in that abalone shell? I bit the inside of my cheeks to keep from giggling.

She opened her eyes and saw me watching. Perhaps my resistance was too much even for her, or maybe my time was up, but Lyssa stood and gestured toward the door. As I followed her down the hallway, I scolded myself for being a jerk. After all, she was right. People *did* come to Sedona in search of something more. Mystical adventures, right livelihood, healing. PhDs and CEOs dropping out to bag groceries or teach yoga. Divorcées dabbling in tarot cards or tantra. *Failed reporters looking for redemption.*

At the front door, I turned to thank her, and apologized for my skepticism. She nodded graciously.

"But there's something I don't understand. Drugs, sex parties—the temple needed to operate on the down-low. Without social media, how could you reach people?"

"Humans have always relied on social networking, my dear. Word of mouth. Body language. Aura sensing . . ."

I lifted an eyebrow, and she successfully read my body language.

"A Jeep company delivered prospective clients to us."

Another piece clicked into place. It was how he'd known about the saddle trail and the alcove, *next to Ishtar's Spire*. I already knew the answer, but I asked anyway, just to hear Lyssa say it out loud.

"Blue Sky?"

"Yes."

*   *   *

Lyssa's story had the ring of truth, but I needed corroboration. When I left her house, it was nearing eleven, so I headed for Uptown and the history museum. I scanned the Sunday morning crowd for the chatty volunteer docent and spotted her pink pantsuit immediately. She peered up at me, no recognition in her faded gaze, but she readily reminded me of Barbara's maiden name as we stood in front of the publicity still for *Howling at the Moon*.

"Barbie Bellamy. You can take the girl out of Hollywood, but you can't take away the drama." She sighed and shook her head. "We all predicted she and Whittaker were headed for divorce or disaster."

She looked shocked by her own words. Curious, I asked her if she'd known about the Daughters of Ishtar.

"That cult?" She wrinkled her nose and pursed her lips. A herd of seniors entered the movie room, wearing matching lanyards and bursting with questions about John Wayne and Jane Russell. The docent excused herself, visibly relieved at the interruption.

I gave up and went home. I made a sandwich for lunch, barely tasting it as I bent over my laptop. I'd relocated my makeshift office to the sitting area, using the battered footlocker—a relic from Henry's tenure—as a low table while I sat cross-legged on the thick rug. The swamp cooler's ductwork ended at the kitchen's dropped ceiling, but I shifted as close as possible to the blast of tepid air.

A public records search confirmed Barbara Bellamy and Franklin Johnson had married in 1977 in Los Angeles County, divorcing a year later, when "Barbie" was playing a teenage innocent in *Howling at the Moon*. I fast-forwarded through a couple of the episodes, which were enjoying an undeserved half-life on the internet. I couldn't decide whether it was scandal or bad acting that'd sunk the series. The brief marriage, the unsuccessful television career, the goddess circle—all water under the bridge, none of it murky enough for Franklin to leverage Barbara, if that's what he'd been trying to do.

I'd avoided this moment, but I needed to talk to someone else who might shed light on what had happened at the ranch. *Teejay.* I reached for my phone but couldn't bring myself to complete the call. Instead, I returned to the photo I'd taken at Jane's camp. How could I explain the spiral drawing to him when I couldn't explain it to myself?

I sent it without comment, just as the cooler duct made a nails-on-chalkboard screech. I dashed to the wall switch, shutting off the pump, then the fan. Silence filled the loft. Hot air gusted in through the window, and with it a hint of smoke, which I hoped wasn't wafting from the cooler's motor.

I groaned. Climbing onto the roof in the middle of a hot day would be my penance for neglecting maintenance chores. I changed into cutoffs and an old T-shirt and headed downstairs for tools.

The swamp cooler—basically a metal box—was bolted to one side of the roof. I dragged out a ladder from a horse stall and leaned it against the barn, making several trips up and down for tools and parts. Though this side of the roof was shaded by a tall stone pine, the wind was hot, and my hands were slippery with sweat and the sharp-smelling vinegar solution I used to dissolve the lime scale clogging the cooler's pads and hoses.

After reassembling everything, I took a break, draining the bottle of water I'd left sitting on the workbench next to my phone. Teejay still hadn't responded to the photo. Before I could have second thoughts, I scrolled for Ryan's number. I was reluctant to tell him about Jane's camp, yet I wanted to know if he'd heard anything more about Barbara.

He answered, his voice tight. "Can't talk right now, Boston."

"What's—"

"Look northeast."

I stepped out of the barn and started up the stairs to the loft. Even before I reached the landing, I could see the column of gray smoke rising from Wilson Mountain's crown of basalt. I'd been working on the other side of the roof all afternoon, completely oblivious to the alarming sight.

"*Oh no.*"

"Blew up about forty minutes ago. Must've started over-night near Sterling Pass, and it's burning north fast. The canyon's like a goddamn chimney." I heard muffled shouts, the chirp of a siren. "We're going door to door in Pine Flats now." He named a small development with a couple of dozen homes on the north end of Oak Creek Canyon. More sirens screamed in the background.

"Be careful," I said. But he'd already ended the call.

17

I STARED, HORRIFIED YET fascinated. The column of smoke looked like rotting cauliflower, burgeoning whenever the fire found a fresh source of fuel—trees weakened by bark beetles, parched undergrowth, cabins, propane tanks. I tried to stay on task, but my gaze strayed to the expanding gray plume whenever I rounded the horse barn for tools or water. I scanned the eastern horizon for clouds, but today's sky was stubbornly blue. When my phone rang, I welcomed the interruption.

"There's a fire in Oak Creek Canyon," Mark Stillman said. "Two thousand acres already."

"A bucket helicopter flew over a few minutes ago. The wind's pushing the smoke north."

We talked about the effort to control the fire's forward progress until he changed the subject. "How did it go with Lyssa?"

"It was"—I searched for a word—"*illuminating*. And not."

"Want to talk about it?"

About to say no, I decided Mark was the perfect sounding board—calm, nonjudgmental. Not only that, an idea had started to take shape in my mind, and I wanted his input. I gave him directions, then went back downstairs to finish putting away tools.

I heard tires on gravel and saw that Mark had pulled in front of Claire's house—the weedy two-track sloping down to the barn was easy to overlook. I slid the barn door shut, the Willys still outside, and walked to meet him. He was looking at the house, hands on hips, and I tried to see it through his eyes—a gray-green rectangle of slump block, low and unassuming, at least from his angle. He turned as I approached.

"Great house. Definitely a sleeper."

He got it. I smiled. "My aunt's. Most people would wonder why I don't tear it down for a trophy home." I spoke without thinking, then wished I could take the words back, in case he heard them as criticism.

"Don't ever do that. It's a classic mid-century design. Modest but graceful."

"Thanks." I gestured down the two-track. "My place isn't quite as impressive. I've been doing some emergency swamp cooler maintenance."

He followed me down the two-track, pausing now and then to admire Claire's house from different perspectives, murmuring about intersecting angles and butt-glass windows.

"Claire wanted a house where her studio wouldn't be an afterthought. She designed it, but some starchitect in LA helped when it came to drawing the plans. I can't remember his name, except it reminds me of music."

"A. Quincy Jones?"

"That's it."

"Wow. She moved in exalted circles."

"Hollywood." I started walking again. "She met Whittaker Lee on set, and he invited her to Sedona for inspiration.

She ended up buying a lot on the edge of town. Now it's the middle."

We'd reached the horse barn. I was nervous about showing him the loft, and not only because he was an architect. He followed me up the exterior staircase that'd been added in the mid-nineties when Claire converted the barn's upper level into an apartment. From the wide landing, we could see the brownish-gray pall creeping toward Flagstaff. We watched it wordlessly for a few moments.

"The fire won't burn this way," I said, ninety-nine percent certain. *Maybe eighty percent*, I corrected silently as a dark puff exploded, then faded into the larger cloud behind it. "But the smoke will drift down the canyon overnight."

I opened the glass slider that replaced the former haymow door, and he paused, assessing. I waved him in, relieved that at least the cooler was working better. "Go ahead, have a look. I was about to make some iced tea."

While I poured, Mark explored the five-hundred-square-foot space, divided by a low bookshelf that (mostly) shielded the sleeping nook. The sitting area was sparsely furnished with a pair of mismatched lounge chairs and Henry's battered footlocker, which I'd disguised with a scarf. Opposite the slider, a large window looked over the treetops and a slice of Coffee Pot Rock. Only a corner of the main house was visible, lightly screened by a trio of stone pines.

"Nice—like a treehouse. But the bathroom needs gutting." He smiled to take the sting out of it.

"That'd be a pleasure." *Why not?* I had time on my hands. I carried the glasses over to the sitting area and set them on the trunk. "What else would you do?"

"Besides installing AC? Or a mini-split?" I winced as a string of dollar signs danced through my head. He pointed toward my feet. "May I?"

I stepped off the large vintage rya, knotted in shades of rust and gold, that had once graced Claire's dining room. He pulled back the thick rug to reveal the scuffed vinyl underneath, its faux oak sadly unconvincing. "I'd definitely update the flooring." *More dancing dollar signs.* "But structurally, it's sound, and there's a lot of natural light. You could punch out another window to brighten up the kitchen."

His gaze homed in on a framed photo near the entry of the small galley, a black-and-white print of a bent pine, the pale granite of the Sierra behind it. "Ansel Adams?"

I nodded. "Claire collected almost as much art as she sold."

She'd had the photo appraised a few years ago, when she needed money for her medical bills. Then it was worth only a few thousand, so instead she'd ended up selling another chunk of land to a neighbor, leaving a half acre of her original lot. Now I wondered if the photo might bring in enough cash to remodel the loft.

"I have resources and a professional discount. If you're interested, we could come up with a few options, price them out. An update might not cost as much as you think, especially if you have the skills to do some of the work yourself."

Mark's gaze briefly skimmed my bare legs as we sat on the chairs. Instead of changing out of my work clothes, I'd used the time before his arrival to finish storing tools and tidy the sitting area. I crossed my legs, suddenly self-conscious. "I'd like that."

"So . . . tell me about your shamanic journey."

"That's a line you don't hear every day." *Humor—my usual stall.*

"Except in Sedona."

His smile was persuasive, so I told him what I'd learned about the Daughters of Ishtar. "Franklin and Barbara were together before she married Whittaker. He followed her out here, and Lyssa blamed him for the circle's collapse. Apparently, Barbara thought forgiving Franklin was a growth step, and he took advantage."

He leaned back in the chair, closed his eyes. I let him think, or not think, whatever it was he did. After a few beats of silence, he opened his eyes again. "Are you sure it wasn't the other way around? Maybe Barbara was seeking Franklin's forgiveness."

"For choosing Whittaker?" I tested the theory. "She married Whittaker for his money. Alienated his friends. Even drove away their daughter."

He shrugged. "If she was genuinely seeking transformation, as Lyssa claims, it would've been hard for her to move forward without first coming to terms with the past."

The comment was almost offhand. *Almost.* I looked at him out of the corner of my eye as I set my glass on the trunk. "Some things are harder to forgive than others."

"True." His tone was even.

I reached for his empty glass. "More tea?"

"Sure, thanks."

I took my time in the kitchen. When I returned with the tea, he nodded toward my laptop and suggested researching bathroom fixtures. We pulled the chairs closer together, angled the screen so we both could see. It didn't take long to understand Mark had impeccable taste . . . and clients with lavish budgets. After a few false starts, we found a couple of product lines that worked for small spaces and smaller bank accounts. I was bookmarking a web page with sink cabinets when a muffled crash from below got my attention. Our gazes met.

"Probably a pack rat." I grimaced. "They keep outsmarting me."

"Let's take a look. Might be a simple fix."

The sun had dipped behind the horizon, and orange flames flickered through the smoke. An acrid taste hit the back of my throat as I led the way down the stairs. I switched on the overhead bulb, and dust motes floated in the dim light. The former stables were an embarrassing jumble of storage and tools, even with the Willys still parked outside.

I realized my error. "I left the sliding door open this afternoon so I could move the ladder. That's like unrolling a red carpet."

Mark raised a finger to his lips. A furtive noise came from the old horse stalls, where I'd stacked Claire's furniture and covered it with tarps—a luxury condo for pack rats. And pack rats attracted snakes. I approached slowly, kneeling to cautiously lift one corner of a tarp. A sputtering ball of fur exploded from underneath, startling me back onto my haunches. I landed on the dirt floor, and the kitten rounded its back and puffed.

"Oh!"

Mark chuckled, and I glared at him. "I'm not laughing at you." He fought a smile. "Well, maybe a little. *That* is one spicy furball."

The kitten darted back into its hiding place, and a wooden chair wobbled. I stood, brushed myself off, and reached to pull back the tarp. "Should a kitten that small be on its own?"

"Sometimes the mothers take them out hunting. The kittens get tired, then lost."

"Lucky a coyote didn't find it." My heart clenched. More than lucky. Silently, I thanked all the gods and goddesses that I'd ignored the guy at the hardware store who'd advised me to put out rat poison. I couldn't see the kitten in the tangle of chair legs, so I tried coaxing it out with smoochy noises. My answer was an impressive hiss.

"Let me try."

I stepped aside to make room. He'd found a piece of old straw. Sitting cross-legged on the dirt floor, heedless of his light gray slacks, he began slowly trailing the long stalk back and forth. At last, a tiny orange and black paw reached out. He allowed the kitten to capture it briefly before pulling the straw closer, a few centimeters at a time. Within minutes, the kitten forgot its fear and climbed onto Mark's lap.

I melted and knelt beside him . . . only to freeze up again when the kitten spat at my approaching hand.

His voice was soft. "Let her get used to us."

"*Her?*"

"Orange and black. Tortoiseshell cats are almost always female."

"And you know this how?"

"My ex had two cats. The tortie had attitude. She called it tortitude." He gently rubbed the side of the kitten's neck with a finger, and it—*she*—started to purr. "I don't suppose you have any supplies. A box? Blankets?"

"Boxes I have in abundance. She'll have to settle for some clean garage towels."

"That'll work." He glanced at the smartwatch on his wrist. "The grocery store might still be open. You can take her upstairs while I go pick up a few things."

"Okay." I resigned myself to a new set of scratches, but the kitten was docile enough once Mark wrapped her in a towel so only her half-orange, half-black face peeped out. I arranged a couple more towels in a small cardboard box for a cozy bed, but as soon as I got her upstairs and unwrapped her, she scuttled below mine instead.

Trying not to take the rejection personally, I looked for a shallow bowl and filled it with water, setting it near the kitchen. She still hadn't emerged by the time Mark returned, carrying a grocery bag in each arm. I reached for one and unpacked several cans of food, a kitten-sized litter box, and a suspiciously complete array of pet-parenting supplies. He carried the other bag into the kitchen.

"Hungry? I picked up a few things from the deli."

"You *are* a mind reader."

He smiled and shook his head at the lame joke. While I set out plates for the "few things" (small cartons of everything left from the holiday weekend), he opened a can of kitten food and used it to lure her from under the bed.

We were sharing the last sliver of chocolate torte when he nodded toward the photo of Claire, still propped to one side. "Your aunt? You look like her."

"You think? People always said I took after my dad." I leaned forward to reassess. Claire and my father were nothing alike, other than a shared gene for red hair. Though the black-and-white photo didn't show it, hers was a blaze of glory, while my father's—like mine—was dark with auburn undertones.

"A little resemblance around the jaw, but mostly the look in her eyes. Assessing, confident. You were close to her?"

I nodded. "My parents? Wrapped up in each other. Claire was like a beacon on a stormy sea."

Though I'd nearly forgotten my mother's birthday tomorrow, I hadn't forgotten how often she and Claire had clashed over the years. Now it was as if the two women were at war inside me. No wonder I couldn't settle on a path forward. Like my mother, I craved security, the sense of *home* I'd found here with my aunt. But I also wanted to be more like Claire, bravely embracing change, seeing opportunities instead of setbacks.

"Claire was so . . . fearless. Even in the way she took on cancer. She left home when she was a teenager. Hitchhiked to California and worked her way through art school. She used to tell me she tried being a flower child but found the lifestyle too restrictive."

"Sounds like an interesting woman." He held my gaze, and after a few seconds I looked away.

The kitten had fallen asleep in her box, probably in a food coma after eating an entire can of something grandly labeled mousse. (While we scooped salads and casseroles from deli containers, I'd made Mark laugh by pronouncing it "mouse.") I nodded toward her. "Shouldn't we take her to a vet? Or to the shelter?"

"It's the Fourth. Everything's closed except gas stations and grocery stores, and they were turning down the lights when I left. Besides, she chose you."

"Uh-uh. I'm hardly ever home." Or at least, I wouldn't be, when—*if*—I got my job back.

"She might be the answer to your pack rat problem."

"I think she needs to grow up a bit first." Mark had picked up a lot of pet supplies for an overnight guest. Was he setting me up? Commitment. Responsibility. It had happened so fast, I didn't have time to consider . . . but maybe that was the point.

He read my thoughts again. "You can reassess in the morning."

* * *

Before Mark left, we stood on the landing and stared at Wilson Mountain, flames glowing like orange fireflies in the darkness, beautiful and horrifying. The image stayed with me when I closed my eyes, so I lay awake, brooding over Mark's comment about the past. The Lees' tangle of jealousy

and manipulation had ensnared others long before the goddess circle. Henry Grisom, once Whittaker's best friend, had
been banished from the ranch. Barbara called him a thief,
but I'd bet Claire's house that Henry hadn't stolen the necklace. Somehow, the shell-and-stone artifact found its way to
Franklin. Maybe he'd used it to lure the killer away from the
party that night.

As I tumbled into a troubled half-sleep, the sound of a
flute pulled me back. I'd been walking barefoot on a dirt
trail, following the cliff dweller toward a wall of stone. He
turned and cocked his head to listen, and I realized the music
was filling my loft. The flute silenced abruptly.

My phone. There was only one reason Teejay would call
this late. I heard the ping of a text message and reached over,
triggering the touch ID.

I blinked at the photograph on the screen. Was I dream-
ing? I blinked again, but the petroglyph was still there, a
meandering spiral surrounded by tiny figures, all carved into
the pink stone and overgrown by green and gray lichen.

His message was terse: **This yours?**

My fingers trembled, and I stopped typing. Memories
of that night in Boston crept in—the night I thought I was
leading a killer into a trap, only to find he was already there
waiting for me. Teejay said he referenced his photos by location, which meant he knew where the petroglyph was.

Was he baiting me?

I hesitated so long my phone went to sleep. I set it on
the nightstand and tried to go to sleep myself, but my mind
was busy trying out various scenarios, all of them ending the
same way—though sometimes the hand that held the knife
belonged to the serial killer, and sometimes it was Ryan's or
Teejay's. For hours, I struggled to break free of the mental
carousel, until the scent of smoke spurred me out of bed. I

switched off the cooler and closed the windows, turning away from the flickering orange light on the mountainside.

Back in bed, I stared up at the skylight, watching as drifting smoke dimmed the stars. I felt a tentative pressure near my feet. The kitten slowly padded her way up my sheet-covered legs, across my chest, then settled herself into the hollow above my shoulder. Her little body felt warm through my thin T-shirt, and my muscles softened. Her faint purr finally lulled me to sleep.

When I opened my eyes again, she was gone. The skylight's rectangle was brownish-gray, the dulled sky heightening my sense of dread. I still hadn't decided what to do about Teejay's message as I swung my legs out of bed and reached for a sarong to tie around my waist.

A black-and-orange ball of fur raced me to the kitchen and settled next to the bright yellow ceramic bowl Mark had bought for her. *Fast learner.*

"Next lesson." She looked up. "Coffee before kittens."

While we ate our breakfasts—oatmeal for me, more mousse for her—my phone pinged. My heart raced, then sank as I read Ryan's warning. The Sterling Fire had doubled overnight, pushing the forest supervisor to issue an emergency order. The entire forest, nearly two million acres, was closing tomorrow. Less than twenty-four hours, and I hadn't found Jane or the spiral.

Pacing around the loft didn't help me strategize. The kitten pounced on my bare toes every time I neared her latest hiding place, a reminder my first responsibility was to get her home. I snapped photos, canvassed the neighbors without success, then called the shelter. After a weekend of illegal M-80s and bottle rockets, the kennels and cat rooms were crowded with frightened strays. Reluctantly, I agreed to keep her while they looked for her owner. I posted photos on social media and sent messages to local veterinary offices. By the time I'd done everything possible to help find her people, I was already thinking of the kitten as Percy—short for Persephone.

Was this what Mark hoped would happen?

She attacked my feet again, so I scooped her up and tried to distract her with the sparkly ball Mark had included in her kitten layette. She had more accessories than a Malibu Barbie.

Barbie.

My thoughts ricocheted back to the Lees and Franklin. How much did Jane know? I could go back to the Tolkien-esque camp and wait . . . The hair on the back of my neck rose. This time I wouldn't go alone. Except Ryan had sent a message saying he was working the roadblock at the entrance to Oak Creek Canyon. Mark had phoned to tell me he was on his way to Phoenix to catch a flight to LA. Sam and Evan usually weren't back from their tours until almost dusk. And even if I could convince Megan bushwhacking through the forest would be a fun way to spend a hot, smoky afternoon, her nonstop chatter might scare Jane off.

I tossed Percy's toy underneath the bed. While I waited for her to fetch it—or not—I picked up my phone. **This yours?** Teejay's message still demanded.

Being a reporter had taught me sometimes you had to shake the tree and see what fell out. I typed my reply. **Yes! Where is it?**

And waited.

18

MINUTES DRAGGED BY. The sparkly toy had vanished, either swallowed by dust bunnies or smothered by a rug. In the meantime, Percy discovered my hiking boots next to the door and attacked the laces with kittenish ferocity. She stopped and ran under the bed when flutelike notes trilled from my phone.

"Feel like a hike?"

A tight knot turned over in my midsection when I heard Teejay's voice, like the die inside a Magic 8 Ball. *Reply hazy, try again.* "Now?"

"Last chance before the forest closes. If you want to go, grab your gear and meet me at the office in twenty minutes. I'll drive."

"Okay, sure." While waiting for my instincts to kick in and tell me if I was crazy to go with him, I filled a water bottle, Percy trailing me to the kitchen. I dumped a can of food in her bowl, partly out of guilt for leaving her on her own again, partly to distract her while I laced my boots. We'd been together less than twenty-four hours, and already I was shaping up to be a terrible pet parent. *Foster* parent. I left the swamp cooler on for her but made sure the windows were secure.

At the stoplight, I waited for a long convoy of fire trucks and hotshot crew carriers, emblazoned with the names of strike teams, arriving from points across the west. Cars and SUVs streamed in the opposite direction, most carrying out-of-state plates and disappointed vacationers who'd come for bright blue skies, not a dirty gray smoke ceiling. The Sterling Fire—now five thousand acres—continued its march northward.

When I pulled up at Blue Sky's entrance, it was barely four, but Harmony's silver compact rolled past, and she slid down her window to wave. Gina sat alone behind the reception counter. About to apologize for missing the Grannies' performance during the city party, I stopped at her expression. Deep lines had settled around her mouth, and her eyes were red and swollen.

I walked around the counter and rolled a chair next to hers. "I saw Harmony leaving."

"You know I always try to look on the bright side." I nodded. "We've had so many cancellations. She said it's because we're cursed, and I'm afraid I lost it. I told her to go home. I sent Megan home, too. And"—her inhale stuttered—"the sheriff just called off the search for Barbara Lee."

My heart squeezed. "It's been six days since she disappeared."

"Poor Barbara. She loved to dance."

"I didn't know you were friends. Was she one of the Grannies?" As Gina slowly shook her head, awareness dawned. *Of course.* Gina had been one of Steve's first hires. "You were a Daughter of Ishtar?"

A flush crept up from her neckline. "When I moved here, I didn't know a soul. I met a woman my age at one of the crystal shops, and we got to talking about our exes, how hard it was to bounce back after so much disappointment. I'd just turned forty, and it felt more like a millstone than a mile-stone. There I was, new town, new job . . ."

"Lonely."

She nodded. "When she invited me out to the ranch for a new moon ceremony, I thought, why not? I wanted a fresh start, and everyone there was warm and accepting."

And so she'd embraced the circle's teachings. I found it hard to imagine Gina succumbing to drugs, sex, and New Age music, but as she described her journey from hope to disil-lusionment, I realized the experience had soured her. "Then Frank Johnson showed up. He managed to get his hooks into all of us. I should have been immune to Svengali types—I'd just divorced one of them, after all—but I was completely fooled."

"You were working at Blue Sky then?"

A fresh batch of tears filled her dark eyes. "Steve had just taken over the business and wanted to expand. It seemed like a good idea to offer trips to the ranch, but when Frank got involved, I should've guessed how it would play out. It's all my fault. The gossip nearly ruined us."

I heard footsteps in the hallway and spoke quickly. "Is that why Steve left?"

Before she could answer, Teejay entered. He and Gina exchanged a look. Almost imperceptibly, he shook his head.

"Ready to go, Delilah?"

"I'll follow you in the wagon." I was relieved when he didn't object. With Gina as witness, I asked where we were headed.

"Dry Creek. We can park at the old compactor site and hike across The Flats, then walk down the creekbed until we find your spiral. We've got plenty of time before sunset."

Plenty of time . . . said every stranded hiker, ever. I ignored the knot in my stomach and led the way outside.

* * *

Sedona's former trash dump wasn't a popular trailhead, yet as I pulled up beside Teejay's pickup, I was surprised ours were the only two vehicles here. The red earth beneath our feet was scraped bare, and even with a smoke-dimmed sun, the dirt glittered with remnants of glass and metal. At least the haze knocked a few degrees off the temperature, though the humidity made up for it.

He eyed the liter bottle I slung over my torso. "If you run out, I have extra."

He was wearing a teal-green hydration pack, and I had a feeling its pockets were stuffed with other handy items, Boy Scout that he was. Or wasn't. *Was I crazy to be alone with him?*

His stride loose and confident, he led the way through a spiderweb of old utility roads, bike tracks, and arroyos, all working to wear down the thick reddish layer of Hermit shale. Pockets of shaley soil supported scattered junipers and patches of graying snakeweed or bleached-out grasses. Little brown fence lizards darted across the trail at our feet. Above, a pair of turkey vultures wheeled lazily around a thermal.

If you were zipping by on the highway, seduced by the colorful cliffs straight ahead, you might overlook The Flats. But from the trail, this open piñon-juniper woodland offered long views of Sedona's backcountry, where reddish buttes rose to meet the harder, lighter sandstones that made up the rim of the Colorado Plateau. Decades ago, when the Forest Service leased The Flats to cattle ranchers, a young Whittaker Lee had cowboyed here for extra cash. I wondered if, even then, he'd looked up and imagined himself in a movie.

The viewshed was still mostly unblemished by signs of urbanization. But Sedona's economy was addicted to the crack of tourism, and the broken shale would be easy enough to grade for roads and building sites. When the land exchange was complete, the Forest Service would get its modern visitor center along the highway. The city would annex the rest for retail and lodging. The new tourist gateway into West Sedona would help divert traffic that clogged Uptown and the Village of Oak Creek.

The proposal made a certain kind of sense. Still, my heart ached every time I imagined bulldozers cutting through the red earth, or pictured golf greens spreading like an alien carpet beneath the cinematic backdrop of red rock cliffs and canyons, sucking water from the aquifer below.

Our trail narrowed to hug the side of a ridge, dropping away on the right for views of the Cockscomb, and behind it, flat-topped Doe Mesa. A network of washes, like the one below us, burrowed through The Flats and drained into Dry Creek, which was—as its name suggested—waterless most of the year. Teejay's pace was brisk; keeping up left me little energy to spare for conversation. I'd become nose-blind to the smoke, but I could feel my lungs working harder. We stopped for a break, sitting on an outcropping of pale gray limestone that made a perfect bench. I searched Teejay's face for signs of duplicity, but he was studying the piñon-juniper woodland below.

Telltale dashes of bright green cottonwoods curved through the evergreens, the only evidence of Dry Creek's location. We'd hiked twenty minutes, encountering only a single mountain biker racing back to the trailhead. The knot in my stomach tightened. Was the petroglyph spiral down there somewhere, or had Teejay chosen this lightly trafficked trail for another reason?

"How long since you took that photo?"

He tilted his head, thinking. "Almost twenty years. Not long after I moved to Sedona. I hiked to the Cockscomb, then started following the creekbed south of the old tree farm."

I remembered the area—now a gated development of luxury homes.

"I got a couple of good shots on my last roll before I lost the light. I didn't realize how far south I'd hiked until I started heading back. Pitch dark by the time I found my vehicle."

"In other words, you were lost."

"If you want to get technical about it." He smiled. "I was still finding my way around then."

I sipped my water and did the math. "This was before you started working for Steve?"

"Yeah. I was still into photography." His smile turned wry. "You know how it is—come to Sedona with a dream, end up driving Jeeps."

"Sure." Except I'd come with nightmares, not dreams. Then I remembered what Teejay had said about returning from his last tour in Afghanistan. Like me—and Gina—he'd been searching for some measure of healing. How had the shamanka phrased it? *Yearning to be transformed.*

"Were you part of the goddess circle before or after you started with Blue Sky?"

"Does it matter?" He didn't meet my gaze.

"Gina's blaming herself for getting Steve involved."

"Plenty of blame to go around. But I'll talk to her." He turned then, and the vulnerability in his expression almost stopped me from asking the next question. But I had to know.

"How did that girl end up falling off a cliff?"

His sigh was heavy. "Kayla wanted to go on a vision quest. I told Steve she wasn't ready for it, but she kept at him with questions—how someone should prepare, what to expect—and he wanted to impress her."

"*Steve* took her up to the alcove?"

"Steve knew better than that. When we went to look for her, we found a jar of datura seeds hidden in her sleeping bag.

That wasn't his style." He looked away to stare at the distant cliffs. Their ridges and folds kept the canyons' secrets. Until now.

I shivered despite the heat. "Franklin?"

He shrugged. "He knew about the alcove. Pretty sure he was supplying party drugs, though I couldn't prove it. She'd been out there almost thirty-six hours when we found her. Steve drove her to the hospital and waited until her folks arrived. In the meantime, someone called the sheriff."

"He didn't arrest anyone?"

Teejay shook his head. "Kayla's dad was a Maricopa County judge. He knew the system. He could've sued Blue Sky because we were the ones who brought her to Lee Ranch, but he had no use for a few old Jeeps. He wanted the whole thing to go away. So did Whittaker. We agreed to keep our mouths shut and considered ourselves lucky."

Teejay didn't look like a lucky man. During the past couple of weeks, I'd noted the changes in him as the weight on his shoulders increased. I was sorry to keep pressing him, but I was tired of secrets. "They persuaded the sheriff to back off, but they couldn't stop the town from talking."

"Franklin disappeared for a while, and no one noticed. But Steve grew up here. He couldn't handle the whispers, the knowing looks. He said he was going to stay with a buddy on Maui until the rumors settled down—"

"And never returned," I finished. "The girl? Kayla?"

"She recovered. Pulled herself together and didn't look back, not until last week, when I asked her to release me from our promise."

"That's why you didn't mention the goddess circle when we found Franklin's body?"

He sighed again. "It happened so long ago. It honestly didn't even occur to me Franklin's death might be connected, not until you started poking around. I made some calls, managed to track her down, and she asked to see where Franklin had died."

Creepy. Though I understood the need for closure. "That was her hiking with you in the box canyon."

He nodded. "She wasn't happy about going with me to talk to the sheriff. I told her I'd help her put the ghosts to rest."

The knot in my stomach loosened. Revisiting the past couldn't have been easy for him either. "Why didn't you leave town, like Steve? Why did you stay in Sedona?"

"Same reason you came back. Look." He nodded toward the reddish earth at our feet. Our limestone perch was surrounded by colorful flakes of chert—fossilized sponge. I might have noticed sooner if I hadn't been distracted.

"It's a lithic scatter." My voice hushed. Ancient hunters had waited here, working chunks of stone into points for their arrows while they watched for game to pass below. A few feet beyond, a hair's breadth from eroding over the edge, I saw a rusted can that had been pierced by a church-key opener. Picnickers or cowboys, maybe even Whittaker, had also stopped to rest on this perfect natural bench—all of us connected through the ages.

"Ever feel like you were here before?" I asked him.

"All the time. You good?" He nodded toward the water bottle I was still holding, but I sensed he was referring to much more. I scanned his face, so familiar, and yet . . . I realized then it was impossible to block out the parts of someone you weren't ready to see. Unless, of course, you wanted to stay hidden yourself.

"I'm good." I stashed away my bottle, ready to continue our hike.

When we got to the creek, we found only the ghost of water—bedrock sculpted into basins and chutes, smooth cobbles, rippled sand that had dried to crust. Past floods had scattered boulders and branches across the creekbed, which was edged by brushy growth.

"I'm ninety-nine percent sure your spiral is that way." He nodded south.

"And if it isn't?"

"Then we'll backtrack. If we have time."

It sounded simple. My pulse disagreed, kicking up a notch. Mostly, we think of disasters as cataclysmic, but I'd learned plenty of them snuck up on tiptoe, one small misstep at a time. "Okay. Sounds like a plan."

Our progress was slow. Teejay's photo showed the spiral lit by afternoon sun, but just in case, we searched either side of the waterless creek. We split up to cover more ground, scrambling over rocks and under branches, staying within earshot of each other. The wide channel meandered and turned, then deepened to a narrow canyon as it cut through harder rock. Trees and brush grew above the fractured rim, isolating us from the rest of the world.

The rock I was standing on tottered alarmingly as I swatted at a swarm of no-see-ums drawn to the moisture of my breath. Teejay saw me waving my arms around and crossed the creekbed to offer me a small brown bottle.

"Secret recipe. Cedar gnats hate it."

I rubbed a few drops of the oil blend around my throat, eyes watering at the citrusy and woodsy scent, strong yet pleasant.

"Watch out for snakes," he added before heading back toward the opposite cliffs. I'd already been avoiding hidden pockets of stone and checking branches before moving them aside to look closer at a cliff face or boulder. The careful search took most of my attention, though the occasional scrape of brush or thud of dislodged rock let me know Teejay was still in the vicinity.

Until I realized those sounds had ceased.

A tingle of panic traveled up my legs as I scanned for a glimpse of color or movement. Had Teejay abandoned me? I saw a dark silhouette out of the corner of my eye and twisted to look down canyon. The cliff dweller disappeared around a bend.

I hurried to follow, heedless of branches slapping at my arms and legs, but he'd vanished. I spun around to glance behind me. And gasped. The cliff face was mottled with lichen and streaked by dark brown manganese oxide—desert varnish—except where it had been pecked and chiseled to reveal the pinkish color underneath.

"You found it." Teejay had rounded the bend after me.

"Yes." I laughed, giddy to see my memories made solid. "Isn't it amazing?"

We stood there admiring the large spiral. Its outside turn began with the flute player. Dancers and animals surrounded him, as though they'd gathered to listen—foxes or coyotes, a mountain lion with exaggerated teeth and tail. Here and there, various colors of lichen—orange, acid-green, gray— had grown over the complex scene.

"I remember thinking I needed to come back when the light conditions were better, but then I started at Blue Sky. We need to get Ronnie out here."

"What do you think she'd say?" I wondered aloud. "Is the flute player summoning the animals? Is the spiral a map?"

"She'd say not to pin a meaning on it."

I couldn't help it. I thought of the spiral in Lee Canyon, so similar to this one. Could the two sites be related? Another memory tugged at me. I leaned closer, until the lowest curve of the spiral was at eye level. Everything had been leading me here—my dreams and visions, Jane's drawing, even Franklin's death—*but why?*

I turned to look at the canyon. The sandstone walls rose roughly thirty feet, broken by joints and platforms that held enough soil for clumps of bear grass and small shrubs. The pinkish bedrock at our feet was sculpted and smoothed, scattered with gray and white cobbles. It was lovely, but there were hundreds of spots even more beautiful around Sedona. I took a few photos to help me remember the location.

"We should start back." Teejay sounded as reluctant as I felt. He walked toward a break in the canyon wall, where branches had been laid over a narrow route leading upward. "The Forest Service has been rerouting mountain bike paths around here. This looks like an old trail. Might get us out of the canyon faster."

The trail you know or the one you hope leads you somewhere better—how many times had I faced that choice? Sunset was less than an hour away, another forty minutes or so of twilight to follow. I heard a rolling percussion, so distant I couldn't pinpoint its direction. "Was that thunder?"

"Sounded like it."

We waited without moving or speaking, but the dull rumble didn't repeat. I didn't state the obvious: A storm cell miles away might send water rushing over sandstone and down dozens of tributaries to enter Dry Creek, triggering a flash flood. "Let's get to higher ground."

Decision made, I stepped over the piled branches and started up. The abandoned route was steep and rough, more like a small drainage ditch than a trail, leading through a pocket of fragrant gray-green cypress trees. I placed my boots carefully so I wouldn't dislodge any rocks toward Teejay, following below.

Ten feet from the rim, I called over my shoulder. "It's more open up here."

"That's because someone's been cutting back the brush."
Teejay caught up to me. He reached to pull down a cypress
branch, pointing out the clipped edges.

"I'll thank them later." We still had to find our way back
to the main trail.

I topped out on the rim and paused. The slope was gentle
here, a long rolling rise toward an exposed ridge a hundred
feet away. A light breeze cooled the perspiration on my neck.
The temperature had dropped. I drank some water while I
scanned the trees and brush for a route to the ridge.

My gaze landed on a small piece of metal atop a limestone outcropping, and I thought of the map Ronnie had
shown me. "Is that a site marker?"

Teejay walked over and knelt for a closer look. "Nope.
Climbing anchor. Here's where the other anchor point
was."

I stepped close enough to see a pale gouge in the limestone, raw as a fresh wound. The rim of the canyon was at
least ten yards behind us, and the climb from the creekbed
wasn't that difficult.

As though reading my thoughts, Teejay mumbled, "Odd
place to anchor in."

We looked around. Whoever the climbers were, they'd
been careless, churning up patches of cryptobiotic soil, cutting away scrub oak and junipers to make a small clearing. I
felt a stab of irritation at the disrespect, though I was ready to
move on. "We should strike northeast for the main trail. Or
turn around and hustle back up the creek."

"Yeah. We should." But Teejay's attention was still fixed
on the clearing. He took a few steps, then halted. "Whoa."

I didn't see it at first, hidden among the scattered rocks.
Not until I stood next to him and looked down at the long,
shadowy gash at our feet. "A sinkhole?"

"Didn't know there was one out here, but it makes sense. We were walking over Supai formation rocks in Dry Creek Canyon. Below the Supai layers, it's Redwall limestone."

"Where Sedona's aquifer is?"

"Bingo. Water percolates down and dissolves the limestone, forming caves. Sometimes a cave gets so big its ceiling collapses from the weight of the rock layers above it, creating a sinkhole." He bent almost flat to the ground, peering over the rim into the shadows below. "Someone must have used the anchors to belay down."

In case he wasn't listening, I stressed each syllable. "We can come back tomorrow."

"No, we can't. The forest will be closed." He looked up at me, a smile playing around the corners of his mouth. I opened mine to argue, but he knew how to hook me. "If the spiral is a map, it's pointing here. Look."

CHAPTER

19

THE SINKHOLE FLARED like a lopsided fishbowl, the twenty-foot-long gash hiding a larger cavern below. Teejay pointed across the shadowy depths to its far end. I saw a parade of animals, faded white against pinkish sandstone. *Pictographs.*

My gasp dropped into the shadows. The sinkhole's base—littered with rocks and stunted brush—sloped west into darkness. The east rim looked raw, dangling roots and unpatinated stone suggesting a more recent ceiling fall. Teejay, the geology nerd, pointed this out, an edge of excitement coloring his words.

"Until that section collapsed, the sinkhole would have been almost impossible to see." A light-starved cypress poked up from below, its lower trunk buried by rubble. "We could climb down that tree."

"Seriously?" I tried to see it through Teejay's eyes—the bare limbs a ladder, the broken stone a staircase. My muscles tensed, and I glanced up. The smoke-hazed sky to the north had turned an ominous gray.

"Twenty minutes. That's all." His eyes pleaded.

A wave of vertigo came and went. Twenty minutes was beyond the realm of probability, but . . . *pictographs.* "Okay."

* * *

He made his way down first, testing branches. Dry wood cracked like a gunshot, and my breath caught. He kicked the broken branch out of the way and continued as though nothing had happened. When he made it to the pile of collapsed rock, he looked up at me. "Keep your feet close to the trunk. Three points of contact, like rock climbing."

I started down cautiously, and then my youthful tree-climbing skills took over. I dropped lightly onto the block of sandstone next to him and let my eyes adjust to the twilight tones. The cavity was more than double the size of the opening above us. Nearby, a few dried grasses sprouted up among the scattered rocks and slabs, but the opposite side was bare dirt, shaded by the deep overhang. We scrambled down the mounded rock, Teejay's voice echoing as he rhapsodized about collapsed breccia, hydrology, solution caves. Abruptly, he fell silent.

"What's wrong?"

"Take a look." He raked his phone's light across the sloping floor. It glittered with broken glass, tangled metal, a fine grayish dust. A sharp chemical odor triggered a memory from my crime-reporting days.

"Franklin's lab." I pulled up Ryan's number, then stopped. "No reception. You?"

"Nope. We'll have to climb out to catch a signal. If there is one—reception's spotty around here."

"Where's here, exactly? I mean, in relation to the land trade?"

Teejay looked up, frowned. "The forest boundary is on the other side of Dry Creek. Heading down the creekbed, we'd reach the highway in a mile or two." He looked back at the scattered debris, swore under his breath. "*The land trade.* Surveyors will be all over this area. Franklin was trying to cover his tracks."

"He certainly made a mess of it."

Teejay beamed his phone on a skeleton of metal. "Looks like some kind of hoist went over the edge. Maybe spotlights. Look at all the broken glass." Shards glittered as Teejay swept the flashlight across the scene, but I saw glints of brass, too.

"Bullet casings?"

"Yeah." He aimed the beam farther back, but a long black void at the base of the wall swallowed the light. "That's where the sinkhole drains. Rainwater winds up in Dry Creek, or maybe percolates to an aquifer. Looks like it flowed through a while back, pushed some of this debris around."

"Last time it rained was late April. Evan's naked guy?"

"April twenty-second. Earth Day. I remember wondering if he'd stumbled on some kind of ceremony while he was out looking for UFOs."

"Maybe he stumbled on this. The spot where Evan picked him up is only a couple of miles from here. We should get out, preserve whatever evidence is left."

"The moment we report this, it's off limits. Take photos if you want, but let's keep our distance." He nodded toward the tangled metal. "Ten minutes."

Ignoring a shiver of unease, I nodded and started toward the far end of the sinkhole. Behind me, Teejay said something about another way out. I murmured an agreement, but my attention had already gone to the pictographs.

The gap overhead was wider here, providing enough ambient light for me to make out the faded white marks.

Pictographs here, petroglyphs a few yards away in Dry Creek. Different time periods? Or different cultural groups? I wanted more time to explore, except I'd rather be here with plenty of daylight and an archaeologist—Ronnie Jackson or even Ryan.

Ryan.

The flicker of a memory that had teased at me earlier now burst open. The first time I'd seen the spiral along Dry Creek, I was on horseback. It was the summer after I'd turned ten. Henry had helped trailer the horses down Lower Red Rock Loop Road to the Driscoll ranch. Ryan's dad turned the spit roaster, while his mom and grandmother bustled around the kitchen. Ryan's grandfather was tasked with getting us out of the way for a couple of hours, so we'd ridden up Dry Creek, Whittaker Lee, Claire, and Henry setting a slow pace through the rocky creekbed. I'd trailed behind with the Jackaloons—Ryan and his younger sisters, Steve Nicholson, a few others. Whittaker and old man Driscoll had found the petroglyph spiral when they were cowboying as teenagers, and now they were showing us.

Ryan must have remembered the spiral all along, and yet when I described it to him, he stayed silent. Why? Had he discovered the sinkhole too?

Reflexively, I checked my phone. Still no reception. Worse, my battery had drained below fifteen percent. I switched to airplane mode and stepped closer for a photo. A herd of small deer streamed from a columnar fracture in the limestone, tiny hunters surrounding them with bows and arrows. Shifting for a better angle, I saw that the fracture was actually a gap, like a narrow doorway that led into darkness. The chemical scent of meth was absent here, and a faintly earthy, funky smell emanated from the opening. Above it, barely visible, was a painted human figure, upside down, arms akimbo, as though falling through space.

I locked my gaze on the doorway of stone. "Teejay?"

"Ready," he said, so close he startled me. "I found an easier route up."

"Great. But look at this."

I could feel his breath on my shoulder as he leaned toward the opening. He knelt to pick up a piece of shale, tossing it into the darkness. It landed with a crisp smack.

"Not very deep." Slowly and softly, as though talking to himself, he said, "Some geologists have theorized a series of subsurface caves and channels interconnect below Sedona and the Verde Valley."

"Hm." I couldn't resist teasing him. "Sounds a lot like Harmony's theory there's a crystal cave hidden beneath the lizard's tail near Capitol Butte."

"That's belief, not theory. Let's check it out."

My amusement vanished the moment I peered through the doorway into my darkest dream world. My legs turned to lead. "You first."

He switched on his flashlight and brushed past. "Come on. It's cramped, but solid."

Curiosity overcame fear, and I squeezed through the opening. Ahead, the phone's glow leached the color from the stone. The passage sloped downward, and I bent to avoid bumping my head, stepping carefully on broken stone slabs. Abruptly, Teejay stopped, his phone illuminating a blank wall of stone. He turned right, taking the light with him. I ignored a flutter of anxiety and headed for the faint glow, trailing my hand along the stone wall. The passageway twisted sharply before leading upward. Tiny stones crunched beneath our boots as we climbed.

Teejay aimed his phone through a rough opening. "It's a cave. Ceiling looks stable."

He pointed the beam across the chamber and we gasped simultaneously. The opposite wall was covered by hundreds of handprints in white and ocher, surrounding a dais of stacked rock. On top lay a mummified figure, beside it, a dozen clay bowls and jars, most of them broken.

"Grave goods." Teejay spoke in an awed whisper.

Battery forgotten, I turned on my phone's flashlight, beaming downward. Potsherds lay scattered beneath our boots. We hadn't been walking on bits of stone after all. Stepping carefully, we approached the dais, our phones casting an eerie bluish light over a recumbent figure draped with a disintegrating cotton weaving.

The foul smell was stronger here, and I registered surprise that mummified flesh continued to exude the odor of decay. The scene could have been horrifying, but a sense of calm settled over me even as my eyes filled with tears. This was someone special, perhaps a chief or a shaman. A grandfather or husband or lover—a person who was valued. His community had sacrificed their treasure to carry his story forward, to create this space where time stood still.

Until a graverobber took it away.

"Somebody was here," Teejay said, his voice flat as he beamed his phone over bits of shell and turquoise. "These were part of a larger piece."

"The shell artifact." I thought of Ronnie Jackson's mysterious investigation. "Most of these pots are broken plainware. The good stuff is gone."

"The lights, the hoist . . . this was a major operation. We need to take pictures." I was about to object—photographing the resting figure seemed wrong. Then Teejay added, "For Ronnie, just in case. Then we get out of here."

I aimed my phone's light so he could document the burial. When he'd finished, I turned to go.

And saw another body, slumped near the entrance to the chamber. Head tipped forward, blond hair covering her face.

But I didn't need to look because the smell was clue enough, and I recognized the white clothing, now stained with dried blood.

"I think we found Barbara Lee."

I searched Teejay's face in the bluish light, seeing a reflection of my shocked horror. Wordlessly, he took another photograph before we exited. The cold weight of death pressed at my back as we made our way through the passage again.

The moment we stepped outside, I inhaled deeply. Petrichor—that heady blend of iron-rich soil, tangy saltbush, and *moisture*. A raindrop landed on my shoulder, the tap of an icy finger. I looked up at the sinkhole's opening. The sky was a bruised shade of purple.

"We can climb out here. It's not as deep." Teejay led the way past the rock art.

The wall led almost straight up to the sinkhole's rim, roughly twenty feet above. Here and there, the sandstone had fractured and broken—Teejay's route. Except the route ended a few feet short, where the stone angled inward in a shallow overhang.

He read the doubt on my face. "Easier than it looks. I'll go first. When you get to the last pitch, throw your leg up and over. I'll pull you the rest of the way. Pretend you're getting on a horse." His attempt at levity fell flat.

"Right."

He gripped rock, stepped up to the first foothold, and glanced over his shoulder. "Watch where I put my feet and hands."

When it was my turn to step up, years of yoga classes failed me, and my boot scraped uselessly. I called up to him. "My legs are shorter than yours."

Teejay scuttled back down like a spider and reached out to help me get started. I climbed slowly, raindrops stinging my arms like angry hornets, sending icy numbness through my fingers. I was about five feet from the top when the sun found a crack between the horizon and the pall of smoke and clouds. For a few seconds, light transformed the raindrops to a coppery gold. Teejay smiled at me from where he waited, and I saw the cliff dweller's face briefly superimposed on his.

Then the sky rumbled, the beam of light vanishing like a mirage.

My foot slipped. I started sliding downward, stone banging against my knees, scraping my hands as I reached out to slow my fall. A few feet from the bottom, I lost contact with the cliff, feeling something give way in my left ankle as I landed hard. Pain knifed up my leg when I tried to stand.

"You okay? If you can get to that first edge, I'll pull you the rest of the way." He shifted, ready to scramble back down.

"No, stay where you are." Eyeing the sandstone, slick with water now, I tried to imagine him pulling me up to the overhang. *And then what?* My ankle throbbed. My legs and arms felt leaden. "That won't work. I twisted my ankle."

"I'll call for help. I can get a signal from the ridge."

"Okay." I wasn't sure he heard me. He'd pulled himself over the rim and disappeared. I stared at the sinkhole opening while daylight faded. Above the collapsed rubble, a rivulet of water flowed over the edge. It splashed and echoed playfully as it tumbled onto the rocks.

Thunder rumbled, louder, closer, driving me to my feet. My breath hissed out when I slipped on a wet stone, but I hobbled toward a sofa-sized slab where I could lean back and wait. Something stirred in the shadows below the deep overhang. *Rising water.* I forced myself to look away, to focus on my ankle. I probed around the joint. Fortunately, my boot compressed the injury.

What was taking Teejay so long?

Rain dripped from the brim of my hat and rolled down the back of my shirt. I pulled out my phone, fingers shaking, nails broken and bloody. The screen was cracked, but it still worked—*yay*. My elation drained. So had the battery, now below ten percent. I momentarily switched off airplane mode. *No service.* Unless a satellite happened to pass directly over-head of this narrow hole in the earth, I was cut off from the world. My throat went dry. I reached for my water, but the fall must have stripped the bottle from me. The sling was empty.

I was zipping my phone back into a pocket when a shout came from above. My heart lifted, then turned to ice.

"That you, Boston?"

I recognized Ryan's silhouette, the bulky duty belt around his hips. His concern sounded genuine. But I knew. Behind the charming lopsided grin and flirtatious repartee, he'd been lying to me all along. Franklin might have played a part in this, but he was murdered days before Barbara ended up in her stony grave.

I leaned back against the stone slab and forced a smile, hoping it masked the quaver in my voice. "Ryan! Wow, am I glad to see you. I messed up my ankle. I need help getting out of here."

He reached for his hip, and my breath stopped until his flashlight switched on. He surveyed the sinkhole.

"Thank God we got here in time." A second figure loomed behind Ryan. *Teejay?* Before I could shout a warning, Ryan continued. "I wouldn't have found you if hadn't been for Whitt. He said Teejay planned to frame you and leave you for dead."

Lightning flashed, freezing the moment: Whittaker straightening, tall and vital as a youth, yanking the pistol from Ryan's duty belt. Confusion settling over Ryan's face a split second before Whitt shoved him over the edge.

He landed with a sickening thud, his flashlight clattering down the pile of rubble until it lodged, its beam pointed uselessly skyward. I scrambled over the rocks, ignoring the pain that knifed my ankle, finding him on his left side atop a clump of brittle grass, his forehead bloody. Fingers shaking, I reached to check his neck for a pulse, and he moaned, eyelids fluttering. "Didn't know . . . Sorry." He passed out.

The crack of a gunshot echoed sharply around the cavern. Details from my wilderness first aid class crashed through my mind in panicked waves. *Never move someone with a suspected head injury. Move him before Whittaker shoots again.* I grabbed Ryan's shirt and rolled, landing in a tangle of arms and legs. I went motionless and prayed Whittaker couldn't see us below the lip of the sinkhole.

A dislodged pebble fell from the rim, and then he called out, his voice strong and taunting—the old Whitt. A chill drove into my bones. He was trying to draw me out, moving around the opening to get a better angle. *Like shooting fish in a barrel.*

"I didn't want to hurt Claire's little girl. But you kept poking around, just like her. It wasn't Henry, she said, but a man's got to defend what's his. That's what I told her. That's what I told that slick-ass art dealer. I let Barbara think her gaslighting worked. Then I turned the tables on all of 'em."

Demented—or dangerous? The sound of flowing water covering my movements, I crawled backward into the shadows. I had to make it harder, give him two targets. Trash and duff swirled around my legs. *Something must be blocking the sinkhole's outlet.* The longer I kept him talking, the better our chances of being rescued. Or was I wrong about Teejay too?

"Who helped you?" Echoes scattered my voice. His shot rang to my left, striking the heap of twisted metal.

Scoffing laughter. "Everybody thinks this weak and feeble-minded old man needs help. I played poker with the devil. Bluffed him and damn near beat him too, till you came along."

"There's equipment down here that needed a crew to operate." A loud smack as a bullet entered earth. *Too close.* My hand closed over a rock. I tossed it to my right and scuttled like a crab to the left, biting back a yelp as my kneecap met broken glass.

"Frank owed me for what he and Barbara did to me." Whittaker's voice changed direction, nearer now. "I said I'd turn him in unless he made me a crew of zombies. They'd've worked themselves to skeletons for another taste of meth."

Lightning flashed. Whittaker stood on the edge, legs wide, brandishing the pistol like a gunslinger in one of his westerns. I glanced toward Ryan, his khaki shirt pale in the darkness. I hoped the glare from the trapped flashlight might blur Whitt's line of sight. Then the khaki shape stirred, and fear rose to my throat.

I swallowed it back, tried to distract Whitt. "Did Franklin betray you? I found Barbara's body. She was going to leave you for him, wasn't she?"

A bark of laughter. "Mebbe you're not so smart after all, missy. That cold bitch would've turned on Frank the instant she got her hands on the ranch money. I let the devil take her."

"She found out what you were doing. Is that why you killed her?"

I got another bullet for an answer, splintering stone above my right shoulder. Too close. I made myself small as possible behind the pile of twisted metal, heart hammering. "Water's starting to back up. Pretty soon it will fill the sinkhole and the cave. Destroy every artifact that's left."

The upward beam of Ryan's flashlight turned everything else dark gray, but I sensed the pistol swinging in my direction.

"That cave's stayed high and dry for centuries. Besides, we carried away most of it. Polychrome jars, copper bells, an obsidian knife . . ."

While he bragged about the treasures he'd stolen, warmth flowed through my limbs, rage melting away my fear. *Keep him talking.* "How'd you find it?"

"Chasing after a lost calf. I was just a kid, but I knew that cave was special. Took the shell bird as a souvenir and left everything else the way it was. Kept it secret for years. Told only one soul and got betrayed for my trouble."

Lightning briefly illuminated the rim of the sinkhole. The rivulet had grown into a waterfall. And Whittaker stood next to it looking directly at me.

Oh hell. I squeezed my eyes shut, waited for the bullet.

His shot went wild. I opened my eyes. Whittaker had vanished, my rage vanishing with him, leaving nothing but icy dread as a roar echoed around the cavern, filling my ears. I wondered if the storm was deciding whether to drown us, electrocute us, or bury us in rubble.

I hobbled toward Ryan, water splashing over my boots, hoping I could haul him far enough up the mound of rock in time. He'd levered himself into a sitting position, leaning against a slab of sandstone, his right hand supporting his left forearm, face tipped toward the sky. Lightning flickered over his features.

Then he smiled, and I realized the beam moving across his face was a searchlight.

* * *

I felt warm pressure on my chest and opened my eyes to catch sight of Percy's little black-and-orange face before she tucked herself under my chin. For a few minutes, I listened to her purr and let myself think it had all been a dream.

Then I moved my left ankle, stiff and sore. Fully awake now, I swung my legs out of bed and reached for the brace the hospital had loaned me. Percy raced for the kitchen as soon as my feet touched the floor.

"Coffee first." I found my robe in the bathroom, saw the scratched and bruised face looking back at me from the mirror. I turned away to follow the kitten, my gaze straying to the windows. The cliffs looked scrubbed, the sky brilliant blue.

Sipping coffee, my leg elevated on a chair, I watched Percy devour her breakfast with her usual gusto. While she cleaned herself, I limped around looking for my phone, finding it on the nightstand. The good news was I'd remembered to charge it. The bad news was the spiderweb of cracks, and behind it a long string of missed calls and messages. I didn't feel like talking to anyone.

Instead, I sat on the bed, still in my robe, and thumbed through photos. The spiral *was* real. I'd zoomed out to include the cliffs, the creekbed, and Teejay standing there grinning, unaware what was about to happen a few yards away. While Whittaker took potshots at me, Teejay called in the cavalry—the sheriff's office, the fire department, his buddies on the ropes rescue team.

After the ER doc had finished taping me together, I found Teejay waiting for me in the lounge with a bearded blond Viking who introduced himself as Grady Cleveland. They told me Ryan was in surgery and offered to take me back to Sedona.

Fat drops smacked against the pickup's windshield as the blond Viking drove, the first monsoon storm of the season slowly turning to drizzle. I sat next to him, crashing from my adrenaline dump, the hypnotic back-and-forth of the wipers lulling me into a not-unpleasant fugue state while he recounted the rope team's hike through the dark. "Teejay met us on the trail, but I didn't think we'd find you in time, until we saw the helicopter."

The roaring, the searchlight.

"The sheriff redirected a forest patrol chopper assigned to the fire. They made the short haul. By the time they delivered you to the EMTs, the feds were on their way."

"So fast." The words felt like cotton in my mouth.

Teejay leaned forward from the jump seat behind me. "I called Ronnie from the ER. She and Lisa Vargas tracked down Evan's naked guy. He witnessed the shootout between Whittaker and the cartel members."

"Cartel? Better start at the beginning." My head spun. I tipped it back against the seat, fighting fatigue as Teejay filled me in. The dealer who'd purchased Whittaker's collection was an informant, under pressure from the feds to set up one of his clients, a cartel boss who laundered drug money by reselling artifacts with faked certificates.

"Wait, what did you say?"

"They called him El Diablo." *The Devil.* "He supplied equipment, transportation, guards . . ."

Grady weighed in. "Military-grade gear, armed and dangerous men, a dozen tweakers moving artifacts in the middle of the night—no surprise things went south."

In the confusion, Franklin had slipped away, becoming the UFO watcher's "alien." Teejay finished, "Franklin went to the ranch to warn Barbara, got killed for his trouble."

I frowned, my thoughts as watery as the strobe of lights through the windshield wipers. Grady pumped the brakes, and we crept past a line of emergency vehicles parked near Dry Creek Bridge. A white Forest Service pickup sat a few yards off the highway.

"Ryan's?"

"Yeah. He and Whittaker parked here to hike up the creekbed. I think Whitt was going to pin everything on Ryan until you and I came along."

"Is Whittaker . . ." My throat closed on the question.

His voice was flat. "They're still looking for him."

The three of us rode the rest of the way to Sedona with only the wipers to fill the silence. The images flashing through my mind gradually faded into the gray fog of exhaustion. Between them, Teejay and Grady had to half carry me up the stairs to the loft. I'd been so tired.

Still so tired. The phone slipped from my hand and, for the second time in twelve hours, I fell back against the pillows and into a dreamless sleep.

THE PHONE RANG in my hand, startling me from my
unintentional nap. It was already noon, and Gina
sounded as chirpy as a wren. "Aren't you the lucky one?"

"Yep, nothing but a sprained ankle and some bruises."

"Okay, there's that, but no one else guessed the fifth, so
the monsoon lottery's all yours."

Not quite awake, I remembered our office pool. *July
fifth.* Yesterday was my mother's birthday. I'd called my
father a couple of weeks ago to explain my new job meant
I wouldn't be flying home for the occasion. "She'll be disappointed," he'd warned me, probably an understatement,
but anticipating her reaction didn't trigger me as much as
it used to.

"And that's not all." The coy note in Gina's voice got my
attention. "Are you sitting down?"

I wasn't sure if she was joking, but I smiled anyway. "I'm
sitting."

"Evan's passengers stopped in after their tour. They loved
your aunt's painting. One offered to buy it. He left his card,
an art gallery in Santa Fe. I know you probably don't want
to sell, but—"

"What's his number?" I wrote it down on the notepad I kept next to the bed, adding *Call Ryan* and *Mom's birthday.* "I'll stop by tomorrow. Oh—"

The Willys was still at the trailhead, and I wouldn't be able to work the clutch anyway. Gina read my mind. "Your wagon's here. Megan took Arnulfo and Teejay to fetch the vehicles earlier this morning."

"How?" Though I'd been reeling from exhaustion, I was pretty sure I'd managed to peel off my own pants before falling back onto the mattress last night. I spotted them half underneath the bed and poked at the damp fabric with my good foot. The keys were still zipped into a pocket.

Gina tsked. "They hot-wired it, like a pair of delinquents. Arnulfo says to tell you your transmission is bad."

I laughed. "If he'll put it on the hoist and check it out, the monsoon jackpot is his. More, if he can fix it."

"Speaking of driving . . . The supervisor rescinded the closure order this morning. When can you get back behind the wheel?"

I smiled at her optimism. Or was it impatience? "Tomorrow, maybe. I could drive Gramps with an ankle brace." I pictured Gina bending over the scheduling grid, working out the substitutions.

"Let's make it Friday. We'll limp along without you until then."

"Ha-ha."

Her tone turned serious. "Teejay told me about Barbara. What a horrible way to die, alone in the dark." Heat rose to my face. I'd shed fewer tears for Barbara—someone I knew—than I had for the cave's other occupant. Gina asked, "Do you think Whittaker did it?"

"Maybe." *The devil took her.* Not exactly a confession, but whatever ballistics might reveal, he was responsible.

"What will happen with the land trade?" Gina's sharp query reminded me that while I slept, the world had shifted.

"Hm. The agreement to initiate isn't binding, so . . ." My voice faded as her meaning sank in. "Maybe Steve will change his mind about selling." But I was already thinking about losing my job again and, along with it, any hope of staying in Sedona.

*   *   *

The ER doc had instructed me to rest, so while afternoon clouds gathered along the horizon, I sat at the table with my laptop in front of me and a bag of frozen peas balanced over my ankle. I read through my notes before calling Ryan, still recovering in the hospital after surgery for a punctured lung and broken tibia.

"Up for a debriefing?" I asked.

He sighed. "Been talking to the feds ever since I opened my eyes. What they didn't spill, I figured out for myself."

He addressed some of the questions rattling around in my mind. Not long after she started working for the Lees, Marisol began to suspect Whittaker's "vitamins" had been tampered with. *Franklin*, I guessed, and Ryan agreed. Afraid to confront Barbara, she'd simply switched the pills back, becoming an unwitting accomplice as Whittaker recovered enough to plot his revenge and get back his collection. I heard a hint of grudging admiration in Ryan's voice. "Tough old cowboy. If that Scottsdale dealer hadn't been working for the feds, Whitt might have gotten away with it."

My mouth went dry. "Any updates?"

"Whitt was trying to hike back down the creekbed when the flood hit. Searchers found his body a couple of hours ago."

*   *   *

Ronnie arrived at my door as sunset was fading from Wilson Mountain's crown, a pizza box in one hand, a growler of beer in the other. She searched my face and grinned. "I thought I looked rough."

She'd spent the day following forestry techs through smoldering logs and mud ash to locate a pioneer cabin that firefighters had spotted while digging a firebreak near East Pocket. Though she'd since changed into jeans and a clean shirt, the odor of smoke clung to her, and she'd missed a dash of charcoal across one cheekbone.

We ate on the deck, the scent of garlic drifting on the humid evening air. Percy complained at being left indoors, then fell asleep next to her bowl. Between bites of pizza, Ronnie described how she'd stumbled across the multiagency investigation months ago. "A group of site stewards were helping me keep tabs on internet auctions. They found a listing for a Sinaguan bowl, and we traced it to a dealer in Scottsdale. Long story short, the feds were already onto the guy. They were angling for the big fish, but I wanted to find the dealer's local contact."

"You must've had some ideas."

"Ryan mentioned once that you were friends. I couldn't let on he was my chief suspect." Her cheeks reddened. "I've never been so glad to be so wrong. Seems he was onto Whittaker the whole time."

"Mm." I took a bite of pizza and washed it down with some beer before changing the subject. "Will the feds recover the Lees' collection? Or the artifacts from the cave?"

"Unlikely. Even if they catch up to El Diablo, there's no law against smuggling Native American antiquities out of the US." She dropped her slice of pizza back into the box, as though she'd lost her appetite. "I think the cave may have been the most elaborate burial ever found in the Southwest.

As an archaeologist, I'm furious that such an important piece of our history was stolen to fund criminal activities, but to disturb the spirit realm that way . . ." She stopped, her expression pained.

I'd been curious how Ronnie balanced her career as an archaeologist with her family's traditions. I hoped she'd confide in me someday, but I could see tonight wasn't the time. Voice wooden, she finished. "The scene should be released tomorrow. They removed Barbara's body late this afternoon."

* * *

I expected a restless night, but I slept ten hours straight, soothed by the sound of rain on the roof. The morning was cool, a few mare's tail clouds flicking across an innocent blue sky. Percy and I ate our breakfasts as I listened to KNAU. After another night of showers, the 10,000-acre Sterling Fire—sparked by two teens setting off firecrackers behind a resort—was ninety percent contained. The Type One incident management team had decamped for a wildfire in New Mexico, leaving Forest Service crews to mop up.

I switched off the news. Percy lifted her head and stretched before wandering to the slider. A moment later I heard vehicles approaching on the two-track—Arnulfo in a Blue Sky Jeep, Sam and his VW behind. I started more coffee and waved them up, surprised to see Sam in a tidy polo, like something Chase-like-the-bank might have worn, only with HAYDUKE LIVES! subbing for the usual logo. He sprawled on the deck to play with the kitten while Arnulfo and I sat on the stairs drinking coffee.

The Jeep was a loaner, Arnulfo explained, mine until he found a part for the Willys. As he stood to leave, he reached into the pocket of his Wranglers, handing me a black rectangle about half the size of a TV remote.

"GPS. Found it on the frame."

"A tracker?" He nodded solemnly, and I tried to picture Whittaker placing the device.

The sun was climbing higher, so after the guys left, I went inside and switched on the cooler, got comfortable with my leg propped atop Henry's trunk. I'd gleaned a lot of details from my conversations with Ryan and Ronnie. I suspected Franklin kept the shell artifact as insurance, forcing Whittaker to bluff about it to get El Diablo to return— *playing poker with the devil*. My visit to the ranch probably alerted Barbara, who surprised the two men. But a few points still eluded me. I called Ryan, now recovering at home, and skipped the pleasantries.

"How did Whittaker know we were at the sinkhole?" He was silent, but I'd already worked it out. "*You* put the tracker on my wagon."

His sigh was expressive. "Whitt called me after you found Franklin's body, said he'd seen a Blue Sky Jeep near the ranch a few times. Pothunting, he thought. I told him I'd keep an eye out. I figured it was Teejay, but then I saw the Willys . . ."

Oh, Ryan. I didn't try to blunt the hard edges of my response. "After you put on the tracker, you blocked the exhaust so I couldn't leave. Did you think I killed Franklin too?"

"Of course not, but I knew whoever did wouldn't like you poking around, and I thought a tracker might help keep you safe."

I considered. "It's still creepy, Ryan."

"You have no idea how sorry I am."

That I could believe. If word got out Ryan let another suspect get the best of him, he'd be back pumping toilets or planting seedlings. For now, everyone but me assumed he'd persuaded Whittaker to lead him to the crime scene. His intentions might have been good, but I wasn't ready to let him off the hook. "I'm keeping the tracker. You can explain to the Forest Service why one of their gadgets went missing."

Footsteps pounded up the stairs, and I jumped, knocking the peas to the floor. "Gotta go," I told Ryan, who was still apologizing. When I saw Harmony and Megan on the other side of the glass slider, holding shopping bags from The Market, I pasted on a smile.

* * *

Maybe it was the frozen peas or maybe it was the essential oils Harmony plied me with, but by Thursday afternoon, the staircase was no longer an obstacle. Ensconced in the loft like a princess hidden away in her tower, I'd spent hours on my laptop and cell phone. A flurry of calls to my father began with *mea culpas* for missing my mother's birthday. (Being stuck at the bottom of a sinkhole with a madman shooting at me was apparently a poor excuse.) Now, bolstered by his legal expertise, I was about to make some changes.

I pulled the Jeep next to the front door and limped inside, my gaze landing on the large gap where Claire's painting once hung. After declining the offer from the Santa Fe gallery, I tracked down an old friend of my aunt's. Sharon Costa, a retired art consultant, convinced a former client to triple the gallery owner's offer. By donating the painting to a museum, he'd earn a sizable tax deduction. I hesitated at first, but when Sharon assured me the museum would acknowledge my aunt along with her client, I gave in. Once, I might have regarded the blank wall as a loss—now I could see it as a field of possibility.

"The painting's safe at my place."

I turned. Evan held a cup of coffee toward me. "Thank you. For everything."

After taking the landscape home for safekeeping, he'd removed the frame to confirm the distinctive signature. Maybe Sharon Costa could tell me how my aunt had ended up with an original Maynard Dixon. Prices for his work had soared only recently; even so, the painting was a surprising acquisition, and I suspected it came with a story.

"Where is everyone?" I asked, taking a polite sip. I needed caffeine like a snake needed sneakers.

"Waiting in Steve's office for the big announcement." He nodded toward the ankle brace. "Glad you're back. Phones have been off the hook since yesterday's *Desert Drummer.*"

The Phoenix news weekly was known for its aggressive investigative pieces. It was hard to beat drug kingpins and international artifact smuggling for pure sensationalism, so our minor role had gone mostly unnoticed, other than a coy reference to a pair of Jeep guides who'd foiled the plan. I reminded Evan the reporter hadn't identified anyone by name.

"Everybody loves a mystery." His grin widened. "Of course, they might figure it out when they see your ankle."

"I sprained it going down the stairs at home."

"Right." He winked.

I followed him down the hall, pausing in the doorway to scan the assembled mystics, nerds, teachers, experts, and enthusiasts. These were my people. We shared a passion for Sedona's wild places and quirky characters, the science and history, the breath-stealing vistas that drew people here in droves.

"Are you sure you're ready to drive tomorrow?" Gina's gaze traveled from my fading bruises to my ankle. She offered her chair, but I shook my head.

"Almost good as new, thanks to peas and Harmony." We shared a conspiratorial smile. The red and blue streaks she'd gotten for the Fourth clashed cheerfully with her aqua sundress.

Teejay joined me in front of the desk as we laid out the company's new direction. We hadn't been able to budge Steve from selling, but when I offered a generous down payment (thanks to Claire's painting), he'd agreed to lower his asking price and carry the note. My father was putting the finishing touches on the paperwork. Tomorrow, I'd wake up the proud—and petrified—owner of Blue Sky Expeditions.

"Are you going to keep driving?" Evan directed the question at me. Out of the corner of my eye, I noticed Sam's head of gold-brown curls tilt toward Megan as he whispered something. Cheeks pink, she waited for my answer.

"Sure. I can't let all those geology lessons go to waste." Truth was, I didn't have a better option. When my renters moved out of Claire's house, I'd move in to start rehabbing the loft with Mark Stillman's help. Maybe I'd rent one or both. Maybe I'd decide to sell up and move on. But for now, I needed a paycheck, at least until Teejay and I could make Blue Sky more profitable.

The bells at the front door jangled, and Harmony signaled Sam it was time to leave for his sunset hiking tour. He followed her and Gina to the reception area. The others headed for the garage, leaving me standing next to Teejay. I leaned back against the edge of the desk to take the weight off my ankle.

"Thanks." Teejay's gaze held mine. "I know you could have used that money yourself."

"Easy come, easy go, as Gina would say." I tried to contain a grin, failed. "I've had a lot of time to think. Let's talk to Ronnie, pitch her on some service-oriented tours."

He chuckled. "Sure, but I think she's got her hands full right now."

We talked about Ronnie's plan to visit the cave with representatives from affiliated tribes. We also discussed how vulnerable the ruins and rock art in Lee Canyon would be once Marisol left for her new job at a nursing home in Prescott. We fell into an awkward silence for a few moments, and I could tell something else was bothering him.

He dragged the words out like a heavy weight. "I think Franklin was trying to get help. That's why he headed for the box canyon. To signal me."

I knew better than to tell him to let it go and move on. I was still working on that myself. "It's a terrible feeling, being unable to save someone."

"Yeah." He shook his head, as though to clear it. "How about a sunset drive?"

A lot had changed. My hesitation to get involved with a coworker hadn't. "Can't. I'm meeting some friends in Clarkdale. Let's sit down tomorrow to put together an action plan."

"Okay, boss."

I shook my head. "I'm the silent partner."

His lips quirked.

"Okay, mostly silent."

"We'll figure it out."

* * *

After leaving headquarters, I turned the borrowed Jeep toward Cottonwood. Restaurants and tasting rooms had settled into Old Town's storefronts, and tourists wandered sidewalks as I drove past. Main Street transitioned to highway, and the bracing scent of creosote bush blew in the windows, bringing with it a rush of childhood memories.

Clarkdale's tidy grid of cupcake-cute cottages was laid out a century ago as the smelter town for Jerome's copper mines. My destination was a pale-yellow clapboard building, a former rooming house for bachelor workers, now an anachronism in the midst of a semicommercial neighborhood. Its door, painted a cheerful periwinkle, opened onto a wide veranda. The man stepping outside to greet me looked familiar, though a bit softer around the edges than I remembered.

At fifteen, Pete Simms had dropped off the radar, lost to alcohol and drugs. Even though it was the summer I'd been wrapped up in Ryan, I'd felt Pete's absence. He was the kindest of the Jackaloons, and he'd been the first to accept an outsider all those years before. His cornsilk blond mop was now a thinning dishwater brown, but his wide grin hadn't dimmed at all.

"Del Cooper, I'd recognize you anywhere."

I climbed the creaking stairs without limping, but that wasn't the only reason I broke into a smile. "Even with the bandages and bruises?"

"Because of them. Scraped knees and elbows were your summer look."

I followed Pete through a transomed doorway. A hundred years ago, boarders might have used this small parlor to entertain guests. Now it was lined with books and filing cabinets. I sat on the visitor chair and tried not to fidget. Ryan had mentioned Pete Simms was a preacher, but he'd left out the details. A few years ago, Pete had returned to the Verde Valley to start a storefront church based on AA principles, later establishing a residential recovery program. When he called last night, I assumed he'd seen the *Drummer* and wanted to gossip, but I was wrong.

"So, you're taking over the business from Steve. You always were fearless about jumping into things."

"Me?" I shook my head. "I'm not a Jackaloon anymore."

His gray eyes lit with mischief. "I'd forgotten your aunt's name for us. We *were* fearless. But harmless," he added, "though I wasn't always sure about Ryan. When I heard what happened to Franklin, I reached out to the sheriff's office. The magistrate agreed a familiar face might help settle her."

Seeing the question in my eyes, he explained. "Franklin brought Jane here last winter. He was trying to get her clean, back on her psych meds."

I told him about my conversation with Sam, how Franklin traded pot for stolen prescriptions. Pete confirmed my theory that Franklin had been trying to help Jane for years.

"I wanted to help, too." Pete's pale skin reddened. "She stayed a few weeks, then one night she climbed out a second-story window onto the veranda roof and disappeared back into the forest. I should've remembered how inventive addicts can be, having been one myself."

The escape must have been around the time I'd seen Jane and Franklin argue. "You said Franklin wanted to help her, but he put her at risk. Why?"

"He wanted her parents to step up. He was dying. Liver cancer, he told me." I stared at him. He said gently, "I believe the ME's report will confirm it."

"Does she understand what happened?"

He nodded. "But she's still fragile." He eyed me, seemed to make up his mind. "She's waiting in the common area."

He led the way to a set of French doors that opened into a sunny room. She was seated at a long rectangular table stained and scarred from countless meals, meetings, and art projects. I didn't recognize the girl I'd barely known. Had Ryan? Someday I'd ask, but I planned to let him stew a while first.

Her deep tan had faded slightly, and her aquamarine eyes—exactly like Barbara's, I realized—were clear. Her hair had been cut and shaped into soft layers, making her look closer to her own age, and she was dressed in a pale blue button-front blouse. Demure—unless you happened to notice the edge of a tattoo peeping out below one short sleeve.

"Hello, Janessa." I smiled, and she smiled back.

"Just plain Jane now." She looked down at the table, her fingertips tapping its surface nervously.

I felt my heart twist as memories rushed back. Barbara had saddled her daughter with a name like a starlet's but called her "plain Jane" whenever she wanted to discourage her from playing with *those rowdy townies*. Usually, when the Jackaloons descended, Barbara had insisted Jane stay indoors, over Whittaker's objections.

Poor little rich girl, I'd thought then, though now I understood the Lees' wealth was only a display. Unless Whittaker's will made other arrangements, Jane would inherit the ranch, with all its problems and potential. I hoped Pete would see to it she had wise counsel.

I took a chair at the end of the table. Behind me, Pete quietly closed the door. "How are you feeling?"

"Better every day." She spoke slowly. "I remember you."

"Maybe you remember this?" I held out the photograph I'd brought with me. I'd forgotten about it until Pete called last night.

Two little girls, sitting at the worktable in Claire's studio. I'd protested at being indoors. About seven, I was wearing a pair of dirty sneakers with cutoffs and (Pete was right) bandaged knees, while Jane, a few years older, had on the kind of dress we used to call "grandma bait." Claire had loaned her an artist's smock so she wouldn't ruin it.

"May I?" Jane reached out, the edge of her sleeve riding up. As I handed over the photo, her tattoo caught my gaze, a red rose surrounded by script: *Daddies' Girl.*

I'd puzzled over it briefly a few months ago when I'd given Jane a lift to the grocery store. You can't work your way up from copyediting, then stop noticing things like that. I'd put the misspelling down to a lazy tattoo artist. Now it made sense—a girl with two fathers.

I was pretty sure Pete knew. When I looked past the sun-damaged skin and hair, Jane's parentage seemed obvious. Besides Barbara's pale blue eyes, Jane had Franklin's long nose and Cupid's bow lips.

"I'm sorry about your father," I said gently.

"He was good to me. Whittaker, too, even after she told him he wasn't my real dad." Her face crumpled, and I kicked myself for pushing her. "I tried to return it. It was bad luck."

At first, I thought she was rambling again. Then awareness dawned. "The shell necklace?"

"Cursed. Dad—Whittaker—never should have given it to her. When they sent me away to school, I took it with me."

"Your parents thought Henry Grisom stole it."

"I know. They fired him." She looked down at her hands, her mouth twisting. "I blamed the necklace, but the truth was she never really wanted me."

Afraid of pushing too hard, I let her talk.

"I went to look for my real father in LA. He wasn't ready to be a dad then, so I left. Traveled some." Her expression told me *travel* was probably a euphemism.

"He found you here, in Sedona." Franklin must have reasoned Jane would return someday. That was why he showed up and why he stayed, long after the goddess circle collapsed.

"I asked him to put the necklace back, break the curse. Then *he* saw it. I promised him I'd never tell anyone. It was our secret."

"Whittaker?" She nodded. "He must have been angry."

Her gaze shifted away, and I knew I wouldn't learn any more from her today. I didn't believe in curses, but I hoped the stone-and-shell artifact would be repatriated and some-how restored to balance. It had been stolen—twice. Made into an ornament, used as a bribe, offered as proof of Jane's identity. Friendships broken, lives lost . . .

Jane slid the photo across the table, but I shook my head. "Keep it, if you like."

She gave me a small smile. "I wanted to be an artist like your aunt. I was so happy in her studio. Someday I'd like to feel that way again."

"Someday I think you will." I hoped it was true.

*   *   *

Snakeweed bloomed bright yellow along 89A as I drove home, and the sky was as clear as blue crystal. When I topped the next hill, Sedona's red rocks filled the Jeep's windscreen. My breath caught. Impulsively, I turned onto No Trees Road, slowing as I neared the box canyon.

I stopped on a rise and watched the cliffs shifting from orange to pink to lavender. From here, I could see the tip of the Giant's Claw. Lee Canyon lay hidden beyond: the lonely ranch, the secret alcoves, the goddess watching over all of it, silent as stone. Some of my happiest childhood memo-ries were there, and some of Jane's worst. I wasn't sure how much Pete had told her, but Jane could go home—*if* she'd ever want to live in Lee Canyon again.

As for me, I'd escaped to Sedona hoping to find the rosy childhood I remembered, yet the shamanka was prescient after all. My life had spiraled back to the same questions of trust and betrayal, forgiveness and fear. I could run again, but not from myself. I searched the purpling folds of the rocks, half wishing the cliff dweller would step out of the shadows to guide me. Was he a symptom of a broken mind? Or was he showing me a path to healing?

It was nearly dark when I pulled into the driveway, but I could see the outlines of a vehicle parked near the barn. For a moment, I thought it was a Blue Sky Jeep, and my heart thumped hard. Then I recognized the shadowy figure sitting on the deck.

I parked next to the Tesla. As I climbed the stairs, Mark stood, cradling a puddle of fur in the crook of his arm.

"Hey," he said. We smiled at each other. "I dropped off those flooring samples and tried to put your key back under the flowerpot, but this one wouldn't let me leave. We've been watching the sunset together."

"The shelter called this morning. They have room for her . . . unless I want to keep her."

"What are you going to do?"

I stood there a moment, wondering if the question was as loaded as it seemed. Was I ready? Would I ever be ready?

"I named her Persephone. She's staying with me." I slid open the door and turned to face him, decision made. "Would you like to come in?"

MY SEDONA

THIS BOOK IS a work of fiction. All characters, names, places, and events are a product of my imagination or are used fictitiously. I've employed my writer's license to turn back time for some places (such as the ranger station and The Flats), added commercial Jeep routes, and altered geography to squeeze in locations that exist only in my mind.

On the other hand, Red Rock Fever *is* real—easy to catch and hard to cure. After all, how can anyone resist a place that hits the sweet spot between desert and mountain? Spiritual seekers, big-city dropouts, artists, musicians, and outdoor enthusiasts all rub elbows in this interesting, even quirky, community with three main population centers—Uptown, the Village of Oak Creek, and West Sedona. Beyond town, backcountry canyons reach from the edge of the Colorado Plateau like beckoning fingers, and the clear waters of Oak Creek meander through forest, woodland, and grassland.

Sedona's famed reddish orange buttes and spires eroded from the Schnebly Hill formation—horizontal layers of mudstone, sandstone, and limestone left by a shifting coastline millions of years ago. Rising above the reddish layers are tilted stacks of buff and gold—Coconino sandstone—formed from ancient windblown dunes. In places, the lighter sandstone merges with the reddish layers below, leaving a landscape striped and blended in marvelous hues.

According to the Yavapai or Wipuhk'a'bah, the red rocks are the remains of huge monsters roaming at the dawn of creation. When Anglo settlers arrived in the late 1800s, they named the rocks for castles, kitchen items, and critters. Sometimes newer names have caught on (looking at you, Thunder Mountain), while older ones are lost to time. Here are some of the places mentioned in *Over the Edge* (fictional names are italicized).

Airport Mesa: The Spanish word *mesa* means table, and this flat-topped landform (also called Tabletop) is home to a 5,130-foot long runway perched five hundred feet above West Sedona.

Airport Saddle: About halfway up Airport Road, easy-to-climb slickrock mounds entice view-seekers and the vortex-curious.

Bear Mountain: Said to resemble a sleeping bear, the 6,557-foot mountain offers a challenging hiking trail with views all the way to Flagstaff's San Francisco Peaks.

Bell Rock: Hundreds of seekers gathered here during the 1988 Harmonic Convergence, cementing Sedona's reputation as a New Age mecca. Even vortex skeptics can witness this bell-shaped butte pulling people right out of their vehicles and up its dark red slickrock slopes.

Cockscomb: Look for its angling, crenelated slope west of West Sedona . . . or on the city flag.

Courthouse Butte: This imposing block of sandstone stands next to Bell Rock in the Village of Oak Creek.

Capitol Butte: Guess how long someone's lived in Sedona by their name for this 6,355-foot dome-shaped peak, once known as Grayback and more recently as Thunder Mountain.

Cathedral Rock: A serendipitous mapmaker's error switched names for this graceful cluster of spires with stocky Courthouse Butte. The iconic view from Red Rock Crossing is said to be the most photographed scene in Arizona.

Chimney Rock: Proving that perspective is everything, this reddish formation resembling a fireplace and chimney is sometimes called Three-Finger Rock by folks living west of Dry Creek Road.

Coffee Pot Rock: An entire neighborhood of coffee-related street names was inspired by this prominent West Sedona formation, shaped like an old-fashioned campfire coffeepot.

The Cowpies: No truth in advertising here—these gorgeous slickrock mounds await travelers driving along Schnebly Hill Road or hiking the Munds Wagon Trail.

Doe Mountain: More appropriately called Doe Mesa, this flat-topped butte rises above Boynton Pass Road in Sedona's backcountry.

Elephant Rock: From Uptown Sedona, the west half of Twin Buttes looks like an elephant with an uplifted trunk. (In polite circles, its book-matched east half is referred to as Naughty Boy.)

The Flats: In real life, this area west of town is home to lodging, offices, and a currently defunct amphitheater and stage.

Giant's Claw: Rising up from the back of the *box canyon*, this spire resembles a woman's upturned face when viewed from *Lee Ranch*.

Merry-Go-Round: Now a favorite backdrop for wedding photographs, its semicircle of limestone blocks starred in several western movies during shootouts, a brutal imprisonment, and a cringe-worthy Elvis number.

Mitten Ridge: A dramatic sandstone wall soars above Schnebly Hill Road and Bear Wallow, a stream with seasonal flows. The long ridge is home to Teapot, the Giant's Thumb, Technicolor Corner, and other visual delights.

Schnebly Hill Road: The views are amazing along this primitive dirt road that climbs to the rim. But unless you have a high-clearance vehicle and nerves of steel, it's best to travel via a Jeep tour or on foot via the Munds Wagon Trail.

The Sphinx: This lopsided pyramid hunkers over the east side of Soldiers Pass across from Coffee Pot Rock.

Sugarloaf: Up until Sedona's pioneer days, sugar was sold in rounded cones. Unsurprisingly, there are dozens of hills and mountains across the US bearing this name.

Wilson Mountain: Lava flows covered Sedona's tallest peak (7,122 feet) six million years ago, frozen by time into a crown of dark gray columnar basalt.

ACKNOWLEDGMENTS

After hacking around the publishing jungle on my own far too long, I had the good fortune to connect with a superlative agent, Dawn Dowdle of Blue Ridge Literary Agency. Thanks to Dawn's persistence and grace, I reunited with one of my first-ever editors at Silhouette Books, Tara Gavin.

Tara, your wise and sensitive counsel helped me clarify my vision and strengthen my story—thank you. Thanks also to Crooked Lane's editorial and production team, including Rebecca Nelson and Thaisheemarie Fantauzzi Pérez, who provided a support structure that carried me through the final stages of transforming manuscript pages into a book.

I'm indebted to Sedona's brilliant and quirky community of forest rangers, hikers, healers, artists, scientists, guides, and seekers who've shared their knowledge and insights over the years.

Thanks especially to my yoga family—the enduring power of our collective practice keeps me grounded even when my head is in the clouds. I'll be forever grateful to Ruth Sraddhasagar Hartung and Rama Jyoti Vernon, who embodied gentleness with strength, wisdom with humor. You live in my heart.

Most of all, I'm grateful to my husband Richard for shaping the safe, creative, and joyful space we live in every day.

I wrote this story with loving memories of my parents, who taught me the joys of dirt roads and picnics in the desert. Thanks to them, I'll never stop exploring.